Also by Pamiela Berenson

Picasso's Envy

Praise for *Picasso's Envy*

I couldn't put this book down. I read it in a day and a half.

— Jo Sargeant

You have an exceptional way with words, thoroughly enjoyable and the 'psychological thrills' really crept up nicely. Thank you for the pleasure of reading your book! Great work!!!

— Vasanti Craig

Picasso's Envy was great reading. No chances of guessing the end. I was eager to read what came next. Really enjoyed the book.

— Roberto Valera

THIRDPLACE WINS

WINS

NO-ONE RUNS FOREVER

Pamiela Berenson

First published 2025 by Pamiela Berenson

Produced by Independent Ink
independentink.com.au

Cover design by Catucci Design
Edited by Victoria Steele
Internal design by Independent Ink
Typeset in 12/17 pt Garamond Premier Pro by Post Pre-press Group, Brisbane

ISBN 978-1-7637276-4-9 (paperback)
ISBN 978-1-7637276-5-6 (epub)
ISBN 978-1-7637276-6-3 (kindle)

To Elsie

ONE

Grace Katherine Mulvaney

Sydney, Australia – 2009

It was a day that was to change my life – again.

I was alone in the office, sitting at our front desk, when the heavy glass panelled doors flew open and in wafted a man who caused me to gasp. Even though we were five floors up, the day's cold wind was still trapped beneath his billowing, beige trench coat. He had presence and the most intense blue eyes I'd ever seen. The man beamed, his smile broad.

Until that day I was having an ordinary Tuesday. An ordinary week, an ordinary month. For me this was good. I had lived constantly looking over my shoulder. Looking to see who might be after me. Was I being followed or watched? But now life was settled, mundane, structured. Intermittently in my life I'd felt this way, but now I was so far physically from my past, I believed I could relax, permanently.

This man strode, not like a customer, but a man on a mission. My gut immediately told me I should feel concerned. He approached the desk.

"You ... Kate?"

He thrust that at me. Not in a threatening way, but not friendly either. Nevertheless, it felt like he'd stabbed me. His tone was not what mattered.

I was no longer Kate. Not for ages.

He'd flung me like a rag doll back into that bad place. Running, running, like when you're in a dream and your feet and legs don't take you anywhere. Weighed down like a beast of burden. Weighed down with my fears. Weighed down by my past actions.

I looked at this stranger and shook myself. I would not have it. No. That beast with his burden could fuck off. Those memories along with it. This man would not dismantle my life.

"Grace Katherine Mulvaney," I heard his voice off in the distance.

My memories quickly vanished. I was back in the office with a lanky stranger standing in front of me. He needed to be dealt with.

"I'm Jackie. Can I help you, Mr ...?"

"But you *were* Kate ... right?"

At that moment I was glad Kimberley and Susie were at lunch.

"Sir ... do you have business with us? Are you lost?"

"Lost you many times, now I've finally found you."

I walked to the door and opened it. I'd regained my composure, outwardly at least. He had to go before I crumbled. I needed 'settled and mundane' to stay.

"Please sit down, Kate."

Holding open the heavy door was making my arm ache.

"I'm not leaving yet, Kate."

I couldn't physically throw him out, so I walked back to the desk and sat.

"Take it easy," he said.

My face must have given me away, but I think it was more the pain in my arm.

"I'm not here to threaten you."

Wasn't he?

He finally sat on the couch.

"A chair opposite your desk would be more practical."

No, it would not.

He got himself comfortable, muttered, "at last." Then removed a shoe and massaged his foot. Returned it.

He didn't look familiar. I shuffled through possibilities, seeking a past where I might have met him. I recalled instances when someone had called Kate and I'd nearly shat myself, but it was just a coincidence. Someone near me with that name. I flicked through pictures in my mind, places where I'd lived. Nothing.

"You don't know me, but I've been looking for you ... for some time. Nearly got to you, then you vanished again."

I didn't normally sit at the front desk. It should have been Kimberley. Where were those girls? Now I wanted them back before this got sticky. But I didn't want him to shoot his mouth off in their presence either.

He sighed a couple of times. He looked thirty-something. Hard to tell, he had that lived-in look. Too young for a heart attack but you never knew.

He leant back on the couch.

"Can I get you a glass of water?" I said, thinking of having to deal with this long body of a man passing out.

"No, no, I'm fine. Changing your name all the time hasn't made the search easy."

It *should* have been very difficult, was my immediate thought. That was the whole point.

I looked at him again. He'd closed his eyes as he leant back on the couch. It was easier to study him. He was tall, willowy, with crazy thick, sandy-brown hair. Generous nose. Clean shaven, no glasses. No, I didn't recognise him.

I got it; it was a practical joke. I'd recently broken-up with a guy, so it could be Oliver being an arse and playing a sick joke. It would have been pure coincidence him picking the name Kate. Oliver didn't know about Kate.

The stranger opened his eyes, looked at me. He must have read something in my face.

"No need to be afraid."

I wasn't sure fear was quite the adjective I was experiencing. It was much more complex than that.

"Really?"

"Nope."

Those eyes held mine. I couldn't look away.

"You're wanted back home," he said.

TWO

Kate/Jackie

The stranger leant forward, elbows on his knees.

"So," he said. "Let's get down to business ... but first ... see these," indicating his feet, "they've travelled a long way looking for you."

He reached down again and pulled off his tanned leather slip-on shoes, both of them this time, then removed bright yellow socks and stretched out his bare feet, fanning his long toes. He began a process of putting everything back on. With considered care he held the heel and toe of one sock, stretched it, then gathered it down and carefully rolled it over his toes, his angular foot, his heel, ankle and up his calf. The sock looked silky, expensive. He moved to the other foot and repeated the process. Then each foot was returned to its rightful shoe. He took particular care not to bend down the backs of the expensive leather footwear. He looked like a vagrant with his wild windblown hair and shapeless coat but clearly held his feet in high regard.

He then smiled at me.

Although his smile was friendly, my skin crawled over every inch of my body.

Where were the girls? I didn't want to ring the police, I really didn't.

"Intriguing," I said. "What is it you want?" He needed to go. "Now you've shared that, Mr Whoeveryouare, I think you'd better leave."

He stood, held out his hand, "Thakit ... Thakit Thirdplace."

Yeah right, and I'd worried about my choice of names. I ignored the gesture.

"It's best you leave, Mr Thirdplace. I don't think you want to hire an animal. That's what we do here. Hire out animals. Dogs, cats, goats, donkeys, trained funnel-web spiders, if that's your thing. We hire to the film and television industry."

"You're right, I don't."

"Then leave. I don't want to have to say that again."

Kimberley, Susie, please don't come back just yet, I prayed.

"Keeping Katherine in the middle is a good idea," he said. "Gives a name rhythm. You must have had as much trouble remembering to answer to your names as we had tracking you. But now I've found you ... as I said, you're wanted back in Ireland."

He tossed that last sentence like you would a ball to a dog. My nerves jangled. I was struggling. This was what I'd feared for years, now it had finally been lain at my feet.

We, did I hear? Not good.

"Back in Ireland?" a voice said behind him.

The girls had returned. Thakit Thirdplace was standing in front of me, blocking my line of vision. While I'd freaked out, my eyes had dropped to my hands.

"We have to leave," Thirdplace said softly to me.

"Yes, you do." I mimicked his tone as I pulled myself together.

"We haven't much time. Now your colleagues are back ..." He turned to look at them and smiled. The girls nodded.

"Ka ... I mean Jackie ... is in a hurry to leave. Think you'll be able to run the place while she's away?"

"Don't take any notice. It's a practical joke, one of Oliver's," I said. The girls looked from me to him and back again.

"She has to go, family matter to attend to," said Thirdplace.

"Of course we can," said Susie.

"You're Irish?" Kimberley said.

I walked past them to the door, pushed it open. He was right behind me.

Growling, I said, "Goodbye, Mr Thirdplace, don't come back."

"No running this time, Kate." He leant into me and whispered. "You are needed ... back home." He straightened. "I'll be back."

So now he's Mr Schwarzenegger.

As I watched him take the lift, my first thoughts were to run. I'd established myself. I was part of a business, I had friends and a social life. But I would flee if I had to. When the business was set up, I'd kept out of the legalities, which meant I could flee at a moment's notice. Now here it was, tied with a ribbon and I didn't want to go anywhere. It was a strange feeling and one new to me. But it was not the time to dwell.

The girls' eyes were wide when I turned.

"Who was that?" they said in unison.

"Cool. A bit old, but cool," said Kimberley. "Amazing eyes."

"What?" I said.

"Well, if Oliver's no longer on the scene," said Susie, "why not? He's good looking. Nice smile." She turned to Kimberley. "He's not old."

I strode to my office, closed the door and slumped in the chair. I wished a drink would work but it never had. Numbness crawled over me.

Who the hell was he, this Thakit Thirdplace? He couldn't be a Gard, even undercover the name was too out there. Private detective?

I searched him on the internet but could find nothing. Perhaps his name was an anagram. I tried but came up with rubbish.

Was there something I'd missed about him? I'd pay more attention next time. What was I saying? There was to be no next time.

Shutting down my fears, I got on with some work.

Try as I might to concentrate, my brain was having none of it. He'd stymied me. My fingers babbled on the keyboard. It was time to go home. Then a thought hit me.

Oh God. Perhaps he'd found out where I lived and was waiting for me?

THREE

Ryan Kelly/Thakit Thirdplace

West Ireland

It was a line I used, telling people my name came to me in a dream. The real story was too long and complicated, not one to tell flippantly. What it did was shift the conversation to dreams in general, offered up like rare artefacts. Focus drifted from me and didn't return.

Kate came into my life sometime after I'd changed my name. When she was born, I was eight. I didn't know her, nor knew she existed. There was just me and my mammy and my brother Colin. My father died from smoking too many cigarettes when I was three. He knew it wasn't good for his health but smoked anyway.

I have few memories of him. While I was a littl'un he'd always been sick. Apparently, he'd been a wildly handsome character and swept my mammy off her feet. The envy of all her friends. Colin knew him, as my brother was older and told me stories of how they'd rough and tumble and kid around. My da's favourite pastime was tinkering with cars.

Back when my father's illness started then progressed, Colin told me mammy spent longer and longer caring for him. She became a zombie. Darkness settled under her eyes. She'd get him comfortable then rush off to work as a cleaning lady. At the end of her day, she cooked for us and looked after da. The kindness of neighbours filled our little house. Friends cared for me and my brother when mammy was late home. She watched the outcome of da's illness take its favours, leaving the remnants of his body to weaken. An oxygen mask hissed and breathed and kept him alive. That sound in our lives I do faintly remember.

Endless races to the hospital, the weeks of his illness turned into months. Through it all, mammy held onto her job. She said her boss was kind and understanding, allowing her the time to care for our daddy. As long as the work was done, she could choose her shifts.

At the end of a day cleaning and after a visit to the hospital, she'd arrive home to ensure Colin and I were okay. Then and only then, she allowed herself the pleasure of sinking into her favourite armchair. Although meant to be asleep, I'd hear her return. Sneaking down the stairs she'd call me over and we'd sit together, me on her lap as she tousled my hair, saying everything would be okay. Although tired, she was happy on those days. There was peace at home, a sanctuary where she could rest, as though she'd had a gulp from the oxygen mask herself.

After my father's funeral the neighbourhood piled into our house for the wake. Even though I was little, I do remember this. I was overwhelmed with the sea of faces that peered down at me. I scrambled through a forest of legs, trying to find my brother or my ma.

I was a stranger that day in our house. I listened to the murmurings that floated high above me. Later, raucous laughter filled the room, pats on my head from well-meaning people which made it sore. Food from moistened mouths fell upon me. Extra supplies of alcohol appeared through doors and windows. Slurred speech increased as did, "ah, sweet boy," ... "he's going to miss his da," and such things. I barely knew him.

When my mother gave birth to me, the neighbours and friends said I was a gift from God. One last hurrah for da.

"It's good to know that bit worked before he got too sick," followed with sniggers and slapping of backs. Covering my ears, mammy said, "Not in front of the boy, please" and moved me to the stairs to watch. Not that I understood. Most of what I remember came from Colin, which became my memories.

My brother was not only my brother, older by eight years, he was my God. He knew stuff. As he grew, he learnt about cars. He liked vintage cars especially. He was very clever with them. Like our da. He'd tinker for hours and, if all his hard work failed, the final tinker was a hearty kick or thump.

"You gotta love 'em, then whack 'em, Ryan, that's the only way to get your way with a motor that's stubborn." Then he'd demonstrate. "Now talk sweetly ... come on darling ... then whack. Not too hard, just enough to let it know who's boss, then before you know it that motor will burst into life."

Our car was ancient and grumpy. I'd repeat what he said as I stood next to Colin holding a flimsy piece of stick. Mostly the stick broke and the car never burst into life. Only my brother Colin could breathe life into a vehicle.

So began my project in our house. Applying Colin's technique, I set about acting as the master fixer. I became a warrior with a stick. I went the extra length and used the principle on all appliances connected to an electricity outlet, as well as others that were not. I concluded at that age, just in case the thing decided not to work, it was best to get in first. Be gentle first, then *whackit*.

I whacked everything so often mammy and Colin called me Whackit Thackit. That added another word to my remonstrations toward the objects that would and wouldn't work.

"Whackit Thackit," I cried as I paraded my stick, my sword, like a medieval lord. On *whackit,* I lifted the stick and came down hard on *thackit.* Mammy soon tired of the amusement as my brother trailed after me, mending what I'd broken. He took to calling me an eejit; Whackit Thackit, the eejit. Eventually the name Ryan was forgotten at home.

By the time I started school, Whackit was also dropped. Thackit became the only name used by my mammy, my brother, the school and the neighbourhood in general.

The teacher was relieved, as there were three other Ryans in the class. Once I knew letters, I decided to eliminate the 'c' as well.

'Thirdplace' I earned.

Although I never won at anything, I always came third. Thakit the Third morphed into Thakit Thirdplace. Soon I became a school mascot. Word spread about my third-place proficiency. When a sports day was being held with another school, bets were placed on me coming third. Secret money was won. My prowess at sports was varied, I mastered none.

Excelling didn't interest me. Being a hero was not my goal. I had no goals. The way things were had always pleased me, provided I was left alone to enjoy them. My mother gave up pushing me and was happy enough that my school reports showed I was doing well despite the 'could try harder.' I achieved the third highest marks in most subjects.

It was only when I got older and had to fill in forms or register for something, that I faltered over my real name. So I changed it legally.

"Are you insane?" said mammy.

"Are you a total eejit?" said Colin.

I knew they both loved me, so I ignored them and went ahead with the formalities. And, in the big wide world, it was much easier to say I dreamt the name.

When my brother became a motor mechanic, he stopped whacking cars and fixed them properly. Colin's natural gift with cars did not filter down to me. I watched him and tried to emulate his skills but just got in the way.

Mammy despaired as I had no idea what I wanted to do in life. I was a nice boy. School friends and adults liked me. I was easy to be with but there was no future in being a nice chap. No money in it.

Pressure was on.

Thakit

Beneath my strong nose, as mammy called it, I was told I bore a lovely smile. This smile could get me through any door, she said, but I had to stay through that door. I needed to pull my socks up and earn that entrance. Job ads, *Good Smiler Wanted*, never came up.

"What about the movies?" I said.

"You have to know how to act," ma said.

"I could learn." I wouldn't shut up about it. "What about advertisements? Everyone smiles in ads."

Mammy took me to a theatrical agency.

"His blue eyes are an asset, but his nose is too big."

Their suggestion I get my nose made smaller, then come back, caused me to lose interest and put paid to my acting career. Mammy smiled.

When I reached my mid-teens, mammy panicked.

Because she cleaned houses, she wanted something better than menial jobs for her son. She had her heart set on my going to university, become something, earn a decent living. That was all well and good and I didn't object, but I had no idea what to study. There were so many things to be interested in. I couldn't decide. Many times at the kitchen table, mammy, bless her, would harp on and on.

"What about being a banker? You're good at maths."

"True, I came third in the school …"

But my brother said that was a wanker's job. As he was God and held more sway than my mother, I decided it was best to leave that one alone. Mammy said it was important to get a degree so I should study something. Anything. Later I could decide what to do.

Yet I couldn't bear the thought of mammy cleaning houses for years while I went to university. It wasn't fair. I wanted to earn money to ease her life. Now that da was gone, her life was a lot easier, but she was getting older and often tired. Colin was off getting married by then with babies on the way.

"You're clever, Thakit," mammy said. "If you applied yourself, you'd be brilliant. Look at your school reports. All good."

"All third."

"*Could-apply-himself* is what you need to take notice of, Thakky. I don't care what you do, you're going to university, getting that degree, and that's that."

"I don't know what to study, mammy."

"Think about what interests you, then look for that course."

"Everything interests me. You know that."

"I don't see you actually doing much."

"All the books I read, ma."

"Reading is only good if it's for study, to get yourself a degree, Ryan."

Ryan – mammy was annoyed.

"I've been too easy on you," she said. "That's the problem. Let you drift. You can't be doing odd jobs all your life. A reliable career with a good income is what will see you through life."

I sat opposite her at the kitchen table where we were having this conversation for the hundredth time.

"I just don't know, mammy." I scratched my head.

"What about the careers adviser at school?"

"Not much help there."

"At least tell me what they suggested."

"Banking, finance, that sort of thing."

"That's good. There's a future there."

"Colin doesn't agree."

Knowing I always took notice of Colin, mammy glowered, muttering she'd give him what for. The next day she went to the school to talk to the Head. Come evening, the kitchen table got another going over.

"It seems your strongest subject is maths and you're good at it. You also don't care about the subject. I was also told you have a very good imagination."

She must have got angry at the Head too.

"How is that going to help him get a job?" she'd asked.

Apparently the Head was as exasperated as my mammy. He told her to get me to close my eyes and imagine anything, anything at all, anything I'd like to do, no limitations.

"So now, here I am, Ryan, asking you."

She told me to sit comfortably.

"Now close your eyes, son and imagine."

Following her advice my mind went wild. I saw myself travelling the world. Each picture was filled with sunshine.

"And what are you doing in the sunshine?"

"I'm looking for someone."

"Oh lord," mammy sounded increasingly frustrated. "Imagine you're working at something. What would it be?"

"I'm tracking someone. Like a cross between a detective and a spy."

"You want to go into the *Garda Síochána* or the Security Intelligence Service?"

I opened my eyes and realised I was at the kitchen table.

"That was so real, mammy."

"You want to join one of the Services?"

"No, I don't think so. Why?"

Mammy slammed her hands down on the table, stood up and said she would find a course and her choice would be what I'd do. That would be that.

I'd spoken with Colin about my life and what I was to do. He was so clear about his own path that he didn't really understand mine or mammy's dilemma.

"She's getting angry with me ... calling me Ryan. I don't know what I want to do. What do you think?"

"I don't know, Thakky, whatever the hell you want."

"She wants me to go to university, but I don't know what to study."

"Just stab at something. Lay all the courses out on the table, close your eyes and stab something."

I needed to close my eyes again. I wondered if this was the traditional path to choosing a career. I gave it a go and stabbed. It was an arts degree.

"But I can't draw," I said to mammy and Colin.

"You'll learn and that's the end of it," she said.

It sounded interesting and wasn't wankersville in my brother's opinion, so I went for a Bachelor of Arts. I had no idea what it meant but mammy thought it sounded okay. It was at least something, she said. My brother was enthusiastic and thought I could become a great artist one day. That surprised me as I didn't know until then he was interested in the subject. Though he did draw a lot himself, mostly futuristic cars. That he thought the subject was okay was good enough for me. I went ahead with the degree. I still couldn't draw. I didn't need to. I dabbled with thoughts of taking studies further, maybe acting or literature. Mammy rolled her eyes. She was happy. I had a degree.

I passed. Third in the class.

FIVE

Thakit

We were a tight knit family of three after da died. With him gone, we became closer. I was raised both by my ma and my brother.

My mammy was very pretty and my brother, good looking. It was said Colin took after our father with his dark brooding looks. He wasn't as tall as me but built with a strong physique. He was practical with a no-nonsense attitude, like our ma.

Then there was me. With good teeth. Blue eyes that neither mammy or Colin possessed and a fetching smile. Tall, skinny and sort of wonky looking, with a nose too big for my face. My hair is another issue. My mother tried controlling it, but it had a mind of its own. I didn't think I looked like either my mammy or my brother. Colin and I scanned over old photographs where an uncle could have been a likeness. Until mammy said it was probably someone before photographs were invented. So we stopped looking.

Kids up the road said the little people had delivered me. When I was little myself this worried me so much I tried to find where they lived so I could meet my parents. Mammy said that was absolutely ridiculous and not at all true.

With all this oddness about my appearance, mammy expected me to be someone special; I'm not sure why or whether my looks were the reason. She didn't have the same expectation of Colin. She didn't need to, I suppose, as he'd always been more serious and achievement oriented. As a child I didn't know about laying out a life path so it could be walked along. I'm not sure Colin ever thought about it either. He just knew what he wanted. Colin never scolded me for not trying hard enough. Possibly he liked the adoration and having me around, doing his bidding. Life was good, whichever way it was viewed.

Did I like school? Did I like living where we lived? Did I miss not having a father? Every day was a day and I loved them all. Not having a father and being born to the little people eventually settled on me like a well-worn cap. Wonky or not, it was what it was.

As for my ma, apart from the time after da died, if she was unhappy, she kept it to herself. She made our lives fun, fashioning games out of everyday occurrences. If she had a boyfriend, I never knew about it. She never brought anyone home. She was happy just to be with us.

SIX

Kate

West Ireland

It seemed so long ago. My past. Distant, as if my early life didn't belong to me. That past where my aunt, my adorable Aunt Iris, belonged. Her memory I still treasure. My mother's sister. How I yearned to talk with her in later years. If she hadn't allowed herself to die, I wondered if I would still be living that life, in that big house.

After my father vanished and when it was clear after a couple of years he wasn't coming back, my ma and I moved into the big house. It was at my Uncle Lachlan's invitation. I was five years old. I remember him being tall and strong with a very direct way of talking. I was a little afraid of him. Mammy wasn't and was very eager to make the move.

A few months after we moved in, Aunty Iris, Uncle Lachlan's wife, took to her room. For reasons I didn't understand, she was not happy we'd joined them. The house was huge and if you didn't want to see someone, or be seen, you could find somewhere else to be. So it seemed strange that we got in the way. If that was the problem. Initially we all ate together, but the atmosphere at the dining table hung like airborne mould, turning greyer and greyer until the delicious food tasted foul.

One day at dinner my aunt made an announcement. I later realised it was a veiled message to my mother. She declared she would no longer be preparing meals and her husband, Lachlan, should get a cook. She and her husband, if he cared to join her, would then eat in the conservatory or the formal dining room. Mammy sniggered. We ate separately from then on. Mammy and I in the large homey kitchen where it was welcoming and always warm. I don't remember either my aunt or uncle ever entering the kitchen again, at least while we were around. The mould vanished.

Once the eating arrangements separated us, I seldom saw my aunt. I missed her even though I barely knew her. I liked her right from the start. Aunt Iris's manner was haughty, but I sensed the warmth beneath.

Uncle Lachlan was not concerned with me. He was neither friendly nor unfriendly. I was there, like a forgotten table lamp. Shine but don't stand out. Unlit, just furniture. He was mostly out attending meetings. Aunt Iris and Uncle Lachlan were social beings and out many evenings a week. Apparently the house had been a jovial place with many visitors. I heard my aunt ran it like clockwork. After we arrived, guests and visitors dwindled. My aunt's and uncle's lives changed. Aunt Iris sank into despair. Beaten.

Young and naïve, with self-interest on my side, I noticed but neither understood nor particularly cared other than wanting time with my aunt.

The energy between my mother and Aunt Iris was electric, but not in a good way. The charge struck like lighting, with both surprise and force, hissing as it flashed, striking hard.

One day shortly after school term started, without telling mammy,

I gingerly knocked on Aunt Iris's door. She called "Come", thinking I was the cook or the gardener. I stood demure and quiet as a mouse just inside the room. She turned and when she saw it was me, a smile broke her face in two.

"Little Katie, come in … come in. Sit with me." The visits from then on became more and more regular until I visited every day.

Not long after these visits began, Aunty Iris got tummy ache. She said it was nothing to do with me and she enjoyed my company. I brought a shine into her day, she said. It was the cook who was trying to poison her. I was in her room one day when Uncle Lachlan popped in.

"Get a new cook, this one is attempting to poison me," said Aunt Iris.

"Why would she do that, Iris?" he said. "There'd be no gain for her, and I don't believe she's a psychopath." He looked towards me. "You realise Katie is still here, don't you?"

"Katie needs to know what's going on. She's an intelligent little girl."

I sat very still, hoping they wouldn't send me away.

"Brianna probably knows that woman," my aunt said. "I bet they're in cahoots." She glanced at me and changed her tone. "Employ someone else. This one's no good. The food belongs in the bin. *I'll* interview them."

"Very well," my uncle sighed and left the room. I loved it when I had my aunt all to myself.

No one was allowed to enter the kitchen while Aunt Iris interviewed prospective cooks. A line-up visited the house, with my aunt interviewing them personally. This was during the day, of course, when mammy was at work and I was at school. Aunt Iris kept me informed of the doings. She asked them all, "Have you ever poisoned anyone?"

Uncle Lachlan said she was silly to ask as they'd hardly admit to it. "I like to see their reaction."

Mrs Gallagher was hired and allowed to stay. She was middle aged and dumpy. Aunty Iris picked her deliberately.

"Then Lachlan won't be tempted," she explained to me. "He's a flirt."

Mrs Gallagher turned out to be a terrific cook and a rock of a person. Eventually she oversaw the running of the house, attending to any number of jobs.

A routine began for me. I'd dump my school bag then run in to see Aunty Iris. Mammy worked five days a week and got home about teatime. I had about an hour with my aunty before she got home. Mrs Gallagher would bring in tea and biscuits or a cake she'd baked and we sat in my aunt's room by the bay window or, if it was warm and sunny, just outside under the eaves. Flowering shrubs in pots sat on slate paving. Iris had the gardener make the area lush and green with an array of flowers in spring and summer.

Aunt Iris's room was large and airy and the bay window overlooked the beautiful garden. Her chosen furniture was picture-book old-world, with doilies and lace tablecloths to protect the table set with fragile bone-china cups and saucers. On her dressing table was a ceramic stand in the shape of a tree on which jewels set in silver and gold hung like raindrops.

Aunt Iris saw me desperate to touch these delicate pieces and finally she could bear it no longer. She picked one from the stand, a sparkling drop earing and clipped it to my ear. So encrusted with diamonds, it pulled on my ear lobe.

She saw how carefully I touched the pieces. Brooches sparkled in the sunlight, earrings dropped like waterfalls or snuggled close to the ear, exploding with colour. She told me about each piece: emeralds, rubies, sapphires both blue and white and diamonds of different carats and colours. Then she placed a necklace around my neck; it was heavy and cool on my skin. I removed it with extreme care, cupping it in my hand like an injured bird. The necklace overflowed from my small palms. It felt so alive, as if it might fly away.

"Katie, you won't break them, I don't mind if you wear them, but only in here," she warned.

"They're so beautiful," I whispered. "I just want to look at them, touch them." It was as if they had hidden lives. "Did Uncle Lachlan give them to you?"

"Most," she said, "some I bought along the way. It seems we share a fondness for jewels, Katie."

"I never knew I did before."

"Take them to the sunshine and see how they sparkle."

I chose an emerald ring. The solitaire stone was set in a circle of little diamonds. Beams of light glinted as I twisted the ring. It was fairyland. Next, I shyly chose diamond drop earrings and watched how the light made the stones smile. Something in me stirred and in that moment, I knew I wanted a collection like hers. I'd make it my life's passion.

SEVEN

Kate

1998

Routine with my aunt was anchored when she arranged for a table and two chairs to be set permanently under the eaves. "Our own terrazzo," she said. It meant we no longer needed to wait for the gardener to set it up.

I'd chatter on about school and if she could get a word in, she spoke about when she went to school. I can't remember too much about her experiences. I wish I'd paid better attention and asked her more questions.

Her health started to deteriorate. She wasn't at all well. One day when devilish pain hit, her face grimaced something terrible. She said it was time for me to leave her alone.

"What's wrong, aunty?"

"Just a bit of indigestion."

Over the days and weeks, the pain grew worse. I begged her to go to the doctor.

"No need. I don't want anyone, man or woman, probing around down there. They're my privates and so they'll stay that way."

"But a doctor would make you better."

"No," was all she said. "And that man is not going to persuade me either."

"What man?"

"Lachlan. He pretends he cares, but I think otherwise."

I learnt to stop talking so much and let her be, that way she didn't send me away. She was happy just to sit and patted my hand from time to time. She became very grey and seemed to age before my eyes.

One day she was talkative, so I grabbed the moment. "Why don't you and mammy get along?"

"We do get along, Katie. I hate her, that's all."

"That doesn't make sense."

"Your mother resented me marrying Lachlan. He was hers, you see, in the beginning. Or so she thought. We all knew one another since time began, that is Brianna and I and Lachlan and Lachlan's brother Liam. When it came time to wed, he liked me the best. She didn't like that and did everything to get him back."

"Didn't she love my da?" I was devastated. That was a bit of truth I knew nothing about. In fact, my da's disappearance was a mystery to me. I didn't remember him except for one photo I'd seen in a drawer somewhere.

"Did she love your da?" my aunty said, "... probably not."

"That's awful, aunty, why not?"

"Your da did love your mammy though. Adored her."

I smiled but felt confused. "Then why did she marry him, if she didn't love him?"

"A lot of people marry people they don't love. They marry for all sorts of reasons. You're old enough to know it's not like in the movies or happy-ever-after stories."

I did know that, but not up close.

"Your da always loved your mammy and before they married, he hoped she was just playing hard to get. Hoped that she cared a little bit for him. Brianna toyed with him. Reeled him in like a fish when he drifted away and became disillusioned. Lachlan was her focus. The day Lachlan and I married was the day she said yes to your da, or asked him to marry her, I'm not sure which."

"Why did he leave then?"

"Hah," said Aunt Iris. She was really spilling the beans. Now she'd started she couldn't stop. "Your da found out she was having an affair."

"An affair ... who with?" I couldn't believe this of my mammy.

"Lachlan."

"But you were married to him."

"That's your mammy. That's why I hate her. She got Lachlan back after all ... and hurt everyone around her." Her face contorted with pain and she shrugged. "And now she's here she can play with him, my husband, as much as she likes. Katie, dear, I don't care anymore." A big sigh expelled some of the pain. "From then on, I didn't much care for Lachlan either. Ego is a powerful thing and he can't resist temptation. He's weak; your mammy's strong."

"But all she does is sit with him, reads to him, in exchange for rent," I said in bewilderment. "They both love literature," I said with urgency. Saying it out loud didn't make sense even though I didn't know much about the world.

Aunt Iris laughed. "Is that what she told you?"

"After da left," I argued. "It was a while after. She struggled to pay the rent and then the company she worked for went broke. She lost her job, remember?"

"Yes, I remember."

"She got another job, but it didn't pay as well ... that's when Uncle Lachlan said we should come and live here. He told mammy it would be nice to have me around, some noise in the house. He said it would be good to have both his girls under his roof. Two sisters together and his niece. He said you'd both like that."

"Did Lachlan tell you all that?"

"No, mammy did."

"And has he ... seen more of you?"

I thought for a moment. "Erm, a bit. Mammy was happy to move in," I gabbled. "She doesn't mind keeping him company and it's only one night a week."

"Aren't I learning a thing or two today," said my aunt.

I was learning a thing or two as well.

"Your mammy is more than happy to pay that sort of rent; in fact, she probably offered." Aunt Iris was quiet for a moment. "She always had to be the best at everything. If I did well at school, she had to be twice as good. She's smart, so all she had do was try a bit harder. She was always the pretty one, the clever one and didn't like it if I shone. She was the youngest, so our parents spoilt her. She was livid beyond measure when Lachlan turned to me. He had tired of her self-interest.

"When your mammy married Liam and had a baby ... which was you," Aunt Iris continued, "she flaunted you before me. Months and months went by and I didn't fall pregnant. We had tests done and it showed I couldn't have a baby. But Brianna knew that. I had a bad fall from a horse years before and it was thought at the time I may not be able to have children. Your mother's gloating was too much for me.

"Even though she was married and gave birth to you, she still wanted Lachlan. So your da left. He was a lovely man ... still is I'm sure, wherever he is. Gentle, quiet and considerate. Too gentle for your ma. Liam had had enough. He said Lachlan could keep the house and Brianna. As they are brothers, the house was left to both of them. He was leaving for good, he said. And he did. Those two brothers lost their friendship, lost you, all due to your mammy's selfishness and need to dominate."

"Why didn't we live here in the beginning if the house was half da's?"

"Your daddy adored your ma, but he wasn't stupid. He knew she still liked Lachlan. He always hoped she'd grow to love him, but he didn't know Brianna like I did. He rented that little place when they married to keep Brianna away from Lachlan. He hoped it would safeguard their marriage."

"They must have been happy back then though?"

"As I said. Lachlan is weak. He had me and as Brianna threw herself at him, he enjoyed the attention. He was out working during the day. Often attending meetings. One of those was meeting your ma. Sometimes there'd be a phone call for him when he was meant to be attending something or other. I grew suspicious. So did Liam."

"What do you mean? Where was he?"

"Attending to your ma. At your house. At lunch times." She gasped with laughter, "Some lunch."

Laughter caused a stabbing pain in my aunt's belly that was so strong she couldn't speak.

"Please, aunty, please see a doctor."

She waved me away. "Run back to Brianna now, dear little Katie," she said in a gravelled gasp. "I've talked enough. I need quiet."

Mammy hadn't visited Iris once since she'd retreated to her room. When the pain got worse, Aunt Iris didn't come out at all. When I think about it now, my aunt never asked after my mammy either. I never mentioned my visits to mammy. She must have known where I went. My homework was never done and I'd spend the evening at it. After one visit when Iris's pain was excruciating, I couldn't hold back any longer.

"Mammy ... please visit Aunt Iris, she's not well. What say she dies and you haven't seen each other?"

"I'm too busy."

"You're not."

"I might catch what she's got."

"I've been visiting her and I'm all right."

"Oh, so you finally admit to it. Well, you're young ... stop bothering me about Iris."

It wasn't long after that my Aunty Iris died. Some said of a broken heart, but the doctors said it was bowel cancer. I heard she could have been saved if she'd sought medical care. I lost my lovely aunt. My support, my best friend, gone. Nothing but a big black empty hole remained. Her patience with my chatter, her company, her warmth, soft and comforting. Her passing left me cold and shivering, deserted. My rock chipped down to rubble.

Mammy didn't want to talk about her. The funeral was awful. Mammy stood at the back with the village tut-tutting and glancing daggers at her over their shoulders. I sat with Uncle Lachlan down the front and wept while he wept. A guttural howl filled the church. He must have loved her; a man could not cry like that unless he did. I was utterly bereft, as no doubt was he. It was the only time I felt close to my uncle.

EIGHT

Kate

At the funeral, a gate closed for me. Gone was adolescence as I stepped into adulthood. It was from then on that I took responsibility for myself. My chatter diminished. With my aunt gone, there was no one to babble with. I became silent, introspective; 'a quiet child', my school report proclaimed.

After a bit I grew friendly with a different group of school mates. Smart-arse girls, the ones who had 'done it', or so they declared. I liked being with them because they stopped me thinking. They pushed me to join their chaos. I told them they were so much fun. They weren't, but it boosted their egos and allowed me to stay. I didn't belong; they knew it, as did I, but it was better than the thunderous silence that inhabited my head. Their noise was loud. Mine was deafening. We smoked behind bushes, although I pretended. It was disgusting, but I puffed and blew the smoke and tried to make smoke rings. Eventually I tired of them, or they of me.

Then I entered my swot period. Subjects suddenly interested me and I wanted to do well at school. I was able to hide behind my schoolwork, which filled the inside of my head and was better than endless giggling. With intense homework there was no time for anything else.

While I was dealing with my grief, Lachlan was dealing with his. He was morose. He decided to wear black, which infuriated mammy.

"You're such a hypocrite," she said to Lachlan one day.

"I actually loved her, Brianna."

At this, mammy gasped, shocked and furious. She acted as if she and Lachlan now had a life together. But if mammy thought that, with her sister gone, there'd be no barriers between them, she was wrong.

We ate in the kitchen again, the three of us, but it was tense and I lost my appetite and grew thinner. Only Mrs Gallagher noticed. She enticed me to eat by making all my favourite treats, but it didn't work.

Mammy carried on being mammy; frivolous, flirty and forcefully cheerful. While Lachlan grunted replies, I knew he wasn't listening. The more he withdrew, the more boisterous mammy became. This drove me and Mrs Gallagher crazy. Stories about the antics of our household must have littered the village. Mrs Gallagher was fond of a story.

Then in the kitchen one morning, Mrs Gallagher announced she would be leaving. We were shocked. I realised how desperate the place would be without her. She was the only one who cared about me. How could she leave?

"No, please don't go, Mrs G," I said. "Please, please stay." I got up from my chair, ran and hugged her. She patted me and left the room.

"Mammy, you're annoying her. And me too. Stop making a fool of yourself."

Mammy looked at me, stunned. "How dare you."

"You could tone it down a notch," said Uncle Lachlan. He got up from the table. "I need to talk with Mrs Gallagher."

My mouth fell open, as did mammy's. Lachlan never criticised Brianna. Sometime later in the day, Uncle Lachlan must have done some serious talking with Mrs G and to my mother. Mammy toned it down and Mrs Gallagher said she'd see how it went.

All that Aunty Iris told me about my mammy had shown its teeth. I became more watchful of mammy's behaviour. She didn't seem to care that her sister had passed or notice how sad Lachlan was – or me for that matter.

After the talk with Mrs Gallagher and the harsh way Lachlan spoke to my mother, mammy changed her ways a little. She showed an interest in my schoolwork and told me how proud she was of me. I didn't really believe she read my school reports or noticed much about me at all, so focused was she on Lachlan. Her new resolve didn't last. Although she quietened down and stopped the outward flirting, she spent more and more time with Lachlan, away from me. Trailing him around the house.

Whether it was the irritating neediness of my mother or his grief, soon enough Lachlan took to the drink. He developed a whiskey habit at four o'clock, then at three and instead of just one drink, it would be two and three, until the hour joined into a single time slot and the glass didn't empty. Mammy had fun with him at first, taking a glass of white wine or a whiskey herself. But she couldn't keep it up and instead tried to get him to stop, or at least slow down. She encouraged him to take walks and they could be seen strolling in the garden together. They looked at old photos. Talked of days past. He didn't want to go for drives. But in the end, nothing worked. Not wanting to miss time with him, my mammy gave up on abstinence and resumed her alcohol consumption.

At weekends I sat with them with a cup of tea in my hand, but I may as well have been invisible. As they were both drunk, their talk of the past became gales of laughter at nothing at all. I drowned myself in homework or went for walks myself. Sometimes I met a friend in the village, but I didn't want to be involved in gossip, so the visits dwindled.

By bedtime Lachlan had usually passed out somewhere in the house and didn't want or need mammy. Iris would have had a chuckle. Finally, Brianna could have him totally without a need for secrecy, but he didn't want her.

There were three people living in that house, all in their separate corners. Mammy stalking Lachlan. Lachlan escaping mammy. And me avoiding them both.

NINE

Thakit

West Ireland – 2001

It was a Saturday, and I remember it was Saturday as both mammy and my brother were home. Colin often visited on his own on a Saturday. The neighbourhood was quiet. A few kids were out kicking a ball around.

Mammy by now, was happy. I had finally graduated from university.

That Saturday, it was like a pause button had been pressed, Colin and I were struck motionless. Driving up our street, and more importantly pulling up at our front door, a big flash black car glided to a halt. To me it was a limo, but Colin said it was just a big, shiny car. Flash cars were not so unusual but this one, with its darkened windows, stood out. They also didn't usually pull up outside our place. The car gleamed in the pale sunshine. Its chrome and polished blackness gave its slow-paced arrival the likeness of a scene from a sci-fi movie. It was so glossy the houses were reflected in its gleaming paintwork. My brother was hysterical with admiration, but he was way too cool to let it show.

"She's grand."

Was all he said.

The darkened windows hid the passengers from view. The driver stepped out. "Is your mammy in?"

By this stage Colin and I were at the front gate, along with the rest of the neighbourhood.

Not acting cool like my brother, I sprinted inside and out the back, interrupting mammy from hanging out the washing.

"Quickly, ma, come quickly." Mammy reluctantly walked to the front of the house and baulked at the door.

"Can I help you?" she said, as the driver by this stage was at the front door.

"Mrs Kelly?"

Mammy nodded.

"Have you a minute?" The driver escorted mammy to the car. She peered into the blackness just as the passenger's window slowly opened.

"If you wouldn't mind stepping into the car," the driver said, "we'll take a short drive to the causeway, away from the neighbourhood."

Colin was giving his full attention to the car, as did the neighbours, who gawped from doorways or hung out from their windows. Colin seemed unconcerned mammy was getting into a stranger's car. Or so I thought.

Colin sprang into life, "No ... no way. Our mother is not stepping anywhere, not without me coming along."

The driver, with questioning eyebrows, looked from the man in the back to mammy.

"I'll be fine, thank you, Colin. I know this man," said mammy. To the driver she said, "I won't be a minute."

Mammy quickly went back inside. She shushed me away as I followed hot on her heels. She sprinted up the stairs. She never did that. When she reappeared, I noticed she'd changed into a nice blouse and was smoothing her skirt as she walked to the door. There was lipstick on her mouth and she'd combed her hair. I was immediately alerted to something special going on. A big black car, a chauffeur and mammy straightening her clothes. All very suspicious.

As mammy walked to the car, Colin stepped forward. "Mammy, I'm worried."

"No, you're not, Colin dear. You just want a ride in the car. Run along now," she said with a parting gesture as though he was some irritating neighbour's child.

Who was she talking to? Run along like we were tiny people. Her manner and voice so changed it sounded quite alien.

"Won't be long," she said with a little wave.

The chauffeur held the door for her and guided her into the back to join a man whose face we couldn't see.

Colin and I stood on the pavement with our mouths open and watched our reflections disappear. I didn't like it. Neither did Colin, though for different reasons, even though he loved our mother as much as I did.

"You're imagining driving that car, aren't you?"

Colin nodded, "... and looking under the bonnet."

"What say she doesn't come back and we're just standing here like eejits?" I said.

TEN

Kate

West Ireland – 1999

Mammy's and Lachlan's life changed. By then I was into puberty. Lachlan seldom took any notice of me during the day but come evening when he had whiskey under his belt, he came for me. He took to wearing a green and yellow, woolly beanie with a yellow bobble. We came to learn this as a sign. He was on the hunt. And not for mammy. He had her. She was not the challenge. At first, I thought mammy might be jealous but she became protective. The nights he skulked around the house wearing the beanie were the nights mammy stayed close to me, keeping me in her room and locking the door.

Tap, tap, tap.

"Come out, Brianna, come out with our little Katie. It's your Lachy wanting to play. Come out, little Katie, it's your Uncle Lachy wanting to play with you," he repeated over and over, his voice thick with booze and lust.

We sat back from the door huddled on the couch, as if like a supernatural monster he might materialise through the walls.

"Come out ... come out and play with your Lachy. Your mammy will show you how. Watch how mammy does it ... then we can try."

Tap, tap, tap.

With his speech sloshed with alcohol, the invitations grew spookier. I clung to mammy's arm. Eventually she got sick of him scaring us, so she dug up her defiance and spoke through the door. "Now be a good Lachy and go to bed. Go on, Lachy, off to bed now." He stopped like a naughty little boy and clomped along the hall.

Another night with her patience diminished and anger up, mammy called through the door, "Get away from us, you disgusting man," then gulped at what she'd said. She still loved him. If she was worried she would lose his favour, they were wasted concerns. By morning he remembered nothing.

The woolly beanie began appearing after dinner, so we had fair warning. The beanie nights became habitual, two or three times a week. He gave up on mammy and called only for me.

Tap, tap, tap.

"Is Katie ready? Can she come out to play. Katie, Kateeee, come out to playeee."

Mammy turned to me one night. "If I'm not here, don't you ever, ever go out, Katie ... never ... when he's drunk or when you see the beanie on his head, keep the door locked ... you hear? Never."

"Yes, mammy."

"Never talk to him when he's drunk. He's a different man and has no reason in his head."

"Can't you tell him to stop?"

"When he's sober, he remembers nothing of the night before. It's just the way he is. Up to a point he can take the drink just fine and then he goes through a gate in his head and a monster walks out. He's a wonderful man but not when the drink gets inside him. He's two different men."

I began to understand why my Aunt Iris said mammy could have him; she'd had enough. My aunt hadn't cared anymore. Why mammy still cared I didn't understand but she always made a fuss of him when he was sober. I kept away from him as much as I could, drunk or sober. He'd always been distant towards me, never played with me when I was little, only occasionally asking me about school. We had little contact.

Lachlan's moods continued, becoming darker. In the mornings he was like grey leftovers. Then the colours changed to brighter hues. For a short period in the early afternoon, he was his old self, even amusing. Although I was nothing to him, his presence was felt by anyone around. He was big, robust and his voice thrilling. Late in the afternoon the man crept into his cave. Later still the monster emerged. Round and round every day. Mammy was always there watching him. Her coaxing smile encouraging him to stop the drink but that got on his nerves. Mammy did not give up; she hung on hoping for change.

I saw the full extent of her days with Lachlan at weekends and school holidays. I believed mammy truly loved him. Mrs Gallagher kept me fully informed with the goings on while I was at school. Lachlan didn't go out and mammy worked part time. To give her fair due, by then she tried to be a mother to me and a carer to him, which took its toll. She could no longer keep up with his drinking and quit herself. Her failure to change him became evident and she grew impatient. Arguments flared. He was never aggressive or violent; more scornful and whiney. Mammy finally reacted when his behaviour sapped her tolerance level.

The sound of doors slamming began, reverberating throughout the house. The walls shook. I took books into Aunt Iris's room and closed myself off. The sound continued, faint and distant. With a warm smile, Mrs Gallagher brought me special treats.

A day or two later I heard the clatter of something breaking against a closed door. Lachlan cackled like an attic dweller. I wasn't scared so much as numb. That day I was tucked away in Aunt Iris's room.

Mammy and Lachlan by then were only interested in themselves. As usual I tuned out and read a book. One night a particularly heated row filled the house. Hiding in Aunty Iris's room, I cracked open the door. First I heard the screaming, then heard mammy storm out of Lachlan's room and run down the stairs with Lachlan following, shouting and flailing his arms. More shouting in the hallway. Creeping along walls, out of sight, I followed them. Doors slammed as their argument moved in and out of various rooms. Finally, at the front door; *bang*. A second bang as a car door slammed. The engine revved into life and the car drove off, spitting gravel in its wake.

I never saw my mammy alive again.

ELEVEN

Kate

Although Aunty Iris had been my best friend and missing her was tragic beyond belief, when my mother died, I hardly knew how to breathe. She was my mother. Tormented as it was, she was my world.

Sadness swallowed Lachlan's face, the blue of his eyes washed away like the tide. His skin sagged, dragging his body along with it. I was still at school, so I had distractions, but I feared going home, expecting drunkenness to permeate every corner of the house. Unexpectedly, Lachlan stopped drinking and spent his time on the computer. He occasionally asked me how something worked. He was constantly on the phone with his accountant looking after his shares and business portfolios. There was much work to be done, he said. I expect he'd let his finances lag after Aunty Iris died and drink replaced his occupation.

The business intensity did not last long. Soon the woolly beanie reappeared. It was late one afternoon and Mrs Gallagher, having prepared food, was about to leave for the day. She reminded me to lock my door after I'd eaten. Without mammy, I had reason to be scared. Taking my dinner into my room, I stayed hidden, sat on my bed, clutched my book and waited.

The quietness in the house filled me with dread. Although the beanie had made its appearance, nothing happened. Expectation of a knock on the door shallowed my breathing. I woke in the morning in a foetal position still clutching my book. I hadn't trusted the calm of the night. Nothing happened but the expectation that something would was unbearable.

I spoke with the gardener on his next visit. Mrs Gallagher must have rung him as he anticipated my request. He dismantled my bed, lugged the furniture downstairs and created a little flat all of my own. The compact home felt safe with a sturdy lock on the door.

Both Mrs Gallagher and the gardener asked if I'd like to stay somewhere else. That filled me with more dread. At least here I was in my own surroundings. I had mammy's possessions around me and Aunty Iris's room I could shelter in. Playing with her pretty jewels was a comfort. No, I did not want to go anywhere.

"Mammy taught me how to deal with him, I'll be fine." Then as an afterthought, "Thank you anyway and please don't spread this around the village." Mrs Gallagher promised. The gardener was not a gossip.

The woolly beanie made its appearance one or two nights a week. Eventually Lachlan's knock started up again and became a regular occurrence. "Katie Kateeee … come out to playee. Your Uncle Lachy has some really fun games … come on, Katie. I know you're in there … Kateee."

I remembered Mammy's words, *Keep the door locked and never ever go out, whatever he says or promises.* Rather than coax or yell at him to leave, I ignored him. Locked in, I stayed quiet as a mouse. Sometimes I found him in the morning asleep on the floor near my door.

Word got out at school about my home life. Mrs Gallagher, I thought, but when I asked her, she reminded me of the day the crowd I'd hung out with came to the house, uninvited. It was after school and Lachlan was well on his way by then although the woolly beanie had not joined him. The girls played up to him, flirted and teased him. He was still handsome in a saggy sort of way. He was putty in their hands.

Soon after, one of these so-called friends asked me what it was like with an older man. "Like this,' I said and grabbed the front of her blouse and pushed her up against a brick wall. I thrust my forearm up under her chin and pressed hard. When she could barely breathe, I let her go and walked off. That changed it for me, I no longer took it on the chin. I developed the beast of a lashing tongue to match my forearm. Nobody bothered me after that. Nobody bothered me at all, friend or foe.

Life in the big house became more and more intolerable.

TWELVE

Thakit

2001

Colin and I stood looking at the space where the car had been. Colin, ever the pragmatist, said, "Shut it Thakky, of course she's coming back." He shrugged his shoulders as if he felt it was a normal morning and sauntered inside.

She was gone for an hour. I'd been watching the minutes tick by. We both leapt up when we heard a deep-throated beep. The motor was so quiet we didn't hear the car stop outside. I was out the front of the house in a giant leap, gripping the front gate. Colin did his saunter thing. The driver opened the door and elegantly assisted mammy out. She was all in one piece. Without so much as a by your leave, she stepped onto the pavement and went inside. We stood watching the car as it pulled away. The neighbourhood was out again gawping, having not missed a thing.

Mammy walked straight into the kitchen, filled the kettle and stood with her back to the table as we sat and waited for her to speak.

And waited.

She turned with the teapot in her hand. "What?"

"What ... what?" I said. "You tell us what."

"What?" repeated Colin.

"He's just someone I used to work for. Don't get agitated. I expect we've given the neighbours something to talk about over the weekend." Mammy put the teapot down. "I'm sorry you couldn't inspect the car, Colin, maybe another time."

"There's another time?" I said.

"I have to get home, mammy, so can you please tell us what's going on," said Colin.

Mammy was teasing us. She smirked as she poured the tea. When she was in one of these moods, I've-got-something-you-want, we had to just wait it out. Colin and I clicked to her game at the same time, so we stirred our tea and ignored her, burning beneath.

"He has work for you, Thakky. To be honest, it spooked me."

Colin and I jumped to this comment, stopped stirring our tea, spoons mid-air and waited once again for her to speak.

"Remember the time we sat at the table and you visualised looking for someone in the sunshine?"

I nodded.

"Well, he wants you to find someone. Well, not find exactly as he thinks he knows where she is, but bring her home, back to Ireland. It will involve travel, being away from home," mammy stressed. "I'm not happy about it."

Colin looked aghast. He looked at me. "You lucky fucker."

"Colin!" Mammy spat.

"Why on earth are you not happy about it?" said Colin.

"Because," said mammy, "it's not a proper job, there are no career prospects. It's play money for a play job."

"It could be my gap year," I said, to make her feel better.

"How many gap years are you going to take? What have you seriously done to find a proper job? Use your degree?"

"He's only just graduated, mammy."

"Only just," said our ma, "only just ... how many years has it been? All you've been doing is piddling around with silly jobs."

"Here we go. I gotta go, tell me all about it later, Thakky." Colin kissed mammy and left.

With Colin gone, I waited again for mammy to continue. She was irritating the hell out of me.

"He's wanting Kate home. She keeps moving around but it's time she came home."

Mammy was talking in riddles. "Not much sense so far, mammy, do go on."

There was an interminably long pause before she spoke. She placed her hands in her lap and sat back into the chair, sighed. "Kate is a young woman, a friend of his family, who was staying with him. They had an argument and she took off. He found her in London. Well, someone found her. At age sixteen, she was living above a club, working as a cocktail waitress. She's now eighteen. She and the club's owner have gone to ground. He's not sure whether she was living, as in cohabiting, with the club's owner, or just staying there."

"Grand ... go on."

"It is not grand, young man. Sixteen. She was a child."

"No, not grand at all. Go on."

"Then just this morning he found out she and the club's owner flew to Trinidad and Tobago. He's missing but Kate's still there, living there under a different name. He wants you to go to Trinidad and bring her home."

"How the hell do I do that?"

"You'll have to use that expansive imagination of yours. I'm not happy about it."

"So you said."

"He'll pay for your hotel and give you living expenses. And the air fare of course. Who knows … getting you out of the house may push you into some sort of reality. He wants you to ring him. He'll go over everything. He'll give you a mobile to use to speak with him."

"Wow." I wasn't sure if this was all a joke, but then mammy didn't have that type of sense of humour. Nevertheless, it sounded ridiculous. "Does he have a name?"

"Aedan."

"Aedan who?"

"That's all you need to know."

"No surname?"

Mammy shook her head.

"Like Madonna."

"Don't be a smart-arse, Ryan. You'll know him as Aedan."

"This is my kind of reality."

Mammy got cross and I couldn't tell if it was with me, herself, so-called Aedan, or just life in general.

"Okay," I said. I sat in a gobsmacked kind of fug. "Wow … grand."

THIRTEEN

Kate

2000

It was late when I left the house. Carrying a backpack and wheeling a small suitcase, I escaped in the dark. Fear must have given me an aroma, as even I could smell its pungency. I worried dogs who knew me would catch my scent and bark. My heart was in my mouth, Lachlan's voice still ringing in my ears. At sixteen, my virginity was intact and there was no way my uncle Lachlan was getting it. At least now he never would.

"Ah, Katie, you're so beautiful, just like your mammy."

That last picture, which held me back and kept me going at the same time; Lachlan leering with a pathetic smile.

I'd walked from the library upstairs clutching a hard-backed book I'd selected. I'd crept as quietly as a mouse, thinking Lachlan had passed out in his room in a drunken stupor.

He hadn't. He was right behind me. The woolly beanie stretched down over his ears, the pompom bouncing. He staggered along the hallway nearly upon me. Before I had a chance to run, he grabbed me, pressed me hard against the wall, his loose, slobbering lips searching mine. His tongue flicking like a lizard's. Sandwiched tight between my clutched book, the wall and Lachlan's boozy body, I wriggled and moved my head from side to side, trying to keep clear of his stinking breath.

"You need to be ready for the world, Katie," he slurred. He pressed harder. "I'm your uncle, Katie, I'll show you … I'll be gentle … you will find it wonderful."

Unsteady on his feet, he wavered. Taking advantage of the minute relapse, I gathered my strength and heaved. With the book I whacked him over his head, forgetting the woolly bobble – the book bounced. My lapse in judgement and his surprise, worked in my favour. I pushed again, with all my force.

"Whooaaah," he staggered, a cry peppered with laughter. He toppled over the top stair and away he went.

From the height of the top step, I had an aerial view. I was rigid with fear, my breath suspended. Barely believing what had just happened, I couldn't move. He lay broken on the floor below, crooked like a Z.

Air gushed back into my lungs. I stood, for who knows how long, not knowing what to do. He lay lifeless. Any second I expected to hear him cackle, "Katie, you're a naughty little girl." But the words didn't come.

I was alone in the house. I was scared, then relieved he wasn't after me. Then fear swarmed over me again. He was dead. He had to be dead. No one keeps still for that long. I had no experience with dead bodies. Death, yes. My mammy, repaired by the funeral parlour after the car accident, my aunt from illness, but not a dead, lifeless body up close and seen on impact. Lifeless, dead and I had caused it.

I crept down the stairs. During his fall, he'd broken a banister. Careful not to trip on pieces of wood, on reaching him I circled, watching, waiting for a movement. The flicker of an eye, a hand suddenly grabbing my leg. Nothing. I pushed my foot gently into his side, onto his leg, his arm, but his body lay still.

My uncle was dead. I had killed him.

My mind brewed with thoughts and finally I knew I didn't want to be around for the outcome. I no longer wanted to be in the house at all. Leave, that's what it came down to. To go where, I didn't know but leave the house was a must.

My thoughts focused into flight mode. In various cupboards and wardrobes, were stored suitcases of various shapes and sizes. They were old and hard to carry. Finally, I found what I was looking for. A newish suitcase on two wheels. I found my favourite backpack and started on my rounds.

First stop, my aunt's room. Since the time she'd passed, nothing had been disturbed. Rather than a sacred monument left in her honour, it was a room no one had bothered to do anything with. Except me. A place where I came for peace and to play with her jewels. To me it had been and still was a place of intrigue, with its quirky little sculptures, drawings and paintings scattered across the walls. Lace doilies covered the dressing table. In the drawers beneath, old lace handkerchiefs lay neatly folded. These had belonged to a long line of grandmothers. From time to time, Mrs Gallagher dusted. She wouldn't allow the cleaning lady to enter the room.

Carefully folding jewels into Aunt Iris's handkerchiefs and doilies, I packed them in my backpack. I found cloth bags protecting expensive leather handbags and took these to protect the other jewellery. I took one small leather handbag, my favourite. The softness of the leather I used to stroke when Aunt Iris had shown me her collection. I packed photos of my mother and my aunt, along with various members of generations passed that I found hidden away in bottom drawers.

Then I checked on Lachlan. He lay as before.

In my room, I pulled out my clothes and laid them on the bed. With winter clothes so cumbersome and taking up so much space, I wore layer upon layer. It was night and cold but provided it didn't get colder, I'd be fine. I packed and repacked, each time eliminating until down to a full suitcase and a bulging backpack. I was never coming back. A decision made while I packed.

In my mother's room was one old photograph of her when she was young, with a man I didn't know. Was this my father? Packing it I decided to inspect when I had time.

In my search of the house, I considered the silver, but it was too bulky, too heavy. My uncle's study gave up a good find. There it was: a thick stash of cash.

Returning to the body at the bottom of the stairs, my uncle still lay in the same position, completely still. With no key, the house seldom locked, I closed the heavy door behind me. I didn't look back. A clear night was given me, so rare to see the stars shine with clarity as if guiding me and sending me luck.

Beyond the village I walked the road that connected to a busier one. At one point I took a breath, realising I hadn't filled my lungs since leaving the house.

A roadside service station shone in the distance. I knew all the risks of accepting lifts, but still I took one. I wanted no record of me on a bus or train until later. Good fortune came with a truck driver who was a good man, more like a da. He must have known I was a runaway. Perhaps he smelt my fear.

"To London," I said, "I have friends there." He took me out of his way to ensure I made the right connections. I wore enough make-up to make myself look older but not too much to look cheap or tarty. My hair was up. I looked classic. I tried not to talk too much, not wanting to expose my fear. Eventually I was in Rosslare and took the ferry to Pembroke and from there made my way to London. My entire trip was made by truck, bus, train and ferry. These last public transport journeys were a necessity. Sleeping when I dared, I was exhausted by the time I reached London and ready to collapse.

Dog-tired as I was, my priority was to find somewhere to sleep.

FOURTEEN

Kate/Pippa

London, England

Barely able to keep my eyes open, I arrived in London with nowhere to stay, no clue what to do and no experience in finding accommodation in a big city or anywhere else. As I left the station, three backpackers walked ahead of me seeming to know where they were going. I followed. We arrived at a hostel. Bright signage lifted my energy. Entering the door, I found the place had a sense of fun, with people coming and going.

Approaching the desk with as much confidence as I could muster, I gave my name: "Pippa Katherine Thornton." Why, who knows? The name simply popped into my head. No, I did not have a reservation when asked for identification, I said I'd been robbed. The receptionist looked at my luggage. I was offered a shared or private room. I took the private with an ensuite and paid in cash. She looked at me askance. *Just been robbed, eh?* She took the cash. The moment I entered the room, I lay down on the bed, fully clothed and slept for ten hours.

Hunger woke me. Retrieving food left over from my journey, I headed to the eating area. Feeling scared and out of my depth, I thought I could learn something from the guests. The majority of backpackers appeared to be on a gap year and came from all corners of the globe. University degrees under their belts or ones they hoped to gain, they spoke of careers either intended or with placements waiting for their return. Overwhelmed, I nodded but offered nothing. I had nothing.

My ambitions in that regard hadn't formed yet. I had no training. I hadn't had time to dream of what I wanted to be or where I wanted to go. Death and distress were all I'd got up to in the scheme of things. What I did have was wealth. Nevertheless, a job was the first thing on my mind.

I was an Irish village schoolgirl plunged into a chaotic universe I knew only from television, movies or books. I had innocence and wonder on my side; everything was new and anything was possible. I discovered I had hope and fortitude in buckets.

Mesmerised as I wandered the city, acclimatising to the traffic noise; the unknown was thrilling beyond measure. Notices adorned windows of cafés and shops for 'casuals wanted'. I walked for hours, totally distracted. The second day I walked with intention in my heart and came across a doorway with a sign: 'WAIT AND BAR STAFF WANTED'. I don't know why I picked that one; maybe it was the small, neat print rather than the blazoned sloppy wording of others. The type looked more professional to my untrained eye. Later I realised the sign was permanent. I got the job. Few questions were asked as they wanted someone to start straight away. There was a uniform that I'd pay for out of my wages.

With my possessions still locked in my room, I worried they'd go missing. My next priority was where to store them. I could hardly wear the jewels with the skimpy uniform I'd been supplied.

My accommodation changed. Someone heard of someone who knew someone working at the bar who had a contact who was looking for someone to share a flat. And not far away. "So where do I lock up my crown jewels?" I joked. The answer was given in jest but was exactly the news I wanted to hear.

"Oh, I keep mine in a safety deposit box," came the reply, mimicking a posh accent.

Wearing the supplied scanty outfit, I began collecting glasses and doing general work no one else wanted. In the early hours of the morning a newly found friend and I walked back to my flat, as she lived nearby.

"How are you liking it?" Tippi asked.

"It's fine, grand," I said.

"You're doing all right." She stopped. "I turn left here. Sleep well, Pippa."

With my past memory still fresh, I slept soundly, knowing there would be no beanie-clad uncle tapping on my door.

At work I said little, watched and educated myself during those early training days. Soon I was promoted to waitressing where tips increased. I was expected to be cute and nice to the mostly male clientele. My experience with my uncle kept me from getting involved. Roaming hands were not allowed – my rules. I learnt how to say nothing but show scorn and a 'naughty, naughty' with my forefinger. The customers loved my rules and my tips grew. The boss liked my pluckiness. It turned the punters on, he told me. As there'd been no complaints, he was happy to keep me on the floor. The boss didn't know money was not my motivation, unlike the other girls. I was marking time and distancing myself from home.

Rumours started that the boss fancied me. He was older. I kept my distance. He was the boss. I didn't think it was true, in any case. Stanley had become single after his wife moved out. An obvious target for the girls. In the not-so-distant past, his family had arrived from southern Italy. He was striking; dark olive skin with heavy eyebrows above dark mischievous eyes and a pronounced nose. Even his lack of height was no impediment.

Although he seemed considerate, I didn't give him a thought beyond being a boss. I didn't have experience with how bosses acted, so I thought him very fair. He was a straight talker, so everyone knew where they stood. I seemed to be the only girl not making a play for Stanley Russo. Getting by each day was all I thought about. I saved my tips and added them to my nest egg.

"Boss or just Mr Russo," he said to call him. Until he started inviting me for lunch in his flat above the club, then I could call him Stanley. I kept the invitations to myself. I told him little of my history – there wasn't much to tell, so he filled in the gaps. My policy of not talking too much proved useful. In fact, Stanley presumed correctly; I had run away from somewhere in Ireland. I also grew sick of the Irish thing, so I learnt to neutralise my accent.

"Pippa," Stanley said one day, "it's time you had legal papers. You don't have to tell me the details, but it's not good for you to be a nameless, stateless person forever."

He gave me the information I needed to obtain necessary papers. When I was going through my mother's belongings, I'd found mine and my mother's birth certificates. I kept these with my jewels. With Stanley's and the girls' knowhow, I applied for a passport. My real identity remained private.

Stanley was about twenty years my senior, I figured. He was kind to me and respected my decision not to sleep with any of the customers. Even the very wealthy ones, as many of the girls did earning good tips, which most of them spent as quickly as they were earned.

"What makes you tick, Pippa?" Stanley asked me.

"I don't," I said, "tick."

"Why don't you move in here with me? I have a big apartment."

"What are you saying, Stanley?"

"I'm saying, move in with me. I like you … a lot."

I remained silent.

"Look, you're not obliged to sleep with me. In fact, you can have your own room. Your own bathroom."

"And my own lock?"

"Christ, Pippa, I'm not a bloody rapist."

I said nothing.

"So you've had a bad experience. Yes, you can have a lock." The pause burst. "Any other demands?"

"No. But what's in it for you?" I asked.

"Oooh, spoken like a true dealmaker … nothing … if you don't want there to be. You'd be company, that's all. To make it fair, you can pay me a nominal rent."

Again, I listened.

"I like having you around. Okay?"

I wasn't so sure about that. I was a kid. He could have the pick of any woman. Why me? All the same, I accepted his offer. The living conditions were much better than the ones I was sharing by then with two of my co-workers downstairs.

My relationship with the girls changed. Or rather, theirs with me. They went mental. Some were envious, some congratulated me, but others were downright mean and nasty. The gossip spread all the way to the clientele. I lived with the boss and they should watch what they said. Most of the clientele were friends or acquaintances of his anyway and it didn't bother them. Mean and nasty crept into my working existence. My things, like bra tops, disappeared just before I was due to start my shift. Mostly I kept my stuff upstairs but if it was only an hour or two between shifts, I left my gear in the crowded changing room. I didn't report any of it to Stanley, hoping it would die down.

The clinch came over something else.

FIFTEEN

Kate/Pippa

2001

Stanley and I shared dinner in his apartment. He was a good cook and he liked to have someone to cook for. On one of the quieter nights, Stanley and I lingered over dinner as I wasn't working that night.

"So, Pippa, will you ever sleep with me?"

"I'll think about it when I'm eighteen."

He laughed. "Always the dealmaker ... and when will that be?"

"I'll be seventeen in one month."

"Jeezus ... you're only sixteen?"

I nodded.

"Why didn't I know this?"

"Nobody asked."

"Shit, Pippa, you're barely legal, especially in a place like this."

He swore to himself. "I'll have to take you out."

"Are you kicking me out?"

"Not out of here, out of the bar."

"I have to work," I said, though I didn't when I thought about all the cash and jewels I had in my possession. Not for a while anyway.

But I had a long way to go in life. The stash was my retirement fund, whatever age that would be.

"I'll get you a job in the office. Train you up in the business. I'm thinking on my feet now, so I don't know what, yet ... fuck's sake," he muttered.

As I wasn't to be kicked out, I relaxed. I was glad to leave the constant haranguing from the girls. Whether it was questions about what he was like in bed to what was my secret. Even if it was praise, I was sick of it. I left my skimpy uniform in the changing room for anyone who could use it.

My passport came through, Pippa Katherine Thornton. Proud as punch, I showed it to Stanley. My correct date of birth proved my age as I hadn't bothered to change that.

"And all this time I thought Pippa was just a name you made up. All the girls do it. And the men too. I imagine many of the clientele are not who they say they are."

I felt mean concealing the truth from him. In that world of false everything, I wasn't sure if he was who he said he was either. He may have thought I hadn't learnt any tricks of the trade yet. It was never discussed again so it wasn't an issue.

"You drive a hard bargain, Pippa. So I have to wait until you're eighteen?" he mentioned once again.

"And then I'll think about it."

He kept his sex life private, never shoved it in my face to prove anything. I'm sure he had one. Women threw themselves at him. No one was sure where I stood. Knowledge leaked out I had my own room and therefore it was thought I might be a relative. Stanley never elaborated and neither did I. Our shared unspoken joke.

I helped him entertain his associates, not knowing who they were. I spoke little, smiled a lot and refilled glasses. Basically the same as my job downstairs. To further teach me and help him out, Stanley showed me his bookkeeping and how he ran the business. He liked to keep things untraceable. He didn't trust the internet. Keeping the police and the tax department on side, he kept two sets of books. His dealings below the line were written by hand and kept in a safe.

Towards the end of my seventeenth year, things got tricky for Stanley. One too many deals. Someone wanted him out of the business, wanted his bar, said he wasn't running things properly. The new guy on the block was taking over. Stanley aged almost overnight. He became edgy and I saw flecks of fear in his eyes. I sensed something was building and packed my bags, living out of my suitcase in my room. I collected my stash from my safety deposit box. My instinct to run was still strong but I had faith in Stanley's timing. He wanted to survive too.

He didn't discuss anything with me but having lived with him, I knew his silent world by observation. I could read him like a book. Then the day came.

"We have to go, Pippa, pack what you can … now. We're being picked up in ten minutes. In-cabin bag size only. Do you have one?"

"What's an in-cabin bag size?"

"Here, I've got a spare."

I'd already updated my luggage and had bought a bag of just the same size. When he showed me, I said, "I have one … already packed."

He looked a little shocked and a tiny smile creased his face. "Good girl."

He was taking me with him. I had expected to run on my own. His concern astounded me. He'd never tried to get into my room and respected my terms. He was a marvel in my eyes.

We flew out that day to Trinidad and Tobago, me as Pippa Katherine Thornton, wearing my winter clothes with summer ones underneath. As before, my new bag was bulging.

Excitement was unquestionable. Fear was Stanley's. I felt blessed to be with him and now knew he'd protect me.

SIXTEEN

Kate/Pippa/Felicity

Trinidad and Tobago

Stanley knew someone who knew someone, and we stayed in this someone's villa out of Port-of-Spain. We had views of the sea. We were both exhausted, but I spent an hour or two looking out across the ocean. It wasn't like the Atlantic Ocean around Ireland, grey with serious intent. This was full-bodied, buoyant and friendly. Blue, not grey. I felt small in the expansiveness of this world, but at the same time felt I belonged in it. It was a similar feeling to how the stars had affected me when I walked out of the big house that night.

With no idea what heat felt like, I was shocked when we landed. I hurriedly pulled off the layers and carried them on my arm. Everything was so different. Faces, smells, sounds. Adventure prickled my skin. Stanley on the other hand, was tired, worried and watchful.

When I came back in from the balcony, Stanley was asleep. There were three bedrooms in this house, all as big as one another, so I took one with a sea view. I wanted the ocean to be the first thing I saw when I woke and the last before sleeping.

I woke early and from the balcony breathed the air, the salty smell of the sea. As Stanley was still asleep, I went back to bed and fell asleep. He woke me with the smell of tea under my nose. Stanley was still on edge even after his very long rest. We were now well into the next day. We had breakfast on the balcony and said little. Eventually Stanley spoke.

"Pippa, I'm in trouble. Big trouble. I don't want you to be involved. I have one request. I know you're not eighteen yet, but will you sleep with me? Then you must go. I'll find you somewhere to live, but you must not be involved with me anymore."

I think at that moment I fell in love with him. I couldn't bear the thought of not being with him.

"I'm not leaving you, Stanley."

"You have no choice. I will not be staying here beyond tomorrow. I can't tell you where I'm going, but I do want you to be safe."

"I'm not leaving you, Stanley."

"You are. There are no terms, conditions or deals on this."

He said nothing more but took my hand.

"Will you sleep with me tonight?" He chuckled and said, "I could say it in Italian if that would sound more romantic."

"I will, Stanley. I'll sleep with you now if you'd like."

Desire and surprise filled his eyes. Did he really think I would say no? Or at the very least, put up conditions?

Our day was spent in and around the villa in the warm sunshine, pretending life was magical and normal. We made love from the moment I said yes. He must have guessed it was the first time for me. Gentle, caring and loving, I was swept into an ocean where we were the only people in existence.

In London our lives had been geared all around his business. To spend a day with him doing nothing was beyond anything I imagined. We swam naked in the pool and drank chilled champagne from the pool's edge, interspersed with making love. That day I'd never felt so warm, so cared for, so totally at one with someone.

I woke feeling sumptuous, the world a different place bathed in a pink glow. Nothing lasts. An icy cold wind blew as reality struck. My Stanley. I could hear him in another room.

"I can't leave you, Stanley," I called from the bed.

He walked back into the bedroom and stood looking at me from the door. He was fully dressed. He came to the bed and held me, cradled me.

"There's a car picking you up in half an hour. I've found a place for you to stay. It's an apartment in a gated community. I've paid two months' rent. You will have to manage from there. I wasn't sure if you wanted to stay in Trinidad and I'm sure you don't know either. I thought two months will give you breathing space." He held me at arm's length, "Pippa ... thank you for making me wait. It was the best day and night of my life. I'll never forget it or you."

I held back my tears, not wanting to waste a moment with him.

"One last thing, Pippa, I've got an EU passport for you in the name of Felicity Doncaster. There are some visas in there too in case you want to take off to the States or someplace."

More tears welled up behind my eyes. I fought them back. I hadn't cried since my mammy died. If I let the flood-gates open, I'd never stop.

I knew he was serious and only he knew how serious the situation was. I could argue no longer. To make his life easier, I respected his wish as he'd respected mine. After kissing and hugging him inside the front door, I walked. Every step dragged as if I was in a bad dream. Each step felt like negotiating my way through thick sticky reeds taller than me. Suddenly the waiting taxi was in front of me. It was the longest walk in my life, I stepped in and left. I didn't look back.

At the new gated community, I used the code Stanley had given me. The taxi took me through those security gates and we entered manicured grounds so immaculate I thought I was in a toy town. I half expected to see a miniature train appear. After the driver dropped me off, I coded into another gate and from there into the building. One flight of stairs and on that floor, another code, then I entered the apartment. I was in.

My new home contained two bedrooms and two levels, with the living area downstairs. There was no view of the ocean, but a small courtyard with plants I didn't recognise around the perimeter. The apartment was furnished, clean and modern. The papers for the rental lay on the kitchen bench.

The end of my seventeenth year and despite all I'd been through, suddenly I knew nothing of the world. Apart from my early life in a big house in a village in Ireland, I knew only Stanley's world. He must have known all along we'd part. Panic set in as I stood in the middle of the living area. As much as I respected his wish, I couldn't let him go. I had to keep an eye on him, make sure he was okay. Perhaps he was still in my vicinity.

The next day I caught a taxi back to the villa, but I could only give directions as I didn't have an address. The driver was an old local and knew every inch of the area. Following my description, we finally found the villa. I asked him to wait out of sight.

Skulking the last bit, keeping close to the roadside shrubs, I snuck around to the back, to the balcony where we'd sat together. The villa was still, the blinds down. It breathed emptiness. I took a risk and stood in sight of the windows. If he was in there, he'd see me.

There was not even a flick of a blind. The tears ran down my face as I whispered Stanley's name. He was gone.

The taxi dropped me back to my apartment. I sat in the lounge room, numb. Life had left me.

SEVENTEEN

Kate/Felicity

2002

It was weeks, not days I stayed in a state of detachment; or so it seemed. My eighteenth birthday came and went. I cried. I couldn't eat. Food tasted like cotton wool. Venturing out, I roamed the streets to places Stanley might visit. I really didn't know where he'd go, I only knew him as a club owner and manager. I didn't even know if he liked the heat, the sunshine or the sea, something I realised I loved. My winter clothes lay forlorn in my backpack, bereft, perhaps never to be worn again.

There was no way to contact Stanley. I bought a prepaid phone; I don't know why. I didn't use it. I had no friends. When that thought hit me, after coming to terms with Stanley's disappearance, I hit another low. Shed more tears. Tears of self-pity, utter loneliness.

Beneath the numbness of my being, lay anger. So deep when I discovered it, I doubled up in pain as it burned. This hate surfaced and raged. Finally hunger came in waves. Hunger may have been there before, but I hadn't felt it. Then it hit me so forcefully I wasn't sure if I had the ability to find a shop or a café. As I walked from the apartment, something felt different.

The day was bright and sunny, and its heat drove out my anger. The shadow of despair lifted. I had to survive; that's what bodies do, survive. I found a café and ate and ate. I'd never eaten so much in one sitting and couldn't remember being so hungry. I ran to the bathroom and threw up. I looked at my reflection as I splashed water on my face. Who was that person: Kate, Pippa or Felicity? I didn't know any of them. They all looked terrible; thin and wan.

The waiter in the café asked if I was okay. Could he help? Kindness brought fresh tears to my eyes. I cried right there in front of him. He let me sit out the back beyond the kitchen.

"I'm okay now," I said as I emerged. "I'll be all right ... thank you."

"Come back if you're not. I finish in two hours. Let me buy you a coffee at least. Something to eat. I know you lost it all."

I smiled. "I'm going for a swim. There's a pool where I live."

"The offer's there if you want it."

That day I taught myself to swim, following instructions I found at the local internet café. Writing it down, I followed the steps, one stroke at a time. First, I learnt to float.

Afterwards, the sun's magic revived me. I burnt as I'd never experienced that intensity before. I didn't care. I found it exhilarating.

Not understanding at the time, I can see how it was baby steps to recovery. Not only from losing Stanley but leaving home, losing my aunt, followed by my mother, fear of my uncle, his death. The exercise gave me an appetite. I gained body weight and muscles as my laps increased.

One morning, waking afresh to the reality I would never, ever see Stanley again, he, in one night had become the love of my life. The nicest man I ever knew and one whom I'd lost. Somewhere there was a blessing in that. A measure for future feelings.

That morning the knowledge hit me that I would continue to live and needed to get on with it.

EIGHTEEN

Kate/Felicity/Caroline

Paying an extra month's rent since Stanley's contribution was nearing its end, I decided to stay in Trinidad. Where else was I going to go? During the following month I looked for another apartment. One empty of tear stains. And smaller. I sold a piece of jewellery rather than use my cash. I didn't have to work immediately, and, besides, I didn't know what to do. I knew a lot about the nightclub business in London, but I didn't want to be involved in that anymore. That was Stanley's world, not mine.

Only eighteen, I felt fifty. What an eighteenth birthday mine had been. Miserable, alone, weepy, barely noticing it had come and gone. When I came out of that gloom at least I had eighteen on my side. My life was ahead of me. My hair was long, and the sun gave it highlights. It hung down my back in waves. I looked okay. It was time I met someone, or people generally.

My first task was a new passport and a few visas while they were at it. I'd learnt a thing or two in London about that. I chose Caroline Katherine Clark. I didn't like the name Felicity and Stanley wouldn't have known my desire to keep Katherine as a middle name. I was also worried Stanley's mob knew of the name Felicity.

While seeking a new apartment, I met someone in the real

estate office as I looked through their listings. A conference had just concluded and people flooded out to the reception area. A man interrupted me, offering assistance. Despite feeling he was being intrusive, I recognised his London accent. At first I was fearful he might be pursuing me. Not in a friendly way. The thought he might be hunting me diminished as it slowly dawned on me he was chatting me up. I wasn't interested but he was someone to talk to. We had England in common, namely London, which was all I knew. There was a café not far and could we continue over a coffee? He saw my hesitancy.

Although Stanley said he wanted to make sure I wasn't involved in his world, how could he be sure he had control over that?

Excusing myself for a moment, out of earshot and sight of the man called Duncan, I asked one of the staff members if they knew him. Yes, they said, he was who he said he was. He was on their books and occasionally consulted for them. She gave me a knowing smile. Whether that was meant to encourage me, I wasn't sure. It didn't but at least I knew he was genuine. He was a property developer and a new building was shortly to be finished. He would be happy to drive me to inspect the show apartment.

Still wary, I took his offer. The two-bedroom apartment was delightful. A little bigger than I wanted but it was hard to find small apartments of any quality. If I could hang on where I was for another month, the apartment would be ready. That arrangement suited me perfectly, I was paid up until then.

"I'll show you others, Caroline, so you're sure."

He took my number and two days later, rang.

"Let's make an afternoon of it and I'll buy you lunch. There are three apartments I'd like to show you." Without giving me pause for breath, he continued. "What do you say? If you give me your address, I'll pick you up at twelve. Or, if you'd prefer, I can meet you at the real estate agent."

I wondered if this was a pattern with me, things happening at lightning speed.

Accepting, I let him pick me up at the front of my building. Duncan talked easily, keeping his personal life out of the conversation. He talked about his passion for real estate and how he'd got into property development. I revealed little of my life. I had no wish to talk about Ireland, or London or how I came to be in Trinidad and Tobago. Rather than make up a pack of lies and worry which was which, I listened. At eighteen I didn't have much else to offer. Again, I decided on the rule I'd come up with when I'd hitchhiked my way out of Ireland. Say little.

At the end of the day, Duncan said, "Don't take this the wrong way, Caroline, but I can show you my apartment; that way you can see the level of quality I put into my places. I use it as a show home and to entertain important clients, so I don't want you to think I'm out to seduce you."

"Am I an important client or a quality assurance officer?"

"Both … what do you say?"

"Okay."

The quality was supreme, offering spectacular sea views. It was worth a zillion.

"… and I've put my heart and soul into it."

He returned me to my apartment building and true to his promise, there was no seduction or even a whiff of it. A few days later, he rang again. This time it was to invite me to lunch, with no mention of further apartment inspections. This was a date. I accepted. I wasn't doing anything else and I felt no threat. Although he showed he was interested in me, there was no harassment. No sly hand groping.

He was overweight and far from good looking, but I felt comfortable with him. He was easy to be with and I was in control. We saw each other regularly.

Then one day, "So who are you really, Caroline?"

"You tell me your secrets then I'll tell you mine."

There the conversation ended and nothing more was said.

I hung out with the people he knew; besides, my social circle plateaued at zero. Slipping into his life was easy. Eventually his personal life emerged. His marriage was over and he had a young son. He didn't hesitate when an offer to work in Trinidad came up. Having left that life behind, I suspected there was nothing left in his bank account. I wondered about time with his son but didn't ask.

He wasn't Stanley, or even someone who glimmered in his shadow, but he gave me comfort. He kissed me and I felt the fear of rejection in his heart.

"Caroline, I've fallen in love with you. I know it's soon, but I fell in love with you that first day I saw you in the real estate office. I'm so scared you don't have any feelings for me, other than as a friend, or that you could love me in the future. Do you think it possible? Could you ... like me ... eventually ... do you think?"

I'd sensed it coming. I was ambivalent I must admit. But I hadn't noticed anything not to like about him.

"I may, Duncan, I may."

Though an acute businessman, I suspected he was a man who accepted scraps from the table of sexual and emotional offerings. His failed marriage stung severely but his issues may have started further back. Stanley had been a great educator for me in the human soul.

The apartment I was to move into still wasn't finished so I rolled over two more months. I wasn't stupid enough to think this was all by chance. Duncan was a developer and a tactician by nature. He was giving me more time to get to know him.

The relationship grew but I was not in love with him. Although I really didn't know what being in love meant. Other than the emotional hurricane that was Stanley, it was only what I'd read in books or movies. This did not shadow any of those. He was amiable and very likable. He was ambitious and ambition was something that I was discovering interested me. To be honest, I wanted company. I was learning about life and life was turning out okay. I accepted when he asked me to move in with him.

NINETEEN

Thakit

Trinidad and Tobago – 2003

The warm climate hit me like a wall as I walked into the bright sunshine of Trinidad and Tobago. New life sprang into my bones. I'd not experienced warmth like it before. It suited me, definitely suited me. I bought new clothes and dressed like a local, as best as I could. Two skinny white legs hanging from long shorts like threads of cotton wasn't going to work until I got a tan. I bought a light pair of jeans. Completing my wardrobe, I bought T-shirts and loose shirts. Shopping, normally something I hated, changes when someone else is paying. However, my upbringing and mammy's voice in my ear took care of being wasteful and not having more than I needed.

Aedan's advice to travel light with only carry-on luggage was invaluable. From passport control, I walked directly to customs and out of the airport. My experience in these matters was non-existent. I settled into the travelling thing, trying to be as cool as my brother would be, but I was excited fit to burst. I remembered Aedan's word: concentrate. It was only then did I consider how far I was out of my comfort zone.

"My contacts have found where Kate is living. It's a simple job, just go there and tell her to come home." End of directions from Aedan. Stupidly I thought it would be that easy.

The apartment where Kate lived was locked behind a security wall, a gated community. A concept I was unfamiliar with. There were dubious characters lurking around who would give a person cause for concern. But there are dubious people everywhere and I wondered if we'd all be living behind locked gates eventually. Kate now called herself Caroline Katherine Clark and by then was living with another man, not the London club owner.

For myself, I settled into a hotel in town. Not too expensive but not too cheap either. Although I was on expenses, I just didn't have it in me to abuse the situation and stay in a five-star hotel. Aedan didn't lecture me about how much to spend on accommodation, but I have my own guidelines. Or rather, as I've said, mammy's. Besides, I wasn't used to loads of money. I was never a person who needed lots of stuff.

There was a township near where Caroline lived and I hung around, drank in a bar or two and frequented the local cafés. There was no way Kate would answer at the locked gated community, so I hoped I'd find her shopping locally. All I had was a photo of Kate when she was about fourteen. No doubt she'd changed her appearance if she'd changed her name. For her to answer her door would have been a lot simpler but that clearly was not going to happen. What the bloody hell was I to do? *Use your imagination,* I could hear my mother say to me.

Then Bart appeared from nowhere. He sidled up to me one day in a bar, and as it turned out, lived practically next door to Kate. A shifty bastard, my instincts told me. "Seen you around," he said. "Tourist, or are you planning to stay?"

Our brief conversation led me to think he was trying to sell real estate. I straightened him out on that.

"I'm looking for a girl, name of Caroline Clark. She recently moved here and I can't get hold of her new apartment number. There are family matters involved," I added to keep him from trying sell me something.

"Caroline?" he asked. "Irish Caroline?"

"Yes."

"Well, you've come to the right man. M'name's Bart," he said, with an accent I couldn't pinpoint but which was English in origin. We shook hands.

Bart, it turned out, enjoyed smearing people with bad gossip, so getting him to keep tabs on Caroline gave him a purpose in life. "She's very pleasing on the eye, in fact a knockout and makes good use of it. That's an expensive piece of real estate she lives in. She could have anyone, any top ace, but she settled on a mediocre one. The property belongs to him. Duncan's a newcomer in the development game. He got lucky, not her."

He gave me the creeps with his fat lips and spittle. He sweated constantly. I wasn't sure what type of business he was in or even if he worked at all. But then I didn't want to know too much about him. If I could just get close to Caroline, on her own, I could speak with her. Bart was all I had.

Aedan had assured me it would require tact.

"When you ring her doorbell, be friendly," he'd said. "Use that smile." Suddenly my smile was important and an asset in providing me with an income after all. But did he know about gated communities?

"Caroline moved in a few weeks ago ... jeez, she's a looker," shifty bastard repeated. The thought of him leering at her made my skin crawl.

"Her boyfriend's name is Duncan Thomson. The place is nice, swanky. They're all nice places," he said. He laughed a slimy laugh, "... 'course they are, I live in one of 'em." His big red lips parted and spread over whitened teeth, exposing a mismatched crown. Laughter spewed. He experienced joy in his own humour.

My idea was to stay incognito until I was ready to approach Kate. I didn't want her to think I was stalking her or to barge right up and scare her off. "The spider and the fly," Aedan had said. I'm not a sneaky person by nature so I had to think about that. "The best way to approach her is gently, quietly." I kept Aedan updated daily, as instructed. Though I quivered every time I had to say there was nothing to report.

Kate wasn't stupid. She would resist going back to Ireland. Aedan wouldn't say why when I asked him. In fact, he was very secretive. I hadn't met him; we'd only talked on the phone. He'd couriered the mobile device I was to use before I left Ireland. He wouldn't answer questions about why she needed to be home, only saying, "I'll tell you steps as you need to know them." So how could I convince Kate? The number of times I questioned Aedan about this finally got on his nerves until he just said, "Use your instincts, just do it," and hung up. Maybe I needed to confer with the little people again.

I used many adornments as disguises. The only thing I couldn't change was my height and frame. Due to the heat, I wore a variety of loose shirts, T-shirts, shorts as my legs tanned, jeans and a light suit. Hats and sunglasses helped. The back-to-front cap gear was also in my 'dress-up' bag. To be honest, I was having the time of my life. I even fooled loose-lips one day as he walked right past me in the street. But I still hadn't seen Kate. Bart was proving less useful than I hoped. I mean, he lived in her community.

"I can tell her you're looking for her if you like. Be no trouble."

"No, best I do that." God Almighty, loose-lips would send her into a deep cave from which she'd never emerge.

Aedan rang me after a several days, sounding casually tense. His breath was heavy and I wasn't sure if he'd just run up some stairs or was anxious. My daily phone calls had lapsed as I'd achieved nothing and there wasn't anything to report.

"Haven't you met Kate yet? What the hell are you doing?"

"It's not as easy as you think, Aedan. She lives in a gated community with a guy who probably keeps her very close. I've been told she's a looker. You didn't tell me that, Aedan. The boyfriend's probably worried he'll lose her."

"You're making excuses. Are you concentrating? Not a strong point, I gather from your mammy. You're not out there to enjoy the sunshine. Don't forget who's paying the bills."

Knowing he'd been speaking with my mam brought me back to my mission. For the moment I'd forgotten mammy was the link with this man. Aedan's hunch was right, I was enjoying the warm climate maybe a little too much. I'd been having so much fun donning disguises and going to the beach and swanning around, I'd lost the intensity my assignment needed. In short, yes, there was a lapse in concentration.

"Aedan," I said. "There's an event I can attend that Kate is sure to be at." It was a real estate conference and Bart, being in the business as it turned out, was attending and could get me in.

"Tread gently, young man. Once you've been introduced, get her alone and greet her with, 'hello, Caroline, I believe we're from the same part of the world.' Don't use Kate straight away as it will scare her off. Think you can do that?"

"Yes, Aedan," I replied like the minion I was.

I saw Bart later and said I'd come if the offer was still open. Slobber-lips practically launched himself at me with glee in his eyes, spraying excitement. "That's great news. She's sure to be there. The invite is for two so you can come with me."

Go as his date? Anticipation drained my new tan. I had no choice.

The morning after the event, I lay in bed ignoring Aedan's calls. I'd been rehearsing my excuses, but they all sounded limp. All I could say was that it was impossible. She was surrounded by people. I wasn't sure if she'd gone into business with her boyfriend, but she was doing all the networking. The boyfriend hung limply by her side. How had the boyfriend managed before he met her? He clung to her, introducing her to everyone. She was a natural, took control and steered the conversation. She was a definite boon to this oaf she lived with. I didn't meet him, but from a distance she showed him up more than if he was on his own. Even Bart couldn't get a look in. She was absolutely stunning in a long red dress that must have been glued to her body. Long dark hair mixed with highlights of coloured sand waved like the sea around her shoulders. That sounds a bit poetic, but mammy sometimes talks like that.

Hello, Kate, ooops, Caroline, we're from the same part of the world, would have reduced me to a cold, forgotten pork pie. Bart attached himself to me intermittently. "I thought you were going to introduce me?" I said.

"Yeah, yeah, just waiting for a gap in the crowd."

It was clear Bart did not have any influence at all.

Aedan's calls relaxed a bit, which meant he was annoyed with me. He suggested I buy a prepaid mobile if I needed to make or receive calls locally. I was not allowed to use his. I had and it rang. It was Bart.

"Morning." He had an urgency in his voice. "You better get over here quick. There's been an incident. Huge fight. Police called and now an ambulance. Get here quick."

Kate/Caroline

Duncan was such a sweet man, living with him was easy. Not a looker, definitely not a looker, but he cared for me. More than that, he adored me. He hadn't long been in Trinidad and Tobago, a little over eighteen months. He wanted a lavish lifestyle and he figured he could do that through property development. He was already on his way. He initiated his rise by the obvious choice, selling real estate. "A good way to get to know the territory," he said. He started through an agency, then networked contacts on and offline. Word of mouth, the most lucrative source.

The majority of his clientele were British expats. He made a name for himself being available and amenable. Some of these people were presumably dodging tax and appreciated those who appreciated their circumstances. Duncan was one of those people who picked out the loopholes. He had a keen mind and was good with figures. Financing was his speciality. I suspected he was dodging something too. I presumed it was tax, but I didn't ask. I think that's what he liked about me. I had a major secret myself and a couple of name changes. I wasn't squeaky clean and didn't want him asking me questions. But he felt proud introducing me to people. He said he liked how I looked and I suspect this gave him a bit of street cred. Overall, he was kind, considerate and didn't push my buttons, except the time he did.

His one failing was his bent on kinky sex. I put it down to his lack of confidence. His escape had been porn and equipment. The porn he accessed on his computer but equipment he went out for. He didn't specifically tell me this. He let me use his computer and his proclivities were so clearly visible I think he was testing my attitude. My uncle came to mind. I did not want an uncle substitute. If I was to live with Duncan, there had to be ground rules. He could do what he wanted but if we were to live together, kinky sex and porn were off the agenda.

"None of that shit with me. Is that understood?" I said. "One request and I'm gone. Shoving porn in my face or doing anything kinky or forceful will have the same result."

"Hon, I don't need any of that with you by my side."

"Fine," I said. We'll see, I thought.

Straight sex was a problem for Duncan. Maybe he'd become used to kinky, or he'd taken up kinky because straight was a problem. Consequently, we didn't make love too often. He may still have gone elsewhere, but I didn't think so.

I had little to no experience myself so couldn't teach him anything useful. I gave myself credit in that I was patient with him. I guess we weren't really suited as he didn't turn me on. In truth, no one had. Except Stanley. But Stanley was my first and only. Duncan knew he didn't do it for me sexually but made up for these shortcomings in other ways. He was generous. He knew I liked stones, as in the jewellery kind, even though I didn't wear a lot. I wore one piece of jewellery at a time, but I liked having the investments. I liked exquisite pieces, like my aunt's, now mine. He watched me as I twirled them in the sunshine, absorbed in their sparkle. He said my smile when I did this lifted his love for me.

Why did I move in with him? He was tender and adored me, as I've said, and I wasn't doing anything else. He didn't want me to work, as in a nine to five job, which unbeknownst to him I didn't have the required skills for anyway. Bar waiting and assisting in running a nightclub were all I had. However, I was a keen learner and watched how Duncan ran his business. I helped him out with his clients when he entertained them. I was the meet-and-greet person who came along for the initial meetings in his business dealings. He loved that I made a good impression with his future clients. Quite quickly I was asked to stay for the duration.

It was a nice life. I was happy enough. No, I didn't want to marry him, although he asked me enough times. "Let's leave it for the moment," I'd say. "No rush." I did think it would be useful having another name. A new name and an extra passport couldn't hurt but I didn't want to commit to Duncan. My sixth sense said no.

Duncan drank little and on the odd times he did, he became a slobberer. Mumbling over and over how much he loved me, slurping wet lips all over my face and neck. To say it sickened me, wouldn't cover it. I walked away rather than tell him to stop and possibly start an argument.

A huge business success came Duncan's way. The biggest he'd had. We all celebrated in Duncan's home, a place where many meetings took place as it was also his show home. Drinking and dancing raged until the early hours. Our last guests left about five in the morning. Duncan was still in party mood and took another swig of rum and orange. He liked to tell himself the orange counteracted the alcohol.

"Enough drink, Duncan," I said.

"Let's keep celebrating, hon."

The look in his eyes warned me we were approaching thin ice. "We've talked about this," I said.

"We're celebrating, hon. You were part of the deal as much as me. It was a big deal we just signed."

"It was, Duncan, and that's great, but drinking doesn't suit you and certainly doesn't do anything for me. Let's go to bed. It's late … erm … no, it's early." I moved towards the bedroom. "I'm tired."

"No … I'm not tired and don't be like that, hon," he said and grabbed me, pulling me back to the couch. "Come on, hon, let's keep celebrating. Let's celebrate you and me."

"No, Duncan. Enough."

He slobbered and rolled on top of me. A heavy weight. "Hon, I love you."

I heaved and slid from under him and moved to get away. "Come on, Duncan, get a grip of yourself."

The alcohol swirling around his brain replaced rationality with stupidity. He undid his fly with one hand and with his other clutched a handful of hair from the back of my head. Smiling and giggling like a three-year-old, he shoved my head down onto his cock.

He laughed and said, "I've got a grip of myself, hon, share my glory …" Giggle giggle.

My face and mouth were muffled. I managed to free my face and yelled for him to stop. "You're disgusting," I said. As I spoke, he got his dick into my mouth again. With his hand clutching my hair and pressing down on my head, I struggled to move. I tried to both bite and free myself.

"Please, honey, do it, I need you. Please, please."

I wriggled and finally wrenched myself free. As I stood, he staggered to standing and lunged for me. He'd never become aggressive before, maybe it was a build-up from suppressing his kinky needs. Even though his pants were down by his ankles, he seized me and went for my hair again. He pushed me against the wall, all the while telling me how much he loved me. I wondered if he saw the irony in his actions. "But I love you, Cas," as he slavered over my face again. His genitals still exposed, he thrust against me, body weight and arms pinning me to the wall. He was a hefty force.

I shoved with all my might and managed to get a space between us. Anger assists strength and intention. I squeezed up my knee and pushed hard into his flabby belly, which gave me room to free my arms. He took a breath, creating an opportunity for me to use extra force. In that moment, I lifted my foot and shoved hard. His pants at his ankles he staggered backwards, the stairs behind him. One foot stepped back and off he went, tumbling head over heels down the stairs. There were a lot of them, and they curved. At the bend he bounced all the way to the bottom.

With his eyes closed he groaned, so I knew he was alive. He formed a Z shape at the bottom of the stairs. A replay of my uncle came flooding back to me.

He was motionless. A faint soft moan, then he went quiet. Oh God, he's dead. I ran down the stairs and approached him carefully in case he was just tricking me and might grab my leg, but he was very still. I was in a panic. I tried pulling up his trousers, but he was way too heavy. I left him as he was. I called his name a few times but there was no response. I pressed into his neck and felt a pulse. I knew about that by then.

The ambulance arrived quickly and when I walked outside to meet them, I was surprised to see the neighbours out in force. At that quiet hour before dawn, any noise saturated the neighbourhood. Our party and subsequent argument must have roared like thunder through the open terrace doors and windows. Then with the ambulance arriving, the gated community never had it so good. I travelled with Duncan to the hospital. I told the ambulance officers he'd had a big night and lost his balance at the top of the stairs. They shrugged and pulled up his pants and zipped him.

I waited at his bedside long enough to learn he would recover.

TWENTY-ONE

Thakit

Taking a taxi after Bart's call, I realised there was no need to ask the driver to get there at lightning speed. That was the only way they drove. I used an unregistered cab as I figured we'd go even faster. We did, like a fired cannon ball. How he didn't get booked was beyond me. Perhaps the police were in their pockets or couldn't give a shit. I took a risk in asking the driver to wait. I told him it would be worth his while and waved dollars at him.

The gates of the community were open as an ambulance had just arrived. Being early morning, the shadows were long and the people milling around were hugging their arms. Dressed in their night gear they must have felt exposed or chilly which seemed impossible to me. How could anyone feel cold in this weather, day or night? The heat was constant. In this quiet neighbourhood, I doubted anything this exciting happened too often. Neighbours were out in numbers, feasting on the event, voyeurism and concern etched on their faces. They edged closer.

I hung out with the crowd and listened to the conversations. Then I rang Aedan. 'Ring if you have something important, no matter the time,' were his instructions. Aedan quickly answered. I walked around with the phone so he could listen. Stairs were mentioned – "he fell I heard" – "big party" – "until all hours." Aedan picked up these snatches of information. Then Duncan's body was covered but, not his head, which I relayed to Aedan.

The ambulance's trolley bed was manoeuvred up the ramp and rolled inside. I was relieved it was Duncan on the bed and not Kate. Then Kate climbed into the ambulance still wearing an evening dress. The doors closed and the ambulance sped away.

Surprisingly, rather than being simply relieved it was not Kate who was hurt, Aedan was more interested in how and why the boyfriend was in hospital. "Fell down the stairs, did they say?"

"Seems so ... drunk after a big party," I said.

"He *fell* down the stairs? Can you check."

"I don't know ... hang on." I moved with the device through the crowd. "Can you hear?" I asked Aedan.

"Yeah, yeah, it's a bit sketchy but keep going."

A group of neighbours discussed the event with Bart. "I heard her say he fell down the stairs" – "definitely that's what she said" – "heard her telling the ambulance driver" – "we're next door and the noise of a row came through our back patio" – "huge party" – "she seems okay," said another.

I repeated what I'd heard in case he'd missed anything. "That's crap," Aedan said.

"What's crap?"

"That he fell down the stairs. She pushed him. I'll bet my money on it. Stay there, Ryan. Line up a taxi and wait. She'll be back in the hour and catching a cab to the airport."

"What are you talking about? Why would she do that?"

"Trust me, I know her. She'll be going to the airport. Don't let her out of your sight and get on the same flight." He hung up.

Bart came up to me as my mouth hung open. "Yeah, it's shocking all right," he said.

"Not now, Bart. I have to go back to my hotel. I'll be back as quick as I can but ring me if you see her come back."

An hour, Aedan said. I needed to check out of my hotel, grab my stuff. Yes, I could do it.

Returning to the townhouse, I sat in the cab across the road, hoping I hadn't missed her. Bart saw me and came over.

"No, she hasn't left, she hasn't come back yet. She'll probably stay at the hospital for a while."

I assured him I'd be okay from there and thanked him. I didn't need Kate to see him talking to a taxi when she got back. Helpful, some of the time, but I wasn't sad not to see Bart anymore – that's if Aedan was correct. Twenty minutes later, a taxi pulled up and out spilled Kate. She moved quickly. Within twenty minutes she reappeared, dressed to travel in casual non-descript clothes and wheeling a small bag. My taxi followed all the way to the airport. Now I was interested in Aedan. Who the hell was he that he knew what went on in Kate's head?

She checked onto a flight to Panama City. I tagged right along behind.

TWENTY-TWO

Kate/Caroline/Pippa

Panama City

Duncan mumbled his way out of his blackout while in the ambulance and became fully conscious, although still groggy. He was in terrible pain, groaning with every movement. Once in the hospital, he was injected with something, became drowsy and soon fell asleep. I stayed to hear the verdict. "He has two broken ribs and a broken arm. Fortunately, nothing too serious. His drunkenness probably saved him. He would have been relaxed when he fell. He'll mend."

I, on the other hand, would not. That was it for me.

From a selection of taxis hovering outside the hospital I chose an unregistered one. I wanted to get home as fast as I could. Promising a good fare, I knew he'd make the journey in half the time. I instructed the driver we would go on to the airport and to wait. I withheld the fare as a safety precaution to avoid someone nicking my cab or the cab just driving off. I packed my in-cabin bag with essentials. A few clothes, all the jewels Duncan had given me, plus his jewels, plus his stash of cash. I figured I'd earnt it, having both lived with him and helped his business grow. I didn't trust the safety deposit boxes in Trinidad and had kept my hoard hidden in his house. As the property was very secure, I took the risk. It was a great risk, but I doubted Duncan had reason to search his own place and he knew better than to go near my stuff.

Duncan would not have reason to believe I'd leave that quickly. When he gained full consciousness and sobered up, he would lie in the hospital bed wondering about our future. He would know he'd broken the rules if he remembered anything at all through the alcohol. His realisation would come quickly when hour after hour and into days, I didn't visit.

Somebody from the neighbourhood probably saw me leave with my bag so he'd find out soon enough. I saw another taxi waiting in the street. A frightening thought crossed my mind that it could be one of Stanley's thugs, or someone after me. My paranoia was showing itself again.

At the airport, I checked into the first flight out of Trinidad with one eye on the board and the other looking over my shoulder. It was the usual crowd that you get at airports: locals, tourists, businesspeople. I did notice some tall dick dressed like he thought the locals dressed. Tourists do that. At one point, I caught sight of him looking at me. Our eyes briefly met but I figured it must be one of those eye flicks that happen. I didn't see him again.

The first plane out was to Panama City and as she'd entered, Pippa Katherine Thornton left Trinidad.

On that first flight with Stanley, I discovered I loved flying. It was the feeling of sitting at very high altitude, the exhilaration of just being and putting your fate in the hands of one person. Risky, but relinquishing control felt good. Besides, if you choose to fly what other option does a person have? This did come as a surprise to me. There's nothing you can do except read or watch something or sleep. Or just do nothing. Which is what I chose. A time of nothing, a void, a time to restore.

I lay low in Panama City in a classy hotel, still in the void. The feeling was delicious. I felt totally safe, confident there was only a small margin of error someone was on my trail. I was wealthy, healthy, in no hurry, the past just that, in the past. I took a look-see of the city on a hop-on hop-off bus. Sightseeing didn't interest me beyond the city sights, so I lay by the pool and read a book. Peace came upon me. The recent past eased out of me. I swam in the pool, letting the water wash away the last of the bad taste in my mouth. I ate little and when I did it was either by the pool or from room service. I stayed an extra day and on day five, I woke ready to move on. At the hotel I saw a brochure. Hawaii. Why not?

Pippa Katherine Thornton left Panama City.

TWENTY-THREE

Thakit

Panama City

Kate took the airport bus to a chain hotel in Panama City. I got out, together with other passengers, and moved along to the reception desk. Two assistants were on duty and I was in the next line, one person back from Kate. I gasped when she checked in as Pippa Thornton, her London name. The name I was told she used at the club. Sensible. I checked in as me.

With Kate ensconced in a swish hotel in Panama City, me alongside, I was able to dive into my bag of tricks and change into worn blue jeans and a white T-shirt. My hair struggled into a short ponytail, topped off with a back-to-front baseball cap.

On the plane I'd had time to think. Not that I was interested in their relationship, but was Kate concerned for the poor bastard lying in a hospital bed? My short observations and knowledge from Bart led me to think the guy adored her. Why was she doing this? They'd had a row, sure, but ditching him in hospital seemed a bit rich. I wondered how she treated people she didn't like. Had their relationship just been a convenience for her? She must be a mean sort of person to leave like that.

"Four nights," I said as I heard Kate say three. An extra day in case she changed her mind. I didn't know how alert she was and if she'd seen my face on the plane. Who notices one person in a crowd of hundreds? I wondered if she was concerned about leaving Trinidad so quickly. But I daresay Duncan wouldn't be after her from his hospital bed. He probably didn't even know she'd left yet. Kate seemed nonchalant as I watched her in the queue. The authorities in Trinidad, as far as I knew, would have no reason to follow her, disloyalty not being a crime.

Three uneventful days were spent in Panama City. Kate sat by the pool and read a book, pecked at bar food or used room service, I assumed. I didn't see her in any of the restaurants in the evenings. She went walking one day and took a hop-on hop-off city bus tour. As she only carried her handbag, I knew she was coming back. I waited for her return in the grand reception area. She went straight to her room and stayed there.

To be noted, I was on a strict 'observe only and follow' instruction. In the last conversation with Aedan, he expressly asked me not to approach her. "Just follow her. Wait until she's settled." I had no idea how Aedan got his previous information on her whereabouts and there was no point pressing him on that. He made it very clear all I needed to know was what he told me.

I kept in touch with Colin and mammy. Colin was especially excited by my exploits. "You lucky fucker," he repeated many times, but he wasn't curious about who I was following or why Aedan was interested in her.

Mammy, on the other hand, was not impressed. "I don't like it," she said over and over. She kept her silence on Aedan's identity.

Kate was back at the pool after her previous day out. Happy hour arrived; she stayed poolside and ordered a drink. I kept up a steady change of clothes. I still enjoyed playing dressing-up. Kate didn't move. When the hell was she going to leave? And where to? I took my guess it would be the following morning.

Waking bright and early, I packed my bag but did not check out. I sat by reception with my bag reading *The New York Times*. Private eyes in old movies hide behind newspapers in hotel foyers. A small mobile device isn't big enough for sleuths where eyes are cast down, unless you hold the thing at eye level and look like an eejit. A sideways or upwards glance over a newspaper is much easier.

Kate appeared at reception with her bag. She took a seat and I figured she must be waiting for the shuttle bus. I checked out and hung out of sight behind a large potted plant with enough gaps in the foliage for me to keep an eye on her.

The shuttle arrived and a small group of people boarded, including Kate. Once I saw her step in, I jumped in a taxi. At the airport I waited out of sight by the shuttle drop-off point.

Cool as you like, Kate walked straight to an airline queue where I managed to get in a few people behind her. The flight was going to San Francisco and then on to Honolulu. I bought a ticket all the way to Honolulu. It was either one or the other. I guessed from the previous flight, she'd be travelling cattle. Seated towards the rear of the plane, I was able to keep an eye on her and follow closely in case she got off in San Francisco.

It was a presumption I made, but was sure Kate, like me, was fond of a warm climate. How exciting her life was, making decisions moment by moment. Thanks to Kate, mine was mimicking hers. She was a person, I was learning, who didn't hang around. When she rested, she rested; when she was on the move, she went. There must have been plans in her head but from my point of view, she was winging life. Did she have an inheritance? Born into wealth? Mine was not to question why, as Aedan reminded me often, so I swam on the surface of knowledge. Who she was I had no idea, but she had sidled into my life making big changes, for which I was thankful.

On the plane I had time to relax and drifted off to sleep until I felt and heard the change in engine noise. We were on descent. Are we sleeping in San Francisco or Honolulu tonight, Kate? She joined the queue to disembark and then moved to the transit lounge. Ah, we're going on to Honolulu. Keeping out of sight, I watched her. She stood at one point and I wondered if she had changed her mind. She was only stretching her legs, before returning to her seat.

As soon as we departed San Francisco, I changed my shirt. Keeping my hair in a ponytail, I discarded the hat. I had about five hours for another nap. Refreshed by the time the engine noise changed, I was firing on all cylinders, ready to sleuth.

When we arrived, Kate took the shuttle bus, which fortunately was packed, so I stepped in too. Maybe she wasn't rich. Maybe her base person was ordinary. Her travel preferences certainly indicated that, although she was fond of up-market accommodation. We alighted at another ritzy hotel, right on the beach-front. I, along with others, joined her at reception. Not hearing how long she'd checked in for, I decided on three nights.

In my room I changed my look and went to the pool and waited. And waited. Finally I asked reception if they could ring my friend Pippa Thornton as I was supposed to meet her. They had no Pippa Thornton registered. Caroline Clark? No. Felicity Doncaster?

"No ... your friend, you say, sir?" I was sounding weird and bringing attention to myself, so I let it go. I stayed another night, first checking the various restaurants and the pool bar, then venturing out to local restaurants and cafés. She'd gone. I'd lost her. Fuck.

Fucked or not, I stood on the balcony and breathed in the sea air, the warmth and excitement of it all. Colin was so pissed off. He couldn't give a rat's arse that I'd lost Kate, just that I was there, and he wasn't.

"You bastard, it's pissing down here."

"So you can experience it more fully, Colin … let me describe it to you again."

"Feck off," he said and hung up.

How rude, I'll have it out with him when I get home. A smile as wide as the beach I was looking at, spread across my face.

I rang Aedan, holding the phone from my ear so his ranting didn't bust my hearing. I did catch him say he was disappointed in me, that he thought I could handle the job. That left me wondering why he would think that. He didn't even know me. My mammy worked for him, was all. He must value his employees. Maybe he wanted her to go back and work for him.

After booking a flight home for the next day, I went out and got rat faced. Artfully, I requested a late hotel departure and appropriate flight out. Getting up early was not likely to happen.

Tail between my legs, at least mammy was pleased to see me, even just to berate.

"You can now go out and find a proper job. Use that degree."

"Yes mammy. Until such times I'm going back to the job I already have."

Up went the arms as my dear mammy harrumphed away in disgust.

TWENTY-FOUR

Kate/Pippa

Hawaii

On my arrival in Honolulu airport, I stood to the side of the flow of passengers, deciding if it felt right to spend time there. Families passed hanging on to their excited children, spangled-eyed honeymooners glided past. Businesspeople with harried expressions fast forwarded to the exit.

My sense of dread at being followed had diminished. I could never be absolutely free, but I was comfortable. I was breathing. My decision to give Honolulu a go had been a good one. After all, who gets to go to Honolulu on a whim? I decided to make the most of it. There were sure to be enough people I could easily lose myself amongst.

The shuttle from the airport dropped off at a number of hotels and I decided to take my pick by look and location. I alighted with others at a swanky one and chose a room with a beach and ocean view. Entering the room, I dropped my bag and walked to the balcony, breathed in the view and Hawaiian air. It smelt good – but I didn't fit. It was too much. I wanted subtle. I wanted calm. I grabbed my bag and took the lift down to reception. Not charged, I checked out, hailed a taxi and headed back to the airport.

Looking at the board I saw a flight to Kauai due to leave in an hour. The name had a nice ring to it. Plus it began with a K, my favourite letter.

From the air the islands were so tranquil, jewels in a setting of iridescent blue. The short flight was in a smaller plane. I looked down and felt exhilarated, free and very optimistic for reasons I could not explain. Maybe it was the space I saw.

Taxis, shuttle buses and chauffeured limousines lined up outside the airport. Without thinking, I walked past the taxis and shuttle buses and spoke to the driver of a limousine.

"I'd like a drive around the island, please."

"All around?"

"Show me the interesting bits."

I was used to tropical plants in Trinidad but I never tired of them. The driver took me along coastal roads, stopping at lookout points and descending through winding lush valleys. I was hooked.

"Do you know of a place to stay? I don't want swanky, I don't want big, something small and intimate. Maybe you know a place personally?" I thought he hadn't heard me and finally he clicked his fingers.

"Got it ... Joan. You'll love her. She has a little place, separate but close to where she lives. I'll take you there. It might be booked but she doesn't bother a lot of the time. Shall we go there now?"

We pulled into a winding driveway off the main road. Bougainvillea sprawled free as we drove the short distance to a quaint house. It looked like additions had been randomly built. The driver, Al, introduced us. Joan shook my hand, clasping her other hand over mine. "Joan Havel," she said with a little giggle in her voice.

The room, more like a small hut with a separate bathroom, was available and I could take it as long as I liked. She showed me around the immaculately clean and tidy accommodation. "I always keep it ready but I'm particular these days with who comes and stays." I immediately loved the place. It fitted me like a glove. I paid a month in advance. She then invited Al and me to have tea.

After tea, thanking and waving goodbye to Al, I felt at ease and totally relaxed. The weather was warm, so I decided to take a swim. The beach was a short walk across the main road and along a pathway. I dried off in the sun. I lay spellbound on the sand watching the ebb and flow of the waves; free, warm and in a place that felt like home. The letter K had worked its charm. The world and my cares washed away completely and now, cleansed and revived, a new person emerged from the water that afternoon.

Joan Havel was an Anglophile, although she'd never set foot outside Hawaii. She had dreams, she said. I didn't correct her when she thought my accent was English. Why shatter her illusions? In any case, she said, she was too old to travel that far, so it was wonderful England was visiting her. I assured her she wasn't too old, but I sensed it was more a case of loving where she lived and having accessible daydreams. The little house she'd named 'Buckingham Place'. She felt 'palace' a little ostentatious. I loved her immediately for her sense of grandeur.

The house, a fifteen-minute walk from the beach, suited me fine. Most people wanted to be on the beach. Set back and a little too far from town to be popular, Buckingham Place was quiet and paying a month in advance, the rent very reasonable.

Besides, I thought, who would ever find me here?

TWENTY-FIVE

Kate/Pippa

Kauai – 2004

Every afternoon Mrs Havel, "Please call me Joan," invited me in for afternoon tea where she served home-baked cake or scones. I felt a little under scrutiny at these teas but nevertheless, she was warm, friendly and naturally hospitable. Joan had a son in Hawaii and a daughter who lived on the East Coast of the US. She showed me pictures of her Lilly, Lilly's husband and the grandchildren.

"Oh lovely," I said. "You must be so proud." I didn't want to listen to endless stories about extremely smart grandchildren, but I sat with her and let her chat flow over me as white noise. There was a quality of sitting with my aunt about her.

"My son is a bit of a disappointment," she said. "His marriage broke down and I would so love to have grandchildren I could see every day." She said this with a glint in her eye. Oh God, I thought, he must be in my age group.

On Sundays, Joan made extra-special preparations for lunch when Cooper usually joined her. They owned a small apartment in Honolulu where Cooper lived during the week. Coming home for

Sunday lunch was a ritual he seldom broke. She showed me photos of her son, so I knew what to expect.

As I was not keen to get involved with anyone else or have them pushed on me, I declined invitations to join that lunch. As she persisted, after a couple of weeks I relented. Joan was so adorable I accepted to please her.

The photos didn't do him justice. In walked Mr Baywatch. Sporty beach people were not really my type, but I wasn't sure what was my type. I had started out so young I had never stopped to consider male types. Cooper was tall. Tousled, sandy hair crowned his head atop a fit, tanned body. Women must be falling all over him.

By the end of lunch, he emerged as a funny boy-man who played down his intelligence, to the point of securing it under lock and key. I wasn't sure if this was an act for his mother or that's just what he did. Not for a moment did I think he was a doozy with no smarts. Maybe he played that to get the advantage. I wondered if he'd had some boyhood experience that left him deciding it was best to use the dumb friendly approach and as an adult it had become habitual. Mr Baywatch looked like a beach bum, but, the big surprise, he was a jeweller with a business.

"What?" I was suddenly shaken into what he'd said. While Joan scrutinised me, I had been analysing her son and not paying attention to the conversation.

"Yes, he's a jeweller," said Joan, "and a very good one."

"Really?" I said.

"Why do people always say that?" Cooper said.

"Because you're such a sweet boy, Cooper," his mother said, patting his hand.

Like his mother, he was easy going and although I wasn't looking for another relationship, we fell into a friendship and hung out together. Delight radiated like a halo around Joan.

"He spends so much more time here now you're staying, Pippa."

She trod carefully around me in case she pushed too far and was obviously aware I was only a temporary guest. Cooper came home more and more. Not knowing how often he visited previously, I only had her word for it. We didn't do much; sat around talking, went to the beach, swam. He showed me how to get up on a surfboard. The three of us occasionally ate at a small local restaurant.

Cooper's and my relationship settled into a platonic situation, which suited me. My limited experience with men had left me wary. I was fearful of another Duncan experience, although Cooper was not at all like him – but who could tell?

In small parts, he grew on me until I couldn't wait until he stepped through Joan's door.

My first month had drifted on and I was paying weekly. Without giving it too much thought, I paid for another month in advance and so it went. Joan was delighted. From Buckingham Place, I took to walking down to the beach for early morning swims, weather permitting. Walking along Joan's pathway was a daily adventure. Apart from the bougainvillea, there was a spreading orange-flowered poinciana tree, big wide hibiscus bushes with flowers in pinks and purples, intoxicating smelling plumeria plants, their flowers blooming in various shades of pink, and the ones I loved, dual white and yellow. They were just the names Joan had told me and those I could remember. I asked her for other names.

"They're my companions, dear. I've been told their names, but I can't remember them all. But they are my lovely people who live in and around my garden. We're all great friends. Names don't really matter. If you talk to them as you walk, they will acknowledge you. If you don't believe me, just try it."

I did. At first I felt silly but figured it looked no sillier than appearing to be talking to yourself when actually it was a phone device. I believe the plants did pay attention. I told Joan when I got back and said it reminded me of how the Irish talk to the little people.

"See," she said, "you English are not all mad like some people say."

I let that rest. I believe Joan didn't know or care if there was a country called Ireland. She wanted England and that was all there was to it.

One day I got out a map. She seemed to think the whole area was England and waved away my hand when I showed her the lines marking the countries on the map. "This is Scotland, Wales and Northern Ireland," I said. "And this bit is the Republic of Ireland."

"It's all so small, dear, everyone must be the same."

She believed what she wanted to believe. Her mind was made up. She was stuck on Buckingham Palace, the Queen, the Changing of the Guard and afternoon teas with scones.

I began to wonder if hiding one's true intelligence was a family thing. She, like Cooper, played it down. This seemed to me very un-American. Underneath I knew Joan was as sharp as a tack. She also brought out in me a caring for humanity and the world in general that I hadn't previously discovered. Judgement was not in her bones and the bad side of people was just a wrong signpost read.

At the beach, I read my book as my toes pushed into the warm sand. I interspersed reading with swimming or just lying on my towel and feeling the sunshine surround me. I became lean and brown. I was so thankful to Al for bringing me to Buckingham Place and helping me find heaven.

Joan and I nattered as she prepared dinner. Although I was a paying guest, I helped by clearing up after dinner or putting out the rubbish. The food bill I insisted on sharing. Joan loved to cook and delighted in preparing the meals. There was no Mr Havel senior. He'd died years back and Joan was happy in her independence.

Over dinner one night, Joan said, "Cooper was worried about me being alone and steered me towards another relationship, but I didn't want to get involved. I loved his father and that was enough for me." However, she mentioned more than once, "it would be so nice to hear the sound of tiny feet pitter-pattering around the place."

TWENTY-SIX

Kate/Pippa/Rose

2005

The weeks turned to months and Joan had reduced the rent. By then I had a little job in town assisting a photographer. I didn't want to work front desk or anywhere in the public eye. Cooper suggested his friend, who was looking for someone part time. The photographer was expanding his business with creative scenic shots. Weddings were his bread and butter and he needed someone for bookings and paperwork. The hours were flexible, any two days a week. I loved it. The studio was on our island and close to home.

Cooper and I grew into an item. We now shared the same bedroom in his mother's home and I stayed occasionally at his apartment in Honolulu on my days off. I no longer paid rent which meant the room was available for rental again. The tranquillity of my existence was so vastly different to anything I could have imagined. There was no necessity for ground rules with Cooper as, being friends first, we'd grown into a pod-like existence. Cooper had no strange sexual proclivities; in fact, he was happy to have sex, or not. He had a fondness for talking. For all his looks, he wasn't a sex-god. He was comfortable and fun.

It did cross my mind he may be bisexual but why that would give him a casual approach to sex, I couldn't say. For some reason, despite my Duncan experience, this didn't cause me concern. I let the thought drift through me. I think I had actually fallen in love with him. How a person can tell, I had no references or anyone to ask. I know being with him was the best, warts and all.

Cooper's attitude to sex did not disappoint me, but it had his ex-wife, who assumed his looks would befit a sexually charged man with a great social life. He was not bothered by either. Cooper and I became best buddies who shared a dislike for 'keeping up with the Joneses'.

A year passed and when Cooper asked me to marry him, it seemed the most natural thing in the world. Joan sighed with pleasure. I did too; as well as a mother-in-law I loved and a man I adored; I'd get a new name. Although my fears of being found were buried deep by then, I still metaphorically looked over and beyond my shoulder from time to time.

"I've always wanted to rid myself of Pippa ... Phillippa," I told Joan and Cooper. "I'd like to be called Rose." They both looked at me as though I'd swallowed a fly. "What do you think? Can you call me Rose?" Their looks continued puzzled.

Cooper was the first to speak. "Well ... um ... you do look like a Rose, name I mean. Yeah," he twisted his head as though I'd just turned upside down, "yeah, it suits you."

"What do you think, Joan?" I said. "Rose Havel ... Rose Katherine Havel. Rose and Cooper. Don't you think that sounds nice?"

"Yes, I suppose, but why? I'm used to Pippa and I like it."

"I've always liked the name Rose. And besides, my name Phillippa was never used, I was always pip-face at school." That was the clincher.

"Of course, dear," Joan shook her head in understanding. "Children can be so cruel with names. Of course, Rose it shall be."

Joan was concerned I'd have no one from my family, or friends for that matter, to invite to the wedding.

"Your parents, I know have passed. What about brothers and sisters?"

"No, Joan, I don't have any family. I'm fine. You and Cooper are my family."

"What about cousins?"

I was uncomfortable getting off the track of the actual wedding and marching back into my history. All along I had avoided that story and was eager to steer the conversation away.

"I'm an only child and no cousins. My aunt died before my mother, with no children."

"Oh, you poor, poor dear."

"Don't feel like that, Joan. I'm fine. I'm happy now and that's all that matters." She wouldn't let it go.

"There must be someone." She paused, thinking through her own family tree. "What about ...?"

"No one, Joan."

"My poor Pippa ... ooh, sorry, Rose. So much tragedy in a young life. Too many deaths for a young girl, plus the fire." She shook her head. "Too much."

I grabbed her hands. "Look at it this way. I have all my tragedies in the past. They're done, finished. I'm entering a life of peace now and you and Cooper have made it all possible."

This little speech was the new me talking. It was quite spontaneous and at that moment, I believed it. The concocted was 'fire story' story to explain how I lost my birth certificate and my personal possessions. Little was saved in that house fire. A story can be told so convincingly, the teller believes it. One must believe to be believed. How could I tell this lovely woman my father left when I was tiny, my mother was her sister's husband's lover and I'd killed my uncle? There was certainly no need for any other misadventures to be shared either. I hoped this put to rest the Havels' desire to visit my homeland (which was England in Joan's mind) and which had been mentioned sporadically.

The wedding was simple with just under a hundred guests including neighbours and Cooper's special business friends. His sister flew over with her husband and their two small children. Joan's house was full of what she craved: laughter and the pitter-patter of little feet. The rental hut being vacant was the answer to the overflow.

We wed on the beach. Dress request was white formal with bare feet in the sand. A flautist piped us from the restaurant along a pathway flanked with palm leaves and shells. White ribbons decorated the improvised chapel of bent palm fronds. I was living the dream, having the time of my life, as a bride is meant to. I'd never dreamt of a wedding, but if I had, that would have been beyond my wildest dreams. I felt I had finally figured out who I was. I had a new name and now a husband with whom I was deeply in love and who was also my best friend. In my new little family was his wonderful mother, who meant as much to me as my Aunt Iris.

We honeymooned on another island for a week but discovered we were eager to get back to our own paradise. Our living arrangements stayed the same, which meant Joan could resume renting the room. Cooper and I paid all the bills, with Joan overcompensating on food and treats.

Mrs Rose Katherine Havel had entered the world.

TWENTY-SEVEN

Kate/Rose

2007

On a walk back from the beach on one of my days off from work, the noise of crazy tourists pierced my solitude. It was that tricky part of the road just before the bend. The local blind spot. A young woman and her male companion yeehawed in the way someone might if let out of confinement. Or thinking they were in the wild west. Definitely tourists, driving a fashionable convertible. This time the tourists read the sign and slowed down enough to see me.

"Hey ... hey," the woman yelled when she saw me. "Pull over, Dave, let's ask this lady."

I walked to the car. "Can I help you?"

"Maybe ... we're looking for a place to stay. Are you a local?"

"Yes."

"This area looks gorgeous. Do you know if there's anywhere around here? A little shack? A room in a house? We don't want a big resort."

A smile eased across my face. I knew just the place. "I do and I happen to know it's free at the moment. I'm going there myself, so I'll show you if you like."

"Hop in," said the woman. "We haven't booked or even looked. We wanted to be spontaneous. Well, I did," she said as I climbed into the car.

My kinda girl.

"I knew we wouldn't have any trouble finding a place," she said to her companion. "... and if the worst came to the worst we could stay in one of those over-prettied resorts ... I'm Jen by the way and this is Dave." She reached back to shake my hand.

The look on Joan's face when I walked the couple over to the house told me she was happy – a sort of, if-you're-happy-I'm-happy kind of look – and gave me the key to let them in. Joan always had the place ready and as always, it was spotless. All I had to do was make up the bed and lay out towels and essentials.

"Joan will handle the money," I said. "She takes care of that side of things." I explained the easiest way to get to the beach and left them to it.

Jen and Dave settled in. Two days later Cooper came home for the weekend.

We fell into our usual routine; Cooper with a beer and me with either a wine or tea with lemon. We sat on the verandah and discussed the days we'd spent apart. I sometimes got a word in but mostly it was Cooper giving me the lowdown on his week, every bloody minute detail of it. But that was Cooper, he liked to tell detail, although he wasn't so good at dealing with it. He had an easy voice, so I enjoyed listening to him though not always the details.

"A young couple walked into the shop," he said. "He had shifty eyes, Rose, you know, makes you sort of wary. He had a strong handshake, a bit too strong, as though he was trying to convince me of something. A man can tell these sort of things."

I let Cooper have that one. It wouldn't have occurred to him that women have an intuition about those things too. But that was Coops, bless him.

"He said he wanted to speak to the jeweller. He didn't seem to think I was for real."

"Cooper," I said, "you don't look like a jeweller."

"So you've said, but I still don't see why."

"Really, Coops," I said, raising an eyebrow, "no one thinks you look like a jeweller. You look like a surfer, a beach bum ... just tell me the story." It was a running joke with his friends.

"Okay," said Cooper. "I introduced myself, then asked their names; where they were from, first time in Hawaii ... you know ... the usual. He was very edgy, and I tried to settle him. John Young, he said, but it sounded like he'd just made it up."

I busied myself with my tea. Fancy that, I thought.

"It was the way his girlfriend looked at him, kinda surprised, when he said the name. Then he introduced his wife as Gina. He said it twice. The second time the full name, Gina Young. She looked doubly surprised and immediately hid her left hand. Like I care whether they're married or not. He had a diamond he wanted valued. Gave me some bullshit story about his aunt having died and left it to him in her will. The family had travelled from around the world for the funeral. Too much information."

"Okay, Coops ... why is his story bullshit?"

"Rose, let me tell the story ... 'Do you want me to take a look?' I asked as I figured he might stand there all day telling me his life story. He absolutely insisted I bring the eyeglass thingy, as he called it, out to the counter. 'Why don't you take a seat,' I said. The girl, Gina shifting from one foot to the other, eyeing me up."

"Was she indeed?" I cut in. "It's about time you got your wedding ring finished, Cooper, and mine."

"Yeah, yeah, builders, plumbers and jewellers, eh? She wasn't eyeing me up in that way. Shifty, like him. I heard John Young say, in a whisper that carried as I moved to get the loupe, obviously so I'd hear, 'He'll swap it. That's what they do. This is not leaving my sight.'

"So I laid out the cloth, making a big presentation of it. This is where it gets interesting. It was a rough diamond. Uncut. Not that a rough diamond is that unusual but unusual enough. This, as well as his nervy attitude, made my antennae shoot up.

"The diamond was genuine. A nice one. Very nice. I asked them if they planned on selling it. He leapt in. 'Whooah,' he said. Truly, just like that, like I was going to snatch it from him. So I asked if they wanted a written valuation for insurance purposes. He got fidgety, so I changed the subject and asked if they were enjoying their stay. His 'wife' gave him a look. The vibration from his jumping knee made the table shake. He attempted to be cool, but it didn't work. 'It is real then? A genuine diamond?' Yes, I said and asked if he had more. 'No, no, just the one.'

"Gina nodded then shook her head and came back to nodding. She didn't say much but I could tell something wasn't right. Maybe she was still in shock she'd just got married. They were Australian, I think."

"Meaning Australians are shifty?" I asked, thinking of our new guests who were also Australian.

"No, Rose, stop it. It was just something I noticed, that's all."

"They thanked me and walked to the door. I asked where they were staying, meaning nothing in particular, but he went weird. Stammered that they were staying with the rest of the family around the coast."

Cooper had finished his story but was still in it.

"What?" I asked.

"Well, I was thinking ... I told you about a heist of diamonds on the loose ... sorry about the pun ... the story's flying around the industry and it's shrouded in rumours and flips every time it gets back to me. I'm thinking, maybe they have them, found them somewhere or even stole them and he wanted to know if his cache was genuine."

"Sounds too fantastic ... describe the couple," I said.

"Why?"

I told him about the Australian couple who'd just moved in.

"We have new guests? Is mom okay about that?"

"Of course, Cooper ... I wouldn't just move people in without checking with Joan." I told him how it had come about.

"When did they arrive on the island?"

"I don't know, Coops, maybe that morning."

"A bit of a coincidence, don't you think?"

"What ... two Australians, the only ones in the Hawaii islands, have landed at our place? Yes, amazing," I said. "Of course they'd be the ones."

"Okay, smarty pants, tell me what they look like."

"You go first."

"He's about five eleven, just under six foot, I'd say. Brown hair, brown eyes that darted around. Nice smile, I suppose, though he was so nervous it was hard to say.

"When they left the shop, they walked towards the car park and did a quick turnaround, went off in another direction. I saw them later when they came back to the rental car ... a red Mustang cabriolet.

"Anyway, he's average build, fit. He had a strong body. You

know, kept himself in shape. She's pretty, sandy coloured hair about shoulder length, slim, maybe five six. Blue eyes ... they kinda sparkled."

"Cooper, I'm getting the wrong vibes here. You're a married man."

He blew me a kiss and said not to be so stupid.

"I'd say they both worked out," Cooper went on. "Maybe they walked away from the car the first time so I wouldn't identify it later?"

"So what are you thinking, Cooper? Ask our guests if they have a bag of diamonds? Who knows, they might be the ones."

"Does that description fit them?"

"Not sure about the sparkling eyes, but yes it does ... could fit any number of couples."

"Yeah, it could ... what're the names of these guests anyway?"

"Jennifer Douglas and David Williams."

"Means nothing, except if they are the ones, proves they gave me false names." Cooper was quiet for a minute, smiling. "Would be a helluva thing if they were the same couple."

"If they're around, you'll bump into them at some stage over the weekend."

"We could ask them in for drinks tomorrow afternoon?" said Cooper.

"Yeah, or better still, I'll invite them to join us for dinner tonight at the Bougainvillea. Joan won't be joining us; she's going to a party."

"Okay, great idea. Can't wait to meet them."

Later that night I was thinking about Cooper's descriptions of the couple. His attention to detail of the woman was one thing, but the attention to the man, another. No, don't go there Kate. But I did.

TWENTY-EIGHT

Thakit

2007

Mammy would have said, 'I told you,' subtly with a touch of cynicism, if she knew I agreed with her. Yes, it was a shame, wasting an arts degree working in a warehouse. I'd risen to manager of my area. It was a job and gave me no stress. A job I'd drifted along with. I didn't see it as a forever job; I didn't want a forever job. Or to be more truthful, I didn't have a clue what forever job I did want. If I went for a career, using my degree, it would mean I had to be serious. I wasn't ready for that. I was still living at home, which mammy liked but which drove her crazy at the same time. She carried on with her usual tirade of what was I doing with my life? I reacted, "Enjoying your company, mammy."

In truth, I wanted to be back sleuthing, checking on Kate; skulduggery suited me. Aedan hadn't spoken to me since my return. When I rang him on touchdown, he grunted an acknowledgement. Not a 'thank you', not even 'stupid tosser', just an incomprehensible grumble. Since then, nothing. I asked mammy twice if she'd heard from him.

"No and we don't want to," was her reply. She wouldn't even give me his surname to enable a search.

Colin's children were growing and as their uncle, I loved them dearly. They were the only humans who didn't make me feel guilty I wasn't progressing in life. Even Colin was turning into mammy.

I worked, came home, read sleuth books and vegetated. On occasions, I rang a friend and went out, or someone rang me, and we went out. The phone rang one Saturday as I lay on the couch reading a book.

"She's living in Hawaii ... married ... name Rose Havel. Do you still have the credit card? You'll need a new phone."

"Aedan?" I bolted upright.

"Who else would it be?"

"Wow, it's really good to hear from you."

"Is it indeed?"

"She got married? Wow."

"Getting married is quite common."

"Yeah ... no ... of course it is." I settled back into a slouch. "Um ... that's great, isn't it?"

"I don't know. She needs to come back home. I need to see her. Think you can manage that?"

"Yes, of course."

"Not of course ... you failed before."

"Events happened."

"Make sure events don't happen this time. A member of her family is seriously ill and she needs to return."

After hanging up, I thought about what he said. His voice sounded different. More strained. Like an old smoker's voice. There were pauses between his words. Perhaps he was the one seriously ill. Perhaps he was the member of the family.

"Mammy," I called from the couch, "is Aedan related in some way to Kate?"

"What?"

"I'm back on." I stretched and walked to mammy who was in the kitchen. "This is great, ma, I can be a sleuth again."

She was emptying the dishwasher. "This is not great, Ryan." Back to Ryan again. "What are you going to do? Throw in the only job you've held on to for more than a week?"

That wasn't fair, but I let it go. "I'll take leave." Which I had.

"If you were working for me, I wouldn't be giving you any leave." Mammy was definitely getting crankier as she got older.

Colin wasn't any happier than mammy. Jealousy bit into him. "You're such a fecking tosser, Thakky. Don't call me if you've only got blue vistas fringed by swaying palm trees to talk about."

With that he hung up. A smile formed on my face.

I flew to Hawaii and on to Kauai, hired a car and drove to the address I'd been given. My God, it was paradise. How could I possibly fail?

TWENTY-NINE

Thakit

Kauai

The winding road to Kate's address was spectacular. Why would anyone want to live in Ireland if they could live here? Flowers had not entered my consciousness until I took that drive. Tall trees with flowers hanging like trumpets flirted with the earth; bushes covered in what looked like yellow butterflies bounced in the breeze, big orange flowers danced in amongst the leaves. And what blew me away, blue ocean blinked through the foliage. I had to stop to take it all in. I'd become quite the romantic. Who knew?

Now would be a good time to ring my brother. No, I didn't want to muddy my day. Like hell I didn't. Lucky for him, the time zone was wrong. I wasn't a total arse. The perfumed air smelt a hell of a lot better than car fumes. A warm breeze soothed and thrilled me at the same time. Returning to my car I put myself back into the sleuth zone and began my mission.

My hire car was a nondescript model in white. Not one that would attract attention. I thought of Colin as I looked at the choices. He'd have gone for the latest Mustang or the biggest Yank tank available. But I wasn't my brother, and I had a job to do, discreetly. I continued the drive slowly along the coastal road. Easily distracted, I mentally snapshotted views through the trees that took my breath away, thinking I'd get married out here too.

Once I'd settled into modest, very blah accommodation, I walked along the beach, dropped my towel on the sand and headed for the water. I needed to acclimatise. To hell with Aedan, he could wait at least one day. Kate wouldn't mind.

Aedan had given me her home address, which I checked out on my way to the beach. It was within walking distance from my motel. I ate breakfast in a small beachside café. My accent was immediately picked up by the waitress, who mentioned that the Irish seemed to like it around there.

"Oh, how so?" I said.

"Well, at least one other does. Rose, she married our local hunk. Stole him from under our noses," the waitress said.

"Is that right, Carol," I said, noticing her nametag.

"Yeah, she stole Cooper's heart. We all like her though, so she's forgiven."

"I'm here for a few days, so I might bump into her."

"You might ... in fact they're booked in for dinner tonight."

"Okay."

My breakfast finished, I had my first opening. My job was almost done, presuming Rose was the Rose I wanted. I had to eat dinner anyway. I'd get talking to her, somehow, explain why she had to leave, easy-peasy.

Another waitress worked the evenings Carol told me. "I have a little boy to take care of," she said, "single mum. Difficult to do nights."

Being totally clueless on the subject with signals of women,

I wasn't sure if this was a come on or she was just giving me information I didn't need or more likely, was hoping for a big tip. Whichever way it was meant, I didn't need complications, although she was very pretty. I gave her the obligatory tip I'd been told about.

It was a presumption I made that Kate, now called Rose and her husband would be dining alone. Why I thought that I couldn't say. So I was surprised to see another couple with them when they arrived that night. Kate and her husband were gorgeous and tanned, definitely an 'it' couple. The other couple, although pale in comparison, were also good looking. But Kate and her husband stood out.

It was a small café by day but at night it became a glamorous, cosy, romantic restaurant, with fairy lights discreetly lighting the trees fringing the building. The subdued music allowed the sound of the waves beyond to blend into the atmosphere.

Dining alone made me obvious, so I asked for a small table to the far side. I had little choice as they were fully booked. They made a table for me by the kitchen door, which suited me on this occasion. I could observe Kate and she would have to pass near to me to use the toilet, or bathroom as it's called here. Her husband was a charmer for sure. It looked as if, from where I sat, the other man was unsuccessfully trying to match his charm. Kate did not visit the bathroom. They finished and left in a group.

Second attempt. Waking in the morning, I thought I'd walk up to the house and introduce myself. Then I changed my mind; no, I wouldn't do that, anything could be going on; rushing off to work, visitors, anything. I could be given the quick brush off. I considered introducing myself and if Kate wasn't there, I could ask whoever answered the door the best time to come back. No, that was a stupid idea. Why had Aedan put all this on me? He obviously had perfectly good intelligence working for him. Had I asked him those questions? Yes, I had, but maybe not so directly. In the end, I was getting myself into such a tizzwoz, I decided against knocking on Kate's door altogether.

Thinking, round and round, I walked back to the café for breakfast. I noticed the other couple from the night before were there. I took a table within earshot, where I overheard them talking of their plans for the day. Their discussion became heated.

"They belong to both of us, both ... of ... us," the woman said. "My handbag's safe."

"No. My jacket pocket. I can check on them. They might fall out of your bag."

"And your pocket?"

"A tight fit. And besides, I look after things better than you."

"Oh, for God's sake. Okay ... what about the safe in the room?"

"Not on your life. They're staying with me and that's that."

Whatever 'they' were, must be small and precious.

They left. Curious as to where they were staying, I sauntered after them for a short distance and watched as they walked along the pathway to where Kate lived. With my towel and book in my bag, I plonked myself down on the warm sand on a part of the beach that, in a short space of time, had become my favourite spot. I got to thinking I should have walked up to them and asked if Kate lived nearby to where they were staying. Damn, I should have thought of that sooner. For some reason I was drawn to the couple and their conversation and wasn't linking my opportunity. It seemed to me beneath the surface, beneath the sunshine and beauty of the place, Kauai harboured shadows.

Shadows crossed Aedan's voice when I rang him.

"What the hell are you doing? It had better not be sitting on the beach. Get to work."

He hung up.

THIRTY

Kate/Rose

To mark the occasion of our important dinner date with Jen and Dave, instead of my usual shorts I wore a dress, and Cooper, long pants.

"Can't wait to see their faces when they meet you, Coops. If they are the couple. I wonder if they'll be Dave and Jen or revert to John and Gina? Let them do all the talking," I said, to use my old rule of staying mute. "Suppose they are who they say they are? There is a chance John and Gina are John and Gina. Intrigue over. If they are Dave and Jen ... well ..."

"My gut tells me not. Intrigue's just begun." Cooper's all-knowing gut was often right.

We originally planned to ask them in for a drink, but we felt there would be less pressure if we met them at the restaurant. On the one hand, we both wanted to meet them and know, but we really didn't want to make our lives too entwined with theirs. The tiny restaurant was full when we walked in. John/Dave and Gina/Jen were already seated. Their faces were a feast of movement; recognition, guilt, indecision and individual thoughts to construct a story.

"This is my husband, Cooper," I hand gestured, "Dave and Jen."

"We've met," said Cooper.

Cool as cucumbers, they didn't mention the previous meeting. It seemed by the time we reached them they'd come to unspoken, individual agreements, do – say – nothing. Everyone's on to the mute rule.

"Everything okay with your room?" Cooper asked.

"Very much so," said Dave. "Lovely spot. All thanks to bumping into Rose."

"We love it," chimed in Jen. "The weather's so warm. We're from Melbourne, which is cold at the moment. We really love this little restaurant too. We had breakfast here."

"They're like family to us," said Cooper, "Mom's friend is the owner." Then Cooper jumped straight in. "How long have you two been married?"

"Oh, we're not married," said Dave, trailing the word married as he realised what he'd said.

I gently kicked Cooper. Not to be deterred he pressed on, "… so not a honeymoon … reason a lot of couples come here."

"No, but maybe we should look at our time here as one," said Jen, looking to Dave.

From what Cooper told me, she'd just got married in the shop. She's Miss Cool Cucumber, I thought.

"What about you two?" Jen asked.

Clever deflection on Jen's part. "I met Cooper here on holiday." We talked generally about holiday romances and mostly agreed that's all they are. I looked at Cooper and smiled. "Sometimes they work."

"Yep," he said, giving me a hug.

"Nice," said Jen.

"Have you decided how long you're staying? Not that there's any pressure either way," I said.

"A few days," Jen said. "Longer if the place is available."

Dave stepped in, "We haven't definitely decided, have we, Jen? We've spent so much time with the family, we may extend our stay another week." Jen's eyes quickened across to Dave. "We may take time for ourselves. See how it goes. There are work constraints to consider."

The elephant in the room was getting bigger by the moment and Cooper couldn't resist. "If you need more money and can bear to part with your diamond, we can always sell it for you. There are always ready buyers for diamonds, especially of that quality," Cooper stated as he tucked into his just served meal.

I didn't notice Jen's and Dave's reaction as I nearly fell off my own perch, my eyes having moved to my just served meal. My foot was getting tired of kicking Cooper. I suppose Cooper had a point. Might as well get that elephant out and walking. In true Cooper style, he decided to hitch a ride.

"Be careful if you plan to sell on the internet," Cooper continued, "you'll be asked to post it. If you post it, you may never see your money or the diamond again. But you'd need authentication papers."

Dave glanced from Jen to Cooper but beyond that they were cool.

"No," said Dave, "no plans to do that."

Cooper was curious beyond his normal level, and I knew he wanted to find out if they had more stones; a lot more, if his suspicions were true. Wondering if they had more and where they kept them if they did, reminded me of a chat I'd had earlier with Cooper. Joan had an over-ride password to the safe in case guests forgot theirs. It was normal practice. I was shocked. The times I'd locked my stash in a hotel safe. Thinking of it gave me the shudders. Just as well I didn't know then.

I'd said, "I wonder if Jen and Dave know that?"

"If they do, they'll carry the diamonds with them," said Cooper.

"Hard to know what they trust or distrust the most. Us, the safe, or losing the diamonds if they carry them around."

With that knowledge, all through dinner I wondered if Jen had the diamonds in her handbag or Dave in his pocket, now that we'd convinced ourselves they had them. Neither of us knew what to look for. Cooper had no idea how many were in the heist and how they'd be carried. Jen's bag was small, which indicated a small heist. Too small in my opinion. On the other hand, I did notice a bulge in Dave's thin, linen jacket pocket.

A sudden prod on my leg shook me off my focus on Dave's pocket. I hadn't been following the conversation.

"Sorry," I said. "I have a thing for linen jackets. I'm always on at Cooper to buy one but I've not been successful so far." Cooper looked at me trying to recollect such a conversation. Inane chatter followed about jackets, which I'm sure Jen and Dave saw through.

As we left the restaurant, Cooper suggested a drive around the island. "... a non-touristy trip." They jumped at the chance. "How about the day after tomorrow? That's your day off too, isn't it Rose?"

"What about the shop?" I said.

"Yeah, no problem. Robert is quite capable. Suit you guys?"

Their nodding heads nearly fell off with the offer.

"Let's say ten," said Cooper as we parted, us to our house and they to the little hut.

Once inside, we giggled like children.

"Dave definitely had them in that jacket. Did you notice the bulge and him nervously patting his pocket?" I said.

"Is that what you were looking at. You practically jumped inside," Cooper chuckled. "So you want me to get a linen jacket?"

"Do you think they twigged?"

"A pet snail would have twigged ... yes ... a bulge? How big?"

I cupped my hands and then compressed.

"That's a bulge," he said.

Cooper had jewellery bags at home, those little black ones, the velvet kind. We tried different amounts of small stones and put them in the inside pocket of one of Cooper's jackets. I judged the bulge.

"That's a lot of diamonds," Cooper said.

"Cooper, what are we doing? ... that look ... I don't know that look. You're up to something."

"I think we're planning to take them, aren't we?"

"Are we?" My blood quickened. This was my territory. Did I have an accomplice as well as a husband?

THIRTY-ONE

Kate/Rose

There was no doubt Jen and Dave had the diamonds, or something they shouldn't have in their possession. Dave was the agitated one. Both Cooper and I thought he was giving the game away with his twitchiness. Cooper thought my looking at his jacket had made him twitchier. How to liberate the diamonds from him? As they weren't theirs in the first place, we told ourselves the cartel wouldn't mind if we took possession.

It presented a challenge for us if Dave constantly carried them on his person. For Jen to carry them in her handbag, Dave would have to trust her. Perhaps he didn't. Either that wedge was between them before they came on holiday, or the diamonds were driving it.

We concocted various scenarios, none involving violence, all involving monkey business. We considered telling Dave the police had paid Cooper a visit at the store; in fact, all jewellery stores. There was a suspected lost diamond heist from a South American cartel who'd stop at nothing to get it back. Jen and Dave should give them to Cooper for him to hand over to the police. But we figured the couple weren't stupid. We began to scare ourselves talking about crazed cartels, so we stopped that one. It might nudge bad luck onto us. We decided on swapping the diamonds for fakes when we took the couple for a drive around the island. Cooper volunteered I should do the swapping. Yeah … right, I thought.

"Provided he wears a jacket tomorrow, he'll have to take it off when we go swimming. Surely he won't want to take them and his jacket onto the sand and leave it there while we're in the water?" I thought on. "They did say they loved the surf, so he'd look a bit silly not going for a swim. So Dave will probably leave his jacket in the car … unless of course he shoves the bag of diamonds down his crotch." I smirked. "Silly … but possible, don't you think? Diamonds *are* waterproof."

"Oh God, this is all getting ridiculous. I doubt he'd do that. Look a bit weird if he swims with a hard-on," said Cooper.

"Okay, so what happens next?'

"You go up to the car and swap them over."

"Oh, I do, do I?"

"You're defter."

"Defter? Is this your inner crim coming out, Coops?"

"You can have left something in the car. Your bikini bottom? Towel?"

We discussed what I could have left in the car and decided my bikini bottom was a logical choice. It was hardly something I could do without.

"Okay, I go up and swap the diamonds. For what?"

"Fakes. Provided the real ones aren't there to compare, an untrained eye wouldn't notice. So you'd have to swap the lot," said Cooper.

"What if they've counted them? What about size?"

"You can count them out. Guess it's best to be on the safe side. I know the size, provided they're around the same as the one I saw. Yeah, that's the thing, they're not polished, not pretty. They're uncut. It'll be more difficult for him to check if what we're replacing them with are fakes. They look a bit like quartz crystal."

"Oh God, Coops, are you sure the one they brought in was real?"

"Yes, darling. I did more than just look at it through the loupe. There are a few ways to check and one of them is ultraviolet light. Also if they're colourless, which this one was. I was taking a while, probably why he was getting so agitated. I wanted to be sure. Don't worry, if they're like what I saw, they're real. If the rest are fake ... that will be a laugh, we'd be swapping fakes for fakes. Also, there's the rumour about the lost heist. They've not been found yet."

"So ... what if Jen and Dave do notice? Who are they going to complain to?"

"It's occurred to me, if we're correct and they have them, the diamonds must have passed through a few hands. I can't imagine a cartel keeping diamonds in a neat little jeweller's bag, if that's what they're in. Perhaps there were more and they've either been stolen again, or ...," Cooper was quiet for a moment, "they've actually done the stealing. We don't know how they got hold of them."

We were both quiet thinking on this when Cooper changed the subject. "I've been thinking, Rose, if we did acquire them and cashed some in, we could take that trip to Ireland. Take mom too. Go to England as well ... show mom Buckingham Palace. You can show me where you come from, show me around. You don't talk much about your life there. I'd love to see it and I know mom would."

"Aren't we jumping ahead of ourselves?"

The mischief bubble we'd cooked up suddenly burst. My world imploded. My inner life just got sucked out like one of those space black holes. No, no, no. That was not a good plan. Cooper noticed my look.

"What's up? You look like someone just stole your diamond heist."

Cooper had gone on about visiting Ireland before, but I ignored him or laughed it off. With a bucket-load of money, I wouldn't be able to laugh it off any longer. He was serious. The idea sickened me. That was another life, another time. Another name. I did not want to go back to Ireland, on any account. I might be wanted and with a different passport I might get away with it, but I'd be constantly checking who might be onto me.

To take my mind off my dread, I asked Cooper to tell me more about the diamonds. He'd only touched lightly on the subject during our chit-chat time. This was unusual. Coops liked to tell all, down to the minutiae. It wasn't likely I'd drifted off, as I did sometimes, but certainly not if diamonds were mentioned.

"The story going around is they went missing on Oahu. It was there that the questioning started. The visits started. Mean nasty types calling on jewellers asking if any uncut diamonds had been brought in. There was threat to their enquiry, like if you say anything to the police, you can forget your knees. Well, I'm not sure that was said, but you know what I mean. Hefty, sinister looking guys skulking around, asking questions, demanding answers in a less-than-friendly manner. By now they could be on any island or out of the country but then the rumours would have stopped."

"Have they asked you?" I jumped in.

"No. But if these mean types discover the diamonds have been found in Kauai and know there's a jeweller living here with a shop front in Honolulu ... well, you don't know. If they discover the finders, the finders will not be the keepers, that's for sure. Nor likely to walk away in one piece. A person would not want to be found to be the finder."

"Wow, that's a threat right there." I shuddered. "Very scary."

"Yeah, if someone is suspected, whether true or false, I wouldn't want to be in that person's shoes. The cartel boss won't be happy. Thing is, it's become a joke. It's like a fishing story when the fish gets bigger with every telling. So far, they've been brought in from South Africa, Columbia, Venezuela and who knows where else. I imagine the cops want in on it too. If we are close to these diamonds … well, maybe it's not a joke any longer."

"If Jen and Dave do have them, how the hell did they get them? Find them? Seems ridiculous. No one gets that lucky," I said.

"I'm not sure luck is the word."

"You know what I mean. It's not like finding a hundred-dollar note."

We were both quiet in our own little worlds. It occurred to me we could be in danger. What of Joan? I've seen the shows, read the books; it's the family that are threatened. My mood darkened further. Although I'm fond of a diamond, I was beginning to think we should let the idea go. Forget about them. I didn't say this out loud. I suspect Cooper was thinking the same. He didn't speak his thoughts either.

The day before we were to take Jen and Dave for a tour around the island, I became quite scratchy. The reality of our plan started to scare me, as a sinister outcome became a possibility. We were getting into the firing line of a lot of bad people. This was not good. Then there was my fear of being hauled back to Ireland, which had poked its head above the waterline. Cooper and I had been living a quiet, peaceful life. I felt safe, and loved, and never wanted to leave.

The weather had changed. Offshore greed had blown in.

THIRTY-TWO

Kate/Rose

The day the four of us took our tour, Dave automatically jumped in the front. I sat in the back behind him and Jen behind Cooper. I used the seating arrangement as an opportunity to keep a close eye on her and Dave. How they moved their hands, where they put them. We were still going ahead with our plan.

It was one of those perfect chocolate-box days; warm, clear sky, the views beautiful, the vegetation showing its full-colour spectrum. Kauai put on its best.

Even in these ideal conditions, Dave failed to relax. Keeping his jacket on appeared strange and highlighted that he was concealing something. That's if you were looking for strange behaviour. I'd noticed a small bulge in his inside breast pocket before he got in the car. Assuming it was the diamonds in Dave's jacket pocket, our plan was on track.

Emotionally, there was a gap between Jen and Dave. He treated her like she was a bit of a loser, in a joking but hurtful way. Giving a look to Cooper when he made these comments. A 'we're the guys' kind of look. He was a good-looking guy, knocking on cool, but his personality let him down. Eejit, is what I thought.

Not wanting to directly suggest he take his jacket off, I indicated how warm it was when Cooper came in on cue.

"This is a beautiful spot for a swim. It's a short walk down to the beach. We can lock our stuff in the back. There are changing rooms and showers, so you don't have to put up with salty bodies afterwards. I know Rose hates that. We have plenty of towels."

"Yeah, good idea," agreed Jen. "The water looks stunning."

Dave remained silent.

We all piled around to the back of the SUV and grabbed our stuff. Dave hesitated.

"Don't you swim?" I asked.

"Sure he does," said Jen. "Come on, lover, it's our holiday."

Dave cast her a fierce look.

Cooper was taller than Dave and did his boy thing, intimidating Dave by standing next to him, looking down on him as he leant against the open hatch. "Come on, last in's a rat."

Last in's a rat? ... sometimes Coops watches too many old movies. That'll never work, I thought, but it did. Dave certainly had the jewels in his jacket. He rolled it carefully, pocket on the inside, hiding the bulge.

We caught up with Jen, who had run on ahead of us. Already changed, Jen was in the water, clearly loving the waves. She wasn't going to be called a rat. Dave, with less enthusiasm, joined her. Cooper and I were right behind them and just as we passed the changing rooms, I yelled,

"I must have left my bikini bottom in the car. It's not in my towel. Back in a sec, you go on, Cooper, I'll catch up. Give me the key." He had one of those waterproof pockets to secure car keys. "Join you in a minute."

I doubted they would have heard but Cooper could explain if they noticed at all.

Sure enough, Dave's jacket gave up the bag of diamonds. To

say I was gobsmacked would be an understatement. Had they counted them? Cooper's confidence in my deftness didn't cover my nervousness and the need for speed. I laid Dave's jacket out like a tablecloth. We'd brought two jewellery bags, one grey and one white to be used as the transfer bag where I put the genuine stones. The diamonds were in a little black jewellery bag. First I poured the genuine diamonds onto Dave's jacket and counted them. Taking two for me I then put the rest into the grey bag. Pouring the fakes onto the jacket, I counted those and put them into Dave's bag. This bag then went back into his jacket pocket and I folded it exactly as he'd done. My hands were jelly. The more I hurried the more I fumbled. "Stop, Kate," I whispered. "Deep breath, girl ... steady." I'd reverted to Kate again which shook me a bit and felt strange. The genuine stones securely in my handbag, I shut the hatch and joined the others.

When I reached the beach I gave a nod to Cooper, laid out my towel and we both ran and leapt into the water joining Dave and Jen. We all lay in the sun after our swim. Dave next to Cooper. We soaked up the perfect tan. We then showered and changed.

In the girls' shower room, Jen said, "you two seem really happy."

"Yes, we are." I felt a confession approaching, nevertheless I asked. "And you?"

"Oh," she said as if an afterthought. "This holiday is a try-one-last-time trip."

"Oh?"

"We're not married," she said.

No kidding, I thought, but said, "That doesn't matter."

"No and yes. We've been together for a few years. We've become a habit. The relationship needs to move on, either off or we get married, or decide to make it for real, have kids, all that stuff."

"Oh," I said, not really wanting to get involved.

"This trip is the decider."

"And how's it going?"

"Nowhere. Exactly the same as in Australia."

I couldn't say 'oh' again, so I said nothing. She seemed satisfied she'd been able to talk, even briefly.

Jen and I joined the boys at the car. We drove a little further and stopped for a late lunch, arriving home by late afternoon. We didn't meet up with them for dinner. Both Cooper and I were exhausted and anxious to look at the diamonds.

Dave had been a bit of pain, following Cooper around like a lost puppy. Jen must be used to that behaviour as she didn't react. He clearly fancied Cooper. I was used to both men and women cosying up to Cooper. He was a likable guy. We casually said we'd have a night out when they were due to leave or before, depending on how long they stayed.

In our bedroom we tipped out the stones. They were so ordinary, I could hardly believe I was looking at a fortune, now I had the time to see them properly. It was certainly a heist. Whoever had lost them would definitely be pissed off.

"What do we do now?" I asked.

"We don't cash them in, that's for sure. We wait. I could sell the odd stone in the shop, but we're closely audited so I have to be careful. Taking them off the island would be the best bet. We might be okay on the mainland. In the meantime, we'll do nothing."

Why were neither of us jumping up and down with excitement? But I for one felt flat. I was worried and couldn't reason why. The wind had shifted. I was in cahoots with someone else. It didn't sit well with me. I hadn't thought about it before, when we weren't rich. As in, yesterday. There was nothing at stake. Now we had worries.

I wasn't comfortable. It was going to be up to Cooper to eke out our haul. Cooper, too, had suddenly become serious. I liked the crazy boy-man but he was now acting like a businessman with solemn commitments and ready to pull away from the kerb.

We couldn't decide where to keep the diamonds. At Cooper's shop they were vulnerable. The house could be turned over. Cooper worried about his mother, as did I.

We had a small safe in the bedroom, small enough someone could steal the whole thing, so we decided to forget that. What we could do and did was bury the safe in the garden.

It was heavy work, but we got it done. A private grassy patch lay outside our bedroom. Cooper took a spade and cut a neat square in the grass, then dug a hole, put the diamonds inside the safe with the door facing upwards. To protect the door of the safe he covered it with a metal tray from the kitchen. Then the dugout earth and square of turf went on top. The excess earth Cooper scattered around the garden. It was the best we could do that night.

We went to bed but now I was lying next to someone I was self-consciously going to watch. I held an uncertainty about him. A distance. A shift. Maybe the uncertainty was about me. I felt Cooper wasn't telling me everything. As I was in the same position, I decided to tell him what I'd done.

"Cooper, I took two diamonds when I was swapping them over in the car. Just in case things, well … in case we lost the lot."

He lay there silently. I waited for an earthquake to hit. And waited.

Cooper was asleep.

THIRTY-THREE

Thakit

Aedan's instructions were driving me nuts: go ahead, approach her, pull back, watch but don't contact her, don't approach. Then, "what do you mean, you haven't spoken to her yet?"

"Have you ever done this stuff, Aedan? It's not as easy as it appears. Believe me, it's not like television or James Bond."

"I found her for you and now you can't carry out a simple task."

Fuck you, I said in my head. "Why don't you get your guys, girls, whoever they are, to finish the job then?"

"Because I want you to do it."

"Why?"

"Thousands of kilometres away, idyllic conditions and you're questioning your job, your easy money, that you agreed to do quite readily. Really? It's raining and miserable, I might remind you, here in Ireland."

"I'm not sure of my next step," I said, annoyed with myself. Only an idiot would complain.

"Why don't you speak with someone at the restaurant, see if you can get an introduction?"

I thought of the pretty waitress. Maybe.

"Are you still there?" he said.

"Yes, Aedan, okay, I'll do that."

"Time is marching on, and I want her back here." He hung up.

He wanted her back. What was she to him? What time was marching on? She must be a relative. I was slipping into murky waters. Worst of all, mammy, who must have known what was going on, wouldn't speak on the matter either.

Another gorgeous day, after a swim and a lie in the sun, having read a chapter of my book, I fell asleep on the beach. I woke ravenous, with Aedan's words buzzing around my head. I shook myself into sleuth mode once again. Lunch at the café and a chat with the manager, someone in charge rather than the waitress.

At the café I asked the waitress, not pretty Carol, if the owner was about.

"No, she has Wednesdays off. Is there something I can help you with? You have a complaint?"

"No, nothing like that. The service is fine and the food," I assured the anxious waitress. "I wanted to ask about someone living in the area. I'm trying to contact someone."

"You'd better come back tomorrow then, I'm not from around here. No, wait a minute, she's not back until the day after. Lucy's over on the big island at the moment. Sure I can't help you with something?"

"No, no, it's a local thing. She's the one, but thanks anyway." I smiled. "Oh, wait a minute ... Carol, one of the waitresses, she's local? When is she on?"

"Her kid's sick, that's why I'm here."

"Oh, that's too bad. Never mind." Hindrances were getting in my way. Aedan would be off his head if I left it for another couple of days. I was back at my original thought: knock on the door. Tomorrow, I'll have an early start.

Across the road and a short walk, the driveway led to a clearing and a house, more of a shack from what I could see. Must be a short-term rental. I'd seen the other couple with Kate, oops, Rose and her husband walk along the same path after the night of the dinner. The house where Rose lived must be further along the driveway.

Suddenly the idea of knocking on Rose's door didn't seem such a good one. I'd lost my balls. Perhaps I never had any? Colin might agree. Mammy also, except she would never be that crude.

Crossing back over the road, I stood in the shade opposite Rose's driveway. I was wearing my sunhat and sunglasses, shorts and t-shirt. Standing there like that I looked a bit weird. People drove everywhere. I didn't know if loitering was against the law. I walked back to the hotel and picked up the car. Perhaps a parked car would be less conspicuous? I parked as close to vegetation as I could and hunkered down in the passenger seat. Now I was really sleuthing. I waited. Unsure what I was waiting for – it could be for my balls to grow. Nevertheless, I'd wait and pick my moment to knock on the door. At least this way my height didn't stand out while I hesitated.

Just as I was getting up my nerve, an SUV carrying four people drove out. Just as well I hadn't knocked on the door. I followed, allowing another car to come between us. If I hadn't been sleuthing, I could have enjoyed the scenic tour. So this is what the couple were on about – they were all having a day out.

They made a few photo stops and eventually parked for a swim. I stood on the top of a low rise by the path that led to the beach. Just as I was about to relax, I saw Rose walk quickly back to their car. As she was on her own, now could be a good time to approach her. That didn't feel right. I so wished I was James Bond. He'd know exactly what to do. Coming out from the bushes to say "Hi" might freak her completely. She fiddled in the back of the car, closed the hatch and walked back down to the beach.

Lunch was their next stop. I had to wait in the car while they ate and was glad I'd brought some food. It also gave me something to do. I couldn't risk reading a book, I might get engrossed in the wrong thing. The four, having finished lunch, drove back with no further sightseeing stops.

Arriving back at my room, I slumped on the bed. My big achievement for the day was to follow them around the island, follow them home and go home myself. There was no moment to approach Rose, apart from the time she went back to the car, at the beach. That had not seemed cool. A strange lanky man coming out of the bushes; I suspected she might have been scared shitless.

On reflection I could have knocked on her door once they were home, but I imagined they'd be busy unpacking the car and getting dinner ready. So when is the right time, Thakit? How was I going to explain all this to Aedan? I decided to leave contacting him. I didn't even ring Colin and gloat.

The little restaurant had me as guest again for dinner. After a few meals, I'd become a regular and was treated as such with a better table. I was surprised to see the other couple dining there also and I was close enough to hear an intense conversation going on. I'd noted their accents were Australian. Obviously on holiday but not enjoying it, even though they'd had a fabulous day out. I kept hearing the words 'Rose' and 'Cooper'. There was little else of interest from the quarrelsome conversation.

With renewed vigour, the next day I parked opposite Rose's driveway again. Here we go. I rehearsed calling her Rose. I opened my car door just as their SUV drove out. From behind my sunglasses, I saw Cooper with a passenger. It was a woman, which had to be Rose. Bugger. I decided to wait for their return. And waited. I read my book for a time, so maybe it was two hours. In that time, no car moved in or out of the driveway. I decided to come back the next day. I figured a parked car opposite or near their driveway for too long could look dubious, even though I'd parked under vegetation again.

The following day I left earlier, parked the car further away and walked. The crunch of my footsteps on their pebbled driveway caused no dog to bark and no alarm to be set off. The house and clearing was beautiful, picturesque in mammy's dialogue and my newly found language. Flowers bloomed everywhere. If this was where Rose lived, it was going to be a struggle to get her back to Ireland.

Framing the front door were flowering, hanging baskets. Everything was gorgeous. Concentrate, Thakit, I told myself. Gulping, I knocked. "Hi," I planned to say, "my name's Thakit Thirdplace and I'm from Ireland." I visualised the reverse situation if someone knocked on our door at home. "Yeah ... so." Defensive, expecting that person to be a politician or a funeral salesman. Maybe they were more friendly in Hawaii.

Still rehearsing, I knocked again. The sound echoed empty. No one was home. I walked around the back calling 'hello', but the place definitely had that no-one-at-home feel. It was a weekday so I guessed they were both at work.

Shit. It should have been all too easy. Exhausted by planning and thinking and being foiled yet again, I walked back to my car and collected my towel. Was sleuthing like this for everyone or just amateurs?

THIRTY-FOUR

Thakit

There was still enough of the day left, so I walked along the sand to my spot on the beach which, although across the road and down a path, was almost in a straight line to Kate's driveway. Oops, Kate again. Getting used to her name changes in my head, was also driving me nuts. Anyway, I contemplated what I should do as I drifted away from my strenuous thoughts into the warm sunshine. The background noise of rolling waves eventually lulled me into a snooze.

Startled by bushes being pushed aside and heavy harrumphing close to where I lay, I elbowed myself up to a slouch. A young woman stormed along the beach, threw her towel down, continued to the water's edge and plunged in. She looked so distraught I had the horrible feeling she was going to drown herself. But there was too much anger. She'd only float. Does anger make you more buoyant? It was something I'd never considered. Even though the place was paradise, people don't always see it that way. Paradise is not where you're at, especially when you're in the state she was in.

I'm no swimmer or lifeguard, but I stood at the water's edge and called out, "Are you all right?"

She turned, surprised, and yelled, "No, I am fucking not all right."

"Can I help?'

She thrashed around in the water for a while, bashing the waves, causing whatever lay beneath to be in fear for its life. She finally walked out and up to me. I recognised her.

"No, I'm not all right, and who the hell are you, anyway?"

"Nobody, well, I mean, I was just lying on the beach and you sounded very distressed. I didn't want you to drown yourself."

"Drown myself, over that fucking piece of shit?"

"No ... I don't expect you would," I said. It was the woman who'd been out with Rose and Cooper and who'd I'd seen at other times with her friend. Although her tears were the angry kind, I never liked to see a woman cry. It reminded me of my mammy, the rare times she cried when she thought of our da. Even as a littl'un, I remembered that. I felt as helpless then as I felt now.

"He left me," she said. "He fucking left *me*. I was going to be the one to leave. The bastard. It turns out he's gay and he's taken off with the guy of the couple we recently met, the couple who own the place where we're staying. We'd just met them, for fuck's sake. We had dinner and then spent the day together."

"Oh."

She flopped onto the sand where I was sitting.

"Gone to the States and with the diamonds, I expect." She gulped. Stayed quiet, which I read as her having said too much. A look of shock crossed her face. "I shouldn't have said that," she said in the quietest whisper.

"Don't mind me, I don't know what you're talking about anyway." But I keenly pocketed that bit of information like it was, well, a rare stone.

We sat together on the sand, quiet for a bit with neither of us making any effort to move.

"He was probably gay all along," she said, "probably denying it to himself, though why in this day and age? Good God, we've now moved into the twenty-first century. His parents are very conservative, perhaps that's the reason. Hiding it from mummy and daddy."

She was having a vent all right. I let her go.

"You know," she spoke to the sea, "sex was never that great, now I come to think of it. There was a distance about him. I've not had a lot of experience, but there have definitely been better ones. Huh, I picked him for security, just like the good girl I am. I'm no better than him, hiding my true self and doing what mummy and daddy expect of me."

She turned to me. I wasn't doing anything, so I was happy to sit there and listen. I felt sad for her. I had become totally absorbed in her story. Kate vanished from my mind.

She carried on like I knew what she was on about, but I realised I was just some spare ear.

"That guy is gorgeous."

"Which guy?"

"Him of the couple we were out with. Cooper. Like something out of the movies. Tall, tanned, good looking, charming." She made a gurgling sound. "Something had to be wrong. I don't mean his being gay. Well, maybe I do. I wonder if his wife knows? She must. Perhaps it's an agreement they have ... maybe it's a marriage of convenience ... he married her to get himself legit and she married him to get a visa."

"Are you a writer?"

"No, I'm fucking not ... but I should be. Make a great fucking story. I'm beginning to think the whole dinner and day out was a scam, though what and why I don't know. It all happened too easily. Too quick. They just sort of ... appeared."

"Who appeared? The couple?"

"Yes, them. She was walking along the road when we stopped and asked if there was anywhere to stay. Well, I did. He bloody wouldn't have the balls. She knew of a place. Of course she did. It was their place. It's lovely ... don't get me wrong. Little shack, cute as a button. We got on well with them and they showed us around the island, took us to little spots we'd never have found ourselves. Rose is Irish but her accent has an American twist. I like to think I can pick accents. Yours, for example, you haven't said much, but I reckon you're Irish."

I nodded with my mouth noticeably zipped, which made her laugh. She had a nice smile. I wanted this woman to talk more, not only about Kate and diamonds, but herself. For a bit she went on a tangent about accents. She was actually very nice and quite funny.

Then suddenly, "Well, thanks for listening. I think I need to go and cry some more and beat the pillow."

"I'll be here. I like this spot, so I'm happy to listen or talk, if you're still around."

"Okay."

With that she left, trailing her towel after her. I stayed a while longer. I wanted to see her again and, presuming she didn't leave later that day, I'd make a point of being at the beach the same time the next day.

It was late afternoon by then. Shite, I'd totally forgotten about Kate.

THIRTY-FIVE

Thakit

That evening, I walked along to the little restaurant. Its name, Bougainvillea I finally noticed. As it turned out, the woman I'd spoken with on the beach was seated on her own. On seeing her, I realised how she'd taken over my thinking. I hadn't given Kate a thought. Suddenly I heard Aedan's voice haranguing me. I pushed him aside and walked over to her.

"Do you feel like some company? I'm quite happy to sit on my own, which I was about to do. So, if you want to be on your own, I won't press."

She was startled but smiled quickly. "Yeah, sit down, join me. You look so different with your clothes on."

"You too ... and very nice I might add."

She was all smiles. "Thank you."

"Did you beat the pillow enough?"

"Yeah, you know, I did. I kept coming back to the fact we weren't a happening item."

She was straight into it. Suited me.

"This trip was meant to sort us out. It sure did. What I've done is come to the conclusion that it's all for the best and I'm glad he's finally out of my life. I'm not glad he stole from me."

"That's not good."

"To be honest, he didn't really steal from me." She paused and I could see her brain churning over, deciding if she should go on. "We found some diamonds ... well, David did."

"Hang on a minute. In all fairness, like you said at the beach, should you be telling me this? You don't know me."

She paused. "I must be naive, too trusting. Maybe you're right ... are you the police?"

"No, I'm not. Nor am I the person who lost them, which is a great shame."

"Should I go on?"

"Up to you. I'm a friendly person and volunteered to listen." She was itching to talk. By now, not only did I want to hear her story, I found her interesting. That genuine kind, not what you say when someone interesting, code for boring. She was very likeable. The story was revealing a depth I'd really not expected, and which might affect my ultimate encounter with Kate.

"They ... the diamonds ... were in the boot of the car we hired," she continued, "hidden in the corner, deep at the back. When David took out our luggage, his finger caught on the string of a little black bag. A little velvety kind of one, like jewellers have. You'd never have spotted it. Black on black, hidden in darkness. We emptied it onto the bed and counted twenty-eight, all about the same size but one or two were larger. To be honest, we didn't know if they were diamonds, but Dave had seen a video about rough and polished diamonds and the process. These weren't polished and looked like little lumps of quartz crystal. Well, you can imagine what was going on in our minds. Imagine if they were real? And if they weren't, why were they in a little black velvet bag, hidden in the boot of a car? David decided to take one to a jeweller and get it valued.

"We were in Honolulu at the time. We sat at the jeweller's while he … Dave … made up a stupid story about an aunt leaving it to him." Jen was talking like a runaway train. "The funny thing is, it turns out the jeweller guy was the husband of the woman, Rose. She's the one we saw on the road and asked if she knew of anywhere to stay that wasn't a touristy place. So, it turns out his mother owns the little place where we're staying." She suddenly asked, "Are you following me? Am I making sense?"

"Erm …"

"Well, anyway, it was a bit embarrassing as Dave had given the jeweller, her husband, false names and said we were married. Of course, at this stage we didn't know the jeweller was her husband. Anyway, once we arrived here, Rose suggested we have dinner and said her husband would be back from Honolulu, where he worked, and that he would join us. You can imagine our surprise and embarrassment, when in walked the jeweller. I was waiting for Dave to 'fess up and he was waiting for me. In the end neither of us did. We just let the conversation drift as though Cooper would accept our lies." Jen leaned forward towards me and said softly, "You know, I don't think he believed us from the outset." She leaned further in. "I think he probably knew there was a bunch of diamonds floating around and knew we had the rest." Jen straightened." That's what I think … he knew. He never believed that story about Dave's aunt."

"So, were they real … well, the one you took in?"

"Yes."

"Wow," was all I said as I didn't want to break her flow. She seemed to want me to say something but as I didn't know what that was, I stayed quiet. Mammy's training.

Jen fired up steam and was off again. "At dinner the friendship snowballed. He's gorgeous, that Cooper. Anybody would fancy him, male or female. He, Cooper that is, has a flirty way about him. Dave must have taken him seriously. Unless he *was* serious. Which he must have been, I guess." She was still babbling and still hurt and very upset. "The whole thing felt controlled, planned ..."

"Hang on ... sorry to butt in, but what was planned?"

"Um ... I suppose I mean their befriending us. I've been thinking it through and it's not how I thought about the evening at the time. We'd been caught out with false names, and it made me feel uncomfortable, but they didn't react, didn't question us. It was like they knew. Dave sat at dinner with a lumpy pocket full of diamonds ... bit of a comedy really. Dave and I were meant to be having a carefree break in Hawaii, sorting out our relationship and instead we got into tense human drama." Jen played with her food. "Rose and Cooper took us around the island, then lunch. They were fun, the day was fun, but underneath I felt they were monitoring us. Maybe it was just that I was on edge about the diamonds. The fact we had them with us. Or Dave did. He wanted to have them on his person. He didn't trust me with them in my handbag. He said I could lose them. He didn't trust safes in rooms either."

"Sounds very complicated."

"Yes, it was ... is. Huh ... obviously those two, Dave and Cooper, were planning a get-away. It's all so bloody clear now. Maybe Cooper left with Dave just to get the diamonds. Poor sucker Dave if that is true. I have a feeling about Rose too. She's an opportunist. She may have put Cooper up to it, the brains behind the setup."

"Why do you say that?"

"She's more complicated than Cooper. She listens a lot, taking it all in. Processing. He's open and up-front. It's all been going round and round in my mind ... I really don't know what to think any more."

"So what happened? You think Dave and the jeweller nicked off to somewhere like California, never to have to work again and live openly gay lives?"

"How did you know? That's exactly what I think."

"Didn't Dave leave you a note or anything?"

"Yes, a note and two diamonds. I guess I'm rich." She looked at me weirdly. "And don't you be getting any ideas. What's your name, anyway?"

"Thakit."

"What?"

"Thakit, long story."

"Another long story. Unless you have to be somewhere, you'd better tell me. Promise I'll listen."

THIRTY-SIX

Kate/Rose

The night of burying the diamonds, I lay next to Cooper, tense with my eyes wide open. Cooper, who falls asleep and stays asleep like a newborn puppy, had woken. The Grand Canyon lay between us.

"What is it?" I said.

"You took two diamonds."

"You were awake?"

"Mmm."

"I can hear you thinking, Coops, what is it? That I took two diamonds?"

"You didn't take them in case we lost the lot. You took them."

"Wow, that's confusing. What's the difference? Is this another side of you I don't know?"

"You took them. That's the difference. Tell me I'm wrong."

He was right but even I hadn't consciously realised that. But at least I told him.

"I told you. Isn't that what matters?"

"Maybe."

Cooper turned over and this time fell asleep. For some reason I'd been put in the cupboard under the stairs where you put people who tell you things and you are not satisfied with their answer. I rolled over and didn't fall asleep.

Sleep escaped me again on the second night and on the third. The following morning of the third night, Cooper still had not gone to Honolulu as was his usual practice. When I questioned him, he said he had business on Kauai. This occasionally happened, but not often. That I had to ask him was strange. Something was up as he was acting oddly. Irritable. Cooper didn't do irritable.

That morning after my third sleepless night, Cooper was up, showered, shaved, all in his normal manner except he was not his usual chatterbox self. After he dressed, he didn't ask me how he looked. He was fond of a second opinion. I instinctively said he looked good. He ignored me and packed his bag.

"Are you back to Honolulu today?"

No answer.

"That's not your normal bag for Honolulu," I said, trying to sound casual, not accusatory.

"It is if I want it to be."

Joan walked in just then and glanced at Cooper and then at me. "What's up?"

"For fuck's sake," Cooper said, "don't you start."

"Settle, son. I've just come to say goodbye for the week. It's what I usually do, Cooper."

"Sorry, mom ... sure."

Cooper pecked his mother on the cheek in his normal manner and then me. Then he was gone.

"What's got into him?" Joan wanted to know.

"Dunno."

"He'll be all right when he gets back. Maybe he's got worms. Used to be the case." Joan left.

What a lovely thought. Thanks, Joan. Before I had time to slay the beast in my mind, there was a knock on the front door. Aha, Coops returning to put things right. But it wasn't.

Stood on the doorstep was a tear-streaked Jen, waving a letter. She walked straight past me and sat on the couch. "Can I have a glass of wine?"

"Wine? Sure, bit early, but no matter. Do I need to join you?"

"Yes. Rose, it's terrible. Read this." She thrust the once crumpled page, now flattened out, into my hand.

Dear dear Jen

I will always care for you but let's face it, love avoided us. We'd mistaken a routine, a comfortable life for love. I think we both knew this holiday wouldn't sort us out and deep down we both recognised there was a missing element.

This may come as a shock to you and certainly to me, although perhaps I've kept the door shut, afraid to open it. Having met Cooper, I now know I am gay. In this day and age, it seems cowardly not to come out. Telling my parents is still going to take an act of extreme courage. Hopefully, with Cooper's help, I can.

We have left for California and I've no idea how long we'll be there or where we'll end up. Cooper has a business, a wife and I have my job, but we'll work it out.

Small compensation, I know, but I've left two stones in this envelope.

Hopefully in time you'll forgive me, and we can be friends once again.

Yours,
Dave

Jen looked at me, waiting for my reaction, any reaction. I had none. Not at that moment in any case.

"You don't look surprised or upset, Rose. Did you know? Did you get a letter?"

I immediately walked around the house. More to satisfy Jen than me. I knew there wouldn't be one. Not Cooper's style. "No, can't find one."

So my flippant thoughts were nudging correct. Gay? How do I pick 'em? He liked to talk a lot, he wasn't overly romantic or sexual, but we had a satisfying sex life. I'd only been with three men and Cooper was definitely better than Duncan. Stanley? Well, Stanley was kept in a private place and could not be brought out for comparisons. Gay? Bisexual? Did I attract men with complicated preferences? Glad of the wine, I took a gulp.

"What are you going to do?" I said.

"Go home." Jen looked dejected. "What else can I do? I'd like to stay and wash all this away. I can't think of a better place than in the sunshine and at the beach. But it would be living memories."

Jen sat nursing the wine and taking gulps while I stood.

"You don't seem surprised." Jen said. "Did you know?"

"No. I guess I'm in shock. He's been a bit strange, especially this morning. He left for work ... Did you suspect Dave?"

"No, but if I think about it ... no ... I don't know. Dave said he wanted to be on his own for a bit over the last couple of days. I didn't think much of it. But now I get it. If you put images on top of something, the image becomes that thing. Which is what I'm doing now, I think. There's something else, something I want to tell you."

This didn't sound good. "Go ahead, Jen ... what is it?" I sat.

"That diamond we showed Cooper, he must have told you."

I nodded.

"We had a bag full of them."

I gave a gulp and looked surprised. The surprise was genuine as I didn't expect her to give up the story.

"When we, rather Dave, was taking our bags out of the boot, sorry, I mean the trunk, from the rental car we hired in Honolulu, he snagged something on his little finger. He felt it swinging. He put the suitcase down and saw a little black velvet bag, heavy for its size. When we got into our room, we tipped the bag onto the bed and out poured all these diamonds. Well, stones of some sort. We thought they looked like quartz crystals.

"Dave checked the trunk again in case there was another bag, or any loose stones inside the car. We expected the car hire company to contact us, but they didn't. They didn't mention them when we returned the car either. Before we took it back, we made another thorough check but found nothing. That's why Dave went into Cooper's jewellery shop with that ridiculous story. We didn't know if they were real. We figured they probably weren't if no one was claiming them."

Jen stopped sniffling. "He's taken them all except the two he mentioned in the letter. He should have at least given me half."

Custody battles. Doesn't take long. At least Jen was thinking straight.

On the other hand, I was not.

We were both quiet in our own worlds.

"Jen, I need to see Joan. Will you be all right?"

"Yes ... actually I feel a lot better having told you everything."

"Joan needs to know. I'm sure she's not aware of what's happened. I have to catch her before she goes out. I want it to come from me in case anyone else knows. Excuse me a moment."

"Yeah, sure." I left Jen sitting with her glass of wine.

Joan had already left, but I needed some breathing space. Time to think. The diamonds. I already had two. Jen's were probably fake. History, my history was repeating itself. A chink had developed that widened beyond a crack. In my mind, it had now become a gaping hole.

Another issue had presented itself. I'd bumped into one of the waitresses from The Bougainvillea. An Irish man had been asking after me.

Time to go.

THIRTY-SEVEN

Thakit

Of course I didn't have to be anywhere. I was happy to tell the story of my name, but more than that, happy to sit over dinner with Jen. I launched into the tale, in an abbreviated form. When I came to the end of that version, I said, "I'm glad he gave you something and, no, I'm not into stealing from damsels in distress. But you do have two stolen diamonds. You might be in danger if whoever lost them are criminals from some cartel in Bolivia or somewhere. Are there diamond cartels like drug cartels? I don't know, but whoever owned them could be unscrupulous sorts. I imagine they've been stolen in the first place. They could of course be people who lost their diamonds somewhere."

"Could be, but they would have been reported wouldn't they? The car rental company would have asked us."

"I'd imagine, like yourselves, everyone wants a piece of the action."

"Wow, I hadn't thought it through. I'm due to leave the day after tomorrow." She looked concerned. "Do you think I'll be all right until then?"

"One can only hope. Really, I don't know. You're from Australia, right?"

"Yes. Where do you live with your Irish accent?"

"Ireland."

"Are you going to rob me on my front doorstep?"

"Only if you give me your address."

"Melbourne. Have you ever been to Australia?"

"No.

"Well, if you ever go, look me up. I mean it. I'll send you my email address."

"Have you spoken with Rose?" I said. "You're right next door."

"I haven't. I'm not sure I want to. We would have something to share, but it may not be appropriate. I imagine she's pissed off. She might blame me. God, I don't know. Maybe I'll just leave it. If I bump into her, that would be fine. I'll be speaking with Joan, the owner, before I go. That's Cooper's mum. I don't know if I should tell her. I don't know what she knows. She's such a sweet, lovely woman ... lives an idyllic life from what I can see. She'll probably ask where Dave is, or not. In any case, I could say he had to go back to work."

We left the restaurant and I told her it was great to meet her. She agreed likewise, smiled and said it was good to have my company for dinner. Before walking away, we made arrangements to meet on the beach the next day. Her last full day before catching her flight. I unexpectedly felt sad. We'd really only just met and my focus in talking to her was to find out about Rose. I found I enjoyed her company and being with her. This was a new experience for me. Sad to say, I'd never been in a relationship, ever. I'd been living in my head, training myself to be totally focused on my mission. Before that, at home, all I could think about was getting back to sleuthing. And before that I took each day as it came. A serious connection with a girl never happened. Since finding Rose, I'd been enjoying my freedom, the money and exotic places. Serious thoughts about a girl would have just got in the way.

However, right then my heart was leaping into my head where mental discipline lay. I reminded myself she was leaving very soon so I could give myself some rein. Enjoy time with her while it lasted. I'd go in hard speaking with Rose, after she left.

Incidentally, I had knocked on Rose's door twice, but no one had been home. I felt relieved, which wasn't how I should have felt. But having to deal with Rose might have interfered with meeting up with Jen.

I reflected on the evening. I'd seen Jen with fresh eyes. She was gorgeous. I hadn't really looked at her before, despite seeing her almost naked on the beach. I liked her straight off when I first saw her going crazy in the water; concern for her welfare is what I thought I felt. I must have become a serious sleuth. A solemn, whacky oddball. How sad was that. I wondered if she saw me as a curiosity. Look what I met in Hawaii, she might say when she was back in her hometown. Like some shell she'd found by the sea.

It was a moonlit night, warm with a slight breeze. Why hadn't I suggested we take a walk along the beach? But then it was best I hadn't. Too much too soon. She was fresh out of a relationship. And I still had a job to do. Taking a deep breath, I sighed out the thoughts.

Jen and I caught up the next day on the beach. There was a whole different feeling that morning. We'd arranged it, so there was intention. Suddenly I was aware of our near nakedness and yet the day before I hadn't considered it. I liked this woman a lot, which wasn't making my life any easier. I am comfortable in my body but with scrutiny, which I was sure I was getting, I am aware of how I look. Skinny legs, big nose; the middle bit's okay along with my feet. I played my nice smile. Did she like me? Did she perhaps fancy me?

We didn't talk much. Perhaps she was brooding so much she didn't notice me other than as an ear.

"Do you think my feet are nice?"

"What?" said Jen.

Why the hell I said that I've no idea. Fill the silence I expect. They are nice feet. It would be good if she thought so too. "Yeah, do you think they're okay?"

"Bloody hell. That's an odd question."

Jen sat up and looked at my feet as I moved them in and out of the sand.

"Yeah. 'S'pose ... yeah they're nice feet." She looked at me like I had a big wart on my nose.

I carried on. "Are you okay, more thoughts drumming through your mind?"

"That's a good way to put it. Yes, pounding, in fact. I can be carefree about it and then I'm not."

I suggested a swim, which changed her mood. As we walked back up the beach, she said, "I've missed out on a holiday and now I want to stay and enjoy it."

"Can you?"

"No, I have to get back to work."

"Would you like dinner tonight?"

I thought she wasn't going to answer. "That would be lovely, yes. A last supper."

"Don't go getting yourself maudlin," I said.

"You're right. It's just so beautiful here and I could stay and stay."

"You can always come back."

"Yes, right again, but would I? A trip like that would be filled with memories. I probably wouldn't."

◆

The following day after dinner, after she left, I felt very empty. I'd never felt an empty like that before. As I've admitted, I'm a novice at the love game. I wanted my brother to talk to. I could Skype him, but it wasn't the same and the time difference didn't fit. I needed to talk to him right then, face to face. Jen and I agreed should I ever go to Australia, to Melbourne, I'd look her up. We had each other's contacts. It all seemed remote, fanciful, but there she was, under my skin.

It was time again to try and meet Kate face to face.

Would you know it, she'd gone, left, vanished – again.

THIRTY-EIGHT

Kate/Rose

I walked back inside. Jen was nearly finished with her wine.

"Jen, I can't find Joan. She must have gone out. Sorry, but I need to be alone right now."

"Yes, sure. I'm leaving this afternoon. I'm all paid up. I was hoping to say goodbye to Joan ... well, never mind. Unless I bump into her before I go."

"Please don't mention this if you do. It's for me to tell her about her son. Promise?"

"Of course. Rose, under different circumstances, it would have been good to get to know you."

If Cooper had been digging, I was sure I would have heard him. The grass square looked untouched. Un-dug. I got the spade from the shed and carefully dug until I uncovered the safe. The combination worked.

The bag was still there. The diamonds still inside. Or were they? Were they fakes? Had Cooper replaced them? Perhaps he'd decided to take them and cash them in after all. It was a gamble, but deep down I believed these were still the real deal. I replaced them with the left-overs from the stash we'd used to replace Dave's. I covered everything over as it was before. That action had helped me cool off. I walked around inside the house mulling over the morning.

How could Cooper do this to me? Why hadn't he spoken with me? We knew each other so well. Though I guess he didn't know me that well or my history. I had secrets. This was probably his. Was this a new trait even he hadn't discovered about himself? For heaven's sake, he'd only just met the guy. It was hard to believe but maybe Cooper was bisexual and the opportunity had not come up for him before. Cooper, so up front, telling all about himself, until he hadn't.

By the time I walked over to see Joan, I was collected and calm. She had returned.

She was making coffee and I let her finish. When she was seated, I interrupted her chatter. Like Cooper, she was fond of a chat. By the time she'd settled, I had my story.

"Joan, I have to go back to Ireland. There's an emergency with a relative, distant relative but they want me over there. I don't know how they found me, but I got a call. I'm leaving this afternoon." Although I didn't possess a mobile phone, we had a landline.

Joan smiled with a quiet giggle. "I knew you had relatives somewhere. Everyone does." She put her cup down. "You look awful, Rose. It must be a shock. Of course you should go. Make sure you let us know how you're getting on. Write a letter like in the old days." She smiled her warm lovable smile.

It felt very wrong to lie to Joan, but I didn't want to hurt her either. She'd never believe the story about Cooper being gay and running away with a stranger. I did not want to be the bearer of that news. Cooper and I had decided not to mention the diamonds to her. We didn't want her with that knowledge if anything went belly up. I was glad I made Jen promise not to tell her. I only hoped she'd keep it.

The same story worked for the photographer, where I worked.

There were plenty of flights out of Honolulu to all sorts of places. I had enough time to clear my safety deposit box, get to the airport and take my pick of destinations. I had my shiny new passport in my married name clutched proudly in my hand. I wasn't sure of a final destination. I picked a flight to Australia that was making a couple of stops.

As I sat in the plane, waiting to take off, I wondered what tempted Cooper to go off with Dave. Not to leave me a note, just disappear. I'd rung his shop and was told Cooper wouldn't be in for a few days. I seldom rang, so the guy minding the store didn't recognise my voice.

Dave was a dick, why would he go with him? Unless it was his dick. You just can't know a person. He'd been weird with both me and Joan for a few days before he left. I realised then why he'd packed a larger bag. Had Cooper taken the genuine diamonds? He must have, if that was his reason for going. But with Dave? Maybe he had swapped them before we buried them? Which meant I had a bag of fakes. My thinking was getting so complicated, I closed my eyes. I concentrated on the thrust of the plane's engines as it readied to take off. Sunken deep in my seat, I felt its force as the plane lifted into the sky.

Scattered in my hand luggage was a stash of cash, some of my aunt's jewellery, plus a heist of diamonds, fakes or not; the rest of my jewellery I wore. Getting the diamonds valued would happen later.

I was a rich woman. I had no need to display it, no need to attract attention, no need to sit in the pointy end of the plane. But I did enjoy a champagne and once we were airborne, I raised a toast, "Here's to you, Cooper."

THIRTY-NINE

Thakit

Kate had gone. I'd missed her again. But I met Joan. She was a delight, just as Jen said. She invited me in for tea, "Just like you have in England."

"Actually, I'm from Ireland, and we do tea too."

Like an annoying fly, she swished the comment away. Although Joan played very sweet, I sensed she harboured an intelligent, strong mind, along with a stubborn streak.

"Before you go saying anything, my son is not gay."

"Erm ... I ..."

"I clean the chalet when it's vacated and empty the bins and I found a torn-up hand-written letter amongst the rubbish. 'What's this?' I said to myself. I felt something was wrong when Jen came to tell me she was leaving, but I didn't want to push it. I know it was naughty, but I pieced the letter together and there it was, a letter from that beastly man she was with. What a scoundrel, drawing my son into the darkness where *he* lives. If Cooper is gay, so be it and it makes no difference to me, but he is *not*. I'm as broadminded as the next person but I won't have lies spread about my son."

Joan leaned forward and adopted a softer tone. "I know my son ... I think he's gone with him for another reason. Diamonds.

That torn letter mentioned stones." Joan sat back. "I'm as aware as the next person, here in the islands, there's been diamonds lost by some drug lord, or in this case, a diamond lord. The rumour is they're from South America or someplace. My son likes to protect me from things, and I let him, but I know what's going on in the world." Joan paused.

"I don't know the story behind it, but I do know my son is fond of a jewel or two. You know Thakit," Joan whispered, "my son can be devious." Then in her normal tone. "There, I've said it."

Squaring her shoulders, strengthened by the telling, she went on.

"We, that is Rose and I, thought he was going to work and presumed it was Honolulu where his shop is. Now I think he was going to the mainland. He goes there often. I imagine he's only gone for a few days, so I shall find out the full story on his return. Now poor Rose has had to go home. She said she didn't have any relatives, but no one has no relatives. One of them is sick. And here you are, confirming that."

Joan was obviously glad she could talk to a stranger on the subject.

"I think they were both up to something. Rose and Cooper, I mean. The mood between them had changed. Instead of being a unified unit, a gap was there, wedged between them. That man, my tenant, had something to do with it, I'm sure. Cooper and Rose were spitting at one another, not like them at all. Like that Dave person's sneakiness had rubbed off on them. The girl was lovely, but the man ... no ... not nice at all. I don't know what's wrong, but I hope it gets sorted out sooner rather than later. So, young man, you'll find she's already returned to England."

My sleuthing skills weren't needed. Where I thought I'd need to coax information, Joan had gallantly thrown open the suitcase, exposing all its contents.

As I was leaving I gave Joan my details. She pressed my hands warmly. "It's been delightful to sit down and talk things through. You're a good listener, Thakit." She paused for a moment. "Such a strange name ... but you have a warm, kind smile, which is heartening. I may see you in England one day."

Once again, heart in mouth, I rang Aedan to tell him Kate had disappeared. "She may be on her way back to Ireland." Not for a moment did I believe that, but it stopped Aedan shouting at me. "So she may show up before I get back."

"Hmmm. Your voice tells me you don't believe a word of it." Aedan paused. "No stairs this time?"

"No."

"Get back here anyway. We'll see if she turns up."

A couple of days later I received an email from Jen saying she'd arrived home safely and how good it was to meet me. She'd forgotten to ask what I was doing in Hawaii; *I'm sorry, it was all about me me me, wasn't it?*

Thankful at the time she hadn't questioned me, but it was about sharing if I wanted to see her again. I had no hesitations about that. Though what I'd tell her required careful thought.

Being home, it was time to reconnect with Aedan. By phone as usual. He wasn't angry which surprised me. In fact, he was quite subdued.

"I feel you're close, Thakit. I'll put my scouts out again. You're costing me a fortune, but I still trust you'll be successful. It's my way of giving you something of the family fortune."

"What the hell are you on about? Why would you be giving me family fortunes?"

"Your ma was a very good employee. It's probably time you came and met me."

He hung up. I sat looking at the phone. Time I talked to mammy and let her know I was about to meet my secretive boss. And let her know it was about time she told me what she knew.

Mammy sat me down at our talking kitchen table. The teapot was hot and full, the milk jug to the side. Okay, it was going to be one of those talks. I sat back and zipped my mouth before mammy suggested I do.

"I used to work for Aedan," she said. "His real name is Lachlan Mulvaney."

"What? Like as in Kate Mulvaney?" My zipping hadn't lasted long.

"That's right. I'll be telling some of the story and he'll tell you the rest. Okay?"

I nodded, fearful if I opened my mouth again it wouldn't shut.

"Lachlan is dying. He's in a wheelchair and has the same disease as your da. He has lasted longer ... maybe better doctors' help. There's no one else left in his family."

"Is he her father?" I said and quickly shut my mouth. "Sorry."

"Uncle." Mammy gave me the story of the family. Two sisters, two brothers, one child. The father left when Kate was a little thing and no one had heard from him since. Kate and her mother Brianna moved into the big house. Both Brianna and her sister Iris died. Short story. Lachlan and Kate were the only ones left. Kate ran away when she was sixteen. Now, because Lachlan is dying, he wants her back before he passes."

His laboured speech at times made sense to me now. How strange, though, that his incredible resources were not enough to find his own brother. Perhaps he didn't want to. There was more to the story there, but I had to let mammy speak in her own good time. She'd gone quiet.

"Is that it? Can I speak?"

"Yes, but not about this. He'll tell you the rest."

Burning questions engulfed me but I had to be patient. I wondered if Lachlan would let me ask questions or would I have to zip my mouth for him too?

Mammy upped from the table then, the conversation over, leaving me hanging.

FORTY

Kate/Rose/Pippa

Sydney, Australia

Huge storms in Sydney prevented the plane from landing and we were diverted to Melbourne. How crazy, the city I wasn't keen to visit was where we landed. I only knew Jen and Dave. Jen was flying to Melbourne. I could have bumped into her at the airport either in Honolulu or Melbourne. It was unlikely but you never knew. Dave was God knows where.

I decided to disembark, like properly get off the plane and take a look-see. I stayed three days. It felt heavy after Kauai. I decided to visit Sydney.

The train took my fancy as I'd see more of the country, though it wasn't a particularly comfortable trip. I transitioned from Rose back to Pippa after I landed. Now I was ready for a new name, a new passport, a new me. The size of the country hadn't dawned on me, nor the hours and hours of travelling, which helped me transition into a new life. One, as yet, I had no idea about.

The train finally arrived in the city's central railway station, not the most salubrious of places. I continued on an inner-city train down to the harbour. I'd read about Sydney while I was in Melbourne.

Booking into one of the stylish and posh hotels close to the harbour, I lay on the luxurious king-size bed and immediately fell asleep. It was evening when I woke. I ordered room service. The next time I opened my eyes it was morning.

The view from my window was of a picture-book harbour, made glorious by sunshine dancing on the water's ripples. Cute green and yellow ferries bobbed back and forth across this harbour to and from places unknown. Places I couldn't wait to discover.

Walking down to where the ferries docked, I bought a ticket on the longest trip. Seagulls screamed and grabbed at leftover food, buskers hawked their wares and tourists flocked to the cruise ship anchored right there in the city. The sights pleased me. I sat up the back on the top deck of a ferry and breathed deeply as we motored into inlets, past exquisite homes, large apartment blocks and many trees. After half an hour or so I said aloud, "This is me," and decided to stay. The city felt robust and vibrant with an overlay of 'whatever'. It suited me.

The sky seemed so big and with this and the bright sunshine, I felt I could let go of Cooper. I'd grown to love that man. Not in the same passionate, out-of-control way I'd so quickly fallen deeply in love with Stanley. There was no urgency with Cooper, no rip-your-clothes-off-now-or-never passion. I knew Stanley as a boss, then as a friend, but it was only that day in Trinidad I felt the full force of passion. Cooper was my best friend, lover and husband. He was easy. But good and bad things come to an end eventually. Everything has its time in the sun.

It was time for a new name. I'd miss Rose, as I especially liked her. However, she'd left town. It's not hard to get a new identity. My first task was to find cheaper accommodation. As it happened, Laurel, who worked the hotel's front desk, was a chatty soul and she and I clicked.

At a loose end, I hung round the quiet reception area in the evenings. Those first few days in the hotel, Laurel helped me with local knowledge, giving me the edge on what to expect. Her professional exterior, so necessary in that swanky hotel, belied her self-effacing, mad-cap character. She had me in fits of laughter with her sharp insight into personalities. Way too accurate when it landed on me. We were like two school-kids who'd discovered the word 'fart'. She owned an inner-city apartment, which was listed as a short-term rental. As it was currently vacant, she suggested I stay there for a bit and she'd rent it to me at mates' rates. It was in a high rise, which is not my favourite, but I was thankful to move out of the fabulous but very expensive hotel.

Without wanting to spook her, I thought she might be a source for a new passport. As I knew no one else, I decided to risk it. I'd ease gently into the subject, skirt the edges and quietly shimmy in. I needn't have bothered. As I said, she could suss out a raw-food eater or an architect of crockery design as easy as spot a fly. "Isn't that just a designer?" I asked. "No," she said seriously.

After she showed me the apartment, I took her to lunch. During the following days, we met for coffee or drinks, depending on her shift. She couldn't risk the whiff of alcohol if she was working, so we only imbibed when it was one of her days off. Then we invariably got smashed. As our friendship grew, it came time to turn to the subject of a new passport.

"Well, finally," she said.

"What do you mean?"

"Well, finally you're asking me what you wanted to ask me all along."

"Am I that transparent?"

"Pippa, I work front desk in an international hotel, I've worked in the travel industry, I've worked in clubs, I know what goes on. Besides, it was nice being softened up. No, you don't look transparent to the untrained eye. Besides, it goes on all the time. Sometimes the passports shown at the hotel are so phony you wonder how they got into the country. Though they could just be the ones they use for hotels."

"And you still let them stay?"

"We have a list and if the name is not on it, yes we do, but you didn't hear that from me."

"You picked me though."

"I just figured you are looking for a new life, or at least a new start."

"Do I have a spooked horse look in my eye?"

"Not that obvious. I'm right, though, aren't I?"

"Yes, you are, on both counts. Can you help?"

"Of course. Let me find out more and then we'll get down to names."

As I walked away, I wondered if this was my moment, the moment I got picked up by Interpol or some international crime organisation, when everything unravelled, starting with Ireland and the manslaughter of my uncle and the jewellery theft from his house. Though I figured the pieces were mine. Then there was the theft from Duncan. Now and again, I've pictured him going for his stash and it not being there. I could see him, prime case for a coronary, going ballistic. He was unlikely to report his missing dodgy money. Or perhaps he went straight out and experienced kinky sex. Had himself whipped.

Laurel and I caught up a few days later. I wondered if she had any news on my passport.

My gut instinct told me Laurel was okay, but my head worried. I could run again, but I liked the place. I was tired of starting over. I thought my life was good in Hawaii but then it wasn't. I thought about Kauai, Joan and reluctantly, Cooper. If I'd stayed? No, I couldn't bear the thought. I'd never been passed over and didn't want to try it. It dawned on me I didn't like confrontation; I preferred to run. I thought about the stash of diamonds. In due course, they would have to be valued. I wondered if I'd carried and securely locked away fakes.

Coming out of my reverie, I noticed Laurel was looking at me. She'd asked me a question and I'd been busy running through my life.

"Where were you? Your face was a novel, with all its peaks and troughs. You're not a good poker player, are you?"

"Bloody hell ... you've sussed me out again. You're having the time of your life reading me, aren't you? No, I guess I wouldn't be a good poker player. I've never tried. Maybe I've relaxed my guard with you."

"Maybe, which is flattering to me. Are you after an Australian passport?"

"Yes, definitely. You can get any nationality?"

"More or less. Something very obscure may not be so easy."

"I hadn't thought about a choice. Australian will be fine."

I bought a prepaid mobile phone and texted Laurel my number. Many days passed with no word from her. The passport seemed to be taking a while but, as I had no other contacts and Laurel had started the ball rolling, it was best to be patient. We planned to meet in a few days for a drink, as Laurel was to start a different shift.

FORTY-ONE

Kate/Pippa/Jackie

With time on my hands and a new city to discover, I walked around different areas, getting to know the lay of the land. Getting a feel for where the people who worked just below the law hung out. And the respectable people, and those who lived and worked above the law in such a clever way no one suspected they weren't at all. Although I now had a contact, in case the passport didn't work out I knew where to go.

It's good to know how a city works, how its public transport runs, how people spend their time. Something drew me to a pub. A force propelled me. Dramatic, I know, but that's how it felt. I sat thinking about not much at all but questioning the reason for the direction I'd been given.

This was something I'd did from time to time. Just sat, blank canvas. It felt as though life was about to take a definitive direction. Something that happened, that I'd learnt about myself. Get out of the way of yourself and life flows. A shift; a new adventure. Just around the corner.

This pub had a beer garden, close to the city's central park and a bus ride from my apartment. I had been walking, taking no particular direction. The pub's lush garden provided shade from the hot sunshine. There I was in the middle of the city, hearing beautiful big white parrots with yellow crests screeching overhead. Other birds, as large as small dogs, walked on long legs amongst the lunch crowds looking for leftovers, digging into garbage bins with curved, black beaks. Someone told me their nickname was 'bin-chicken'. Sounds of birds and traffic filled the air, along with the smell of cut grass and diesel. After Kauai, it was busy, but compared to London, easy going. A middle ground I found comforting.

Having finished lunch, my brain was idling. I'd trained my mind in this way in Trinidad and Tobago when the grief over Stanley consumed me, day after day. The base of my wine glass was cool to the touch and meditative as I circled my fingers around it. It was a weekday, past lunchtime, so there were few patrons. There was no wait service, only a young staff member straightening the chairs and wiping down tables. She came to mine.

"If you'd like anything more to eat, chef is about to close the lunch menu."

"Thank you, but no, I'm fine."

"Are you American?" she said.

Without being aware, it seemed, I'd managed to pick up a US West Coast accent. To be less conspicuous I'd tried picking up a local one. I'd heard the Australian accent was one of the most difficult to imitate. Not wrong. I settled for my own Irish accent which must have mellowed by then. Clearly there were leftovers from Hawaii.

"I spent some time there."

With the cleaning cloth beneath her hands, the young woman leant on my table, bubbling eagerness, excitement in her eyes.

"Oh, where? I'd love to go to San Francisco and New York and, um ... lots of places over there. I'm trying to save but I'm not getting very far."

"Well, it was California." I thought it best to be broad and I knew it would please her.

"How fantastic! Do you think I could get work there?"

"You might have to work illegally if you don't have papers but I'm sure you'd get something." I was sure that's not what this pretty young blonde's parents would want me to say, but it was a casual conversation.

"That's what I think. My brother's in Hawaii surfing at the moment. He keeps moving around, otherwise I'd go over now and stay with him, but mum doesn't want me to go."

She pulled out a chair, looked around and decided she could risk it.

"Do you mind if I sit for a moment? It's our quiet period. I'd love to know about America. My cousin went to Hawaii for a holiday. She loved it, but the holiday didn't go very well for her."

This young woman was so lovely, so good natured and open, I was happy for her to sit. I wondered if I'd been like that. At sixteen, I'd had a fair bit of life thrown at me. Looking back, I was sure I was very naïve and angry. In fact, our age difference wasn't such a gap – she looked about nineteen or so to my twenty-three years, but I felt much older. Experience outpaced age. This kid was adorable; marshmallow on the outside *and* inside, I suspected.

"It would be better if you did have a contact," I said, trying to sound more responsible. "Perhaps you could take a holiday with your cousin?"

"I don't think she'd want to go again. She went with her boyfriend to see if they could patch up their relationship, but it didn't work out. He took off with someone else while they were there. She was heartbroken."

"Sounds like it wasn't Hawaii's fault, only circumstances. Perhaps you could go somewhere else with her?"

"My boyfriend doesn't want me to go either."

"Maybe he could go with you?"

"He's just starting up a business. He's got a property out of town with lots of animals."

"A farm?"

"No, they're animals he trains for film and television. He has a knack with them ... he can train them to do anything."

"Oh, that's different. What kinds of animals?"

"Let me think ... there's Alfie the dog, who is soooo brilliant, he gets lots of work. Pete's training up a couple of bitzer puppies at the moment. Um, what else ... ducks, chickens, two horses ... a miniature horse. He's only just started and it's hard. I'm not much help. He thinks I'm dumb anyway."

"I'm sure you're not ... what's your name?"

"Kimberley."

"Well, Kimberley, you sound very enthusiastic and bright; you need to be encouraged, not put down."

She giggled. "Thank you. But I do some dumb things sometimes."

"Probably nervousness, trying hard to please. We all do dumb things sometimes."

She was quiet for a moment and I thought I saw a tear develop. Oh dear, a raw nerve.

"That's very kind ... um ... what's yours ... name, I mean?"

I hadn't developed the next person I wanted to be, or a name. This was also needed for a new passport. For some reason, 'Jackie' popped into my head, using the 'k' spelling. Why waste a good 'k'? The surname didn't matter right then.

"Thank you, Jackie. You're very wise."

It was my turn to smile. I had to forgive her; she didn't know me. Wise was not a word I'd use to describe myself. I liked her immediately. She was clearly wanting more excitement in her life and to be appreciated, not suppressed. I figured the American dream was a mental escape.

We talked about her boyfriend's business. She didn't sound dumb at all. She knew Pete needed someone to look after the business side of things. She was loyal and supportive and wanted her boyfriend to succeed. She just didn't know how to help him, and he didn't even think of her as potential help.

She pushed back her chair. "I have to get back to work. It was nice talking to you, Jackie. I haven't seen you in here before. Do you come in often?"

"No, first time, but I'm staying nearby, so I'll pop in again."

"I work until mid-afternoon, depending on how busy it is. Maybe I'll see you again?"

"Yes, very likely."

I finished my wine. I felt a seed spring to life.

FORTY-TWO

Thakit

West Ireland

Mammy told me Lachlan was sick, but I wasn't prepared for how sick. Awkwardly sitting in his wheelchair, I could tell he would prefer to be in bed. A nurse hovered.

Never having seen the man before, this was my introduction to a person who had been larger than life in his younger years, from what mammy said. I couldn't imagine it. Oxygen from a Mammy chamber filled his lungs and he spoke slowly. Even with the airflow, it was laboured. The nurse told me he'd had a bad night.

"I could come back another time," I whispered.

"He wants to see you. He's stubborn," she said, with a look of disapproval.

After brief introductions and the shaking of hands, his, very fragile, I waited for him to speak. I knew enough about him to know he wasn't a man for disingenuous pleasantries. And there was no point asking how he was.

"Siobhan rang and told me she'd had an introductory talk with you," Lachlan said.

I nodded. I was still standing, still unsure if I should stay.

"Sit down," he said, with strength he mustered from somewhere. A coughing fit erupted and the nurse came rushing in.

"Don't tire him," she said.

I was about to explain I'd done nothing but thought better of it. He finally stabilised. Vague memories of my father came rushing back. Then the nurse moved my chair closer and left.

He looked at me with his rheumy eyes but with such intensity, I glimpsed the power in the man.

"I'll be brief. I don't have much time or energy. Be patient and don't interrupt. My words may falter but the story won't … nurse?" he called. How she heard him I'm not sure, but she was by his side in a flash. "Get the man a whiskey, and me."

"It's early," I protested.

"You know you mustn't," said the nurse.

"Get it anyway. He and I will need it."

He was quiet for an age, and I thought he had changed his mind about talking to me or wasn't able to. Clearly this was going to take some time. Not only was his speech laboured, but I could tell he had a lengthy story brewing. The nurse returned with two whiskeys. I took a sip. He took a breath.

"I was madly in sex with Kate's mother, Brianna, for years, always in fact, but I never wanted to marry her. Many men wanted Brianna, but I was the one she gave it to."

I wasn't sure if it was his words or the whiskey that hit me. I shifted awkwardly. I wasn't used to this kind of talk and certainly not from an old man.

"I wanted Brianna's sister for marriage. They were both gorgeous, though Brianna was the most beautiful and outrageous of the two. The one with the chutzpah."

Lachlan's breathing apparatus took on extra pressure. The old man was living his memories. "You get what I mean?" His speech laboured and his eyes searched mine.

Not feeling comfortable, I looked away. I didn't want to get into this man-to-man bollocks. Fortunately there were his instructions to obey, stay schtum.

Not discouraged, Lachlan was eager to continue.

"Brianna went after what she wanted and got it. Iris, the quieter one and pretty enough in her own right, was level-headed, unlike her sister. Brianna was aware of her beauty and took it as given she would always get her way. Because of the attention she received, she did well, both at school and socially. Girls her age followed her around, hoping some of her charm would slide off onto them. She was always the one the adults fussed over when she was small. She grew to expect admiration. Entitlement was in her DNA.

"My brother was madly in love with Brianna, seriously in love, not in sex like me or the others. But she barely gave him a second look. I toyed with Brianna but was never serious. She knew that, or at least I thought she knew that. Liam resented me. He wasn't bothered by the others who chased her, as it was clear she thought they were like flies she could brush away. And she did. Like flies, they would return and ply her with attention.

"Marrying time approached and naturally I chose Iris. There was never any doubt in my mind who it would be. Iris and I had been seeing each other, but as the four of us had all grown up together, our closeness didn't stand out. And I'd been out, sewing my oats, as we used to say.

"Iris and I announced our engagement at a party. It wasn't an official engagement party, but we turned it into one. It was obvious to everyone how serious we were, everyone except Brianna. She'd never been defeated in anything and didn't take kindly to it. The shock on her face was palpable. What I'd not expected was her anger. She stormed out of the party. Then the fun started."

Dampened, sarcastic laughter erupted which triggered another fit of coughing. I maintained my silence, wondering why he had chosen me to share this with.

"Brianna said years later she had allowed me to play with her sister, knowing I loved her the best. She didn't want to see it as the other way. The night after Iris and I announced our engagement, Brianna turned to my brother Liam, poor sod. He was so bedazzled by her, he proposed. Or she did. He must have known what everyone else saw, a woman scorned, but he either didn't care or didn't want to see. He told me he thought in time Brianna would grow to love him. He was, as everyone agreed, the better human being of us two brothers. He was certainly much kinder than me, much more sincere and gracious. Why would she not grow to love him?"

The oxygen tank worked hard as it breathed for Lachlan, but he still struggled, coughed and oblivious to my discomfort, continued.

"Iris wasn't as sexually charged as Brianna," he said with a glint as it seeped from his sickness filled eyes.

Did I really need to know all this? Lachlan clearly considered he was a man's man and assumed perhaps, all men were, therefore I would be right there with him. I wasn't. I shifted uncomfortably, in my chair.

He pressed on.

"I admit I married her because she was stable and I knew she would never cheat on me; she would always love me and I hoped, bear children with me. After being tested though, we found Iris could not conceive. Brianna knew this of course. As a teenager, Iris had a serious accident while horse riding. The doctors said at the time, it had affected her reproductive organs and she was unlikely to bear children. I remember the accident. Back then boys were told it was a female matter and it didn't concern us. I remember regularly visiting Iris and shrugging off her illness, too embarrassed to ask.

"In time Iris and I thought about various options but never got around to pursuing them.

"Shortly after Brianna and Liam married, they announced they were expecting a child. Nine months later a baby girl was born. I knew how hurt Iris felt. She suffered and suppressed that pain, bore it like a trooper. She maintained her elegance. Sucked it up. It was the final blow, the final understanding her sister was better than her in all things. She fell into despair, deep depression, and stayed there. Offering her overseas trips and precious stones, her passion, I could not entice her out of her despondency. Brianna was such a bitch. She purposely played with Kate in front of Iris. Of course this upset her. Despite the vengeance Brianna was plying, Iris loved that little girl. I was no use. I didn't intervene."

It was clear Lachlan suffered remorse, but why was he confessing all this to a young man who basically had no interest or connection? It was a good story, for sure, but what was I supposed to do with it? I took another sip of the whiskey and realised my glass was empty.

FORTY-THREE

Thakit

Lachlan summoned the nurse. She must have kept her ear to the door as his voice was so quiet and strained.

"Another for the boy."

Alarmingly, I needed another.

He waited for the nurse to leave. "Sex with Brianna continued, although it had never really stopped. As I mentioned, she was the more passionate of the two sisters but with Brianna, there was an ownership to it. I was the captive. The passion was too strong to stop. After Kate was born, Brianna must have felt she'd done her duty to Liam and resumed our sex feast with all the force she had. Yes, I was weak I know, being a mere male, I couldn't resist."

I cringed inside. Again, why was he telling me. More importantly, why was I listening to this shite? I could have left, but he was a dying man. I couldn't do that.

"When Iris was at home, she shut herself away, eventually moving into her own room. We never had sex again. One day Liam caught Brianna and me mid-carnal embrace. He said he'd wondered where Brianna took her long lunches. He tried ringing her sometimes at work and was always told she was at lunch. His suspicions became verbal. He approached his wife, who flew into a rage. Was he tracking her? Snooping on her? Her outrage made him even more suspicious. The next time he followed her to where we'd moved our assignations. Here in this house. That's where he caught us."

"Hang on a minute. Why weren't they living here? The place is huge?" I forgot for a moment that I was not to interrupt.

"For that very reason. Liam suspected Brianna would continue her relationship with me if they did. My brother didn't have any faith in my morals, quite rightly."

"Your wife just ignored it?"

"She was at work, out, charities, whatever, during those lunchtime sessions. We had it worked out, I'm not proud to say. I'll let it pass, but you promised to stay quiet."

"Sorry."

"Liam left the marriage when Kate was two, maybe three."

Lachlan was labouring. Did he just say Kate? He mentioned Kate before. Zip it or not, I wasn't letting that pass. "Hang on … hang on a minute, Lachlan, Aedan, I'm not sure what to call you. But did you say Kate? As in the Kate I've been looking for? She's your niece?" Mammy was right.

"Yes."

"That's it? Just yes?"

"I'm trying to tell you the story. Please don't interrupt again until I've finished.

"So, Liam and I had a huge row after he caught us. He was sure Kate was mine. She wasn't. Brianna swore on that. We'd been having sex for so long I wouldn't have been able to work it out. In truth, I doubt Brianna could either. But Liam didn't believe me or Brianna. He left. I've never heard from him since. Neither did Brianna or Kate. A couple of years later, Brianna and Kate moved in here."

Lachlan let out a deep sigh.

"How come you haven't got me looking for Liam?" I interrupted again, but this time he didn't reprimand me.

"He's a grown man. What do I say, sorry for shagging your wife? If he wants to disappear, it's up to him. I was wrong and now with everyone dead except Katie, I'm sorry about it. That's the way of it. But he disappeared himself. He knows where I live. The house and the estate are half his.

"Iris got sick a few years later, but locked away in her room, she kept it to herself until it was too late for any doctor to save her. After Iris died, Brianna wanted us to get married. She said after all the years we'd been together, she thought it about time. I didn't want to marry again. For me, everything was the way it should be. Well, not really, it would have been better if Iris was still alive. But I didn't want to add to the mess by getting married again. We argued about it constantly. By that time I'd taken to the bottle and found solace there.

"After one such argument, Brianna drove off in one of her tantrums and ended up crashing the car. Katie was about fourteen. Poor little kid, her father left her, then her aunt dies, whom she was very fond of, and then her mother wraps herself around a tree.

"It was just Katie and me in this big house and I had a drinking problem. Eventually, a couple of years later, we had a big argument and, well ... here I am with wheels as my legs. She pushed me down the stairs and left me for dead."

"Bloody hell ... but that's not a poor little Katie story," I said.

"There was a reason she did that ... I was drunk."

He stopped but I felt the story wasn't finished. "You did something. What happened?"

"Enough. I'm tired."

"What the feck has all this to do with me, apart from explaining why you're looking for Kate? Why would you pick me to look for your niece? You can't leave it there, Lachlan. I can tell there's more. What's going on?"

"Look at me," he said, now angered, "how long do you suppose I'll live?"

The nurse came in and told me to leave, immediately. She must have had a listening device in the room or, the old-fashioned way, a drinking glass pressed up against the wall. Either way, you don't argue with a burly nurse who tells you to watch your language and your manners. As I was heading out, she called after me to please wait for an hour or so. "He needs a short rest. He wants to speak to you further. Mrs Gallagher will give you tea if you go to the kitchen."

He wanted to see Kate before he died. Fair enough. I didn't want tea, so in the pretence of looking for the kitchen I walked around the rest of the house. I walked up the big staircase which was in bad repair. It was obviously not used much these days. The house was a huge pile. And my mammy used to clean this. What a job.

Eventually I came to the kitchen and Mrs Gallagher had tea waiting. "I've met your mammy," she said.

"You were here then?"

"Yes, but she wasn't working here then. She visited once or twice. I liked your mother well enough. Those that came after her were ... well, Iris told me, they couldn't match her. Your ma is a good woman, remember that."

FORTY-FOUR

Kate/Jackie

Christmas had been and gone and, with New Year's Eve passing with its splendid fireworks, we were into 2008. Laurel had invited me for lunch on Christmas Day. At least I hadn't been alone.

In my hand lay a brand-new passport. Jackie Katherine Chittleworth. The inclusion of Katherine gave me courage. I didn't want to let down all the other Katherines I had been, plus those in my lineage. Not all had lived within the law, but they were all strong individuals, resilient, walked tall. As long as I carried the name Katherine, I felt safe, my heritage still with me. Felicity Doncaster was the only name missing Katherine. Stanley would not have known when he wangled that passport for me.

My new passport had a lived-in look. Laurel assured me that was best. Too new could bring suspicion. That logic sounded reasonable, but I thought a person could have a new passport for many reasons. I'd never bothered before about making passports old. Stamps hunkered down amongst the pages, with a few visas yet to be used. It seemed I'd been on holidays around the Pacific Islands.

I returned to the pub on a regular basis and to the table I'd initially sat at. It became my table. If it rained, I was under cover and in the shade, if it was sunny.

Kimberley and I had time at the end of her shifts for a chat. With the cleaning cloth beneath her hand, she would pull out a chair and join me. I learnt of her life and dreams. I was curious about her boyfriend Pete and his business. It was vastly different to anything I'd known.

"He's so busy, he doesn't have time for anything else. His website isn't very good and he doesn't like it if I interfere."

"Is that how the business runs, through the internet?"

"Yes, at the moment. It's not working very well. It's so important to have a good website. We would like to have a physical office as well but that would be expensive. Pete won't get rid of Jimmy though. Jimmy is Pete's brother. He's very different to Pete. He's younger and has had some problems. Pete has been like a father and brother to Jimmy. But Jimmy has no direction and no interest in anything much. Pete says it's a stage he's going through, but I think it's more than that. They lost their parents quite young, and I think it affected Jimmy very badly."

Maybe Pete's stress levels were high, but it sounded like he didn't give enough credit to his lovely girlfriend. How could he not use his bright-eyed, enthusiastic and supportive partner? She told me they'd been together forever, having met at school. They knew each other inside out. It sounded like he took her for granted.

"It's been suggested he gets an agent, but everyone has a different idea. He has a friend who says, 'Don't give away your income to an agent, they'll take all your money. Look at all those film stars who discovered they'd been ripped off for years. Do it yourself, mate.'

Kimberley mimicked the friend's very broad accent. "Pete's split on the idea. Jimmy set up the website. He's supposed to be looking for other ways to advertise, like MySpace, but he doesn't have the same drive as Pete. Pete was hoping it would give Jimmy something to do. Give him an interest, so he could go on and study. It hasn't worked so far. It's putting a strain on Pete, looking after his business and his brother."

I wished there was something I could do to help, but I knew nothing about any of the things Kimberley mentioned.

"Guess I better get back to work. Thanks for listening, Jackie. Sorry if I've dampened down your day. See you next time."

My lunches at the pub became more frequent and I timed them so I could chat with Kimberley. Laurel and I caught up from time to time, and I had no other friends. One rainy lunchtime, I arrived to find someone sitting at my table. I was shocked, not so much by the fact someone had stolen my spot, but my reaction to it. When did I become so set in my ways?

I sat at the table next to 'mine'.

"You can join me if you want," said the occupant. "I notice you usually sit at this table but it's the best table to keep out of the rain. Obviously why you choose it."

"And the sun when it's hot." I smiled.

"Please," she said, "join me."

I pulled out a chair. "I didn't realise I'd become a fixture to be noticed."

"I don't mean any disrespect."

"None taken. I haven't noticed you before. Perhaps I've been deep in thought or daydreaming. Or been sitting on your lap and hadn't noticed. What do you think?"

"I'm usually earlier. I notice you take this table when I'm at the bar, paying. It's my table too." She laughed.

"My name's Jackie, sharer of the table."

"Susie. Do you work around here?"

"No, but I live around here. I'm not keen on cooking and their food is excellent. Is it your lunch hour?"

"Yes, sort of. I work for myself, so I can choose. It gets a bit lonely, so I like to come out for lunch. I rent an office space near here. An old building which was on the to-be-demolished list, but then the owners pulled out for some reason. When cheap rent was offered, I jumped at the chance."

Susie was neat and contained. Clipped short fair hair, highlighted with blond streaks. She gave me the air of being trustworthy, though I don't know why. Maybe it was her composed, eye-to-eye attentiveness.

"I don't like working from home. It's way too lonely and I end up looking at housework that needs doing. And I share with someone else. If she's home and I've taken up the dining-room table, she has nowhere to sit."

"What do you do?"

"I'm an accountant. I also do a bit of website work. I've just started out on my own, so I'm trying to be flexible ... see what takes off."

It sounds trite to typecast, but accountant explained her look. I couldn't help thinking of Kimberley and the website she mentioned.

"That sounds like a full-time job."

"I'm hoping it will be."

"Do you know Kimberley? The waitress here?"

"No. Well I've seen her, of course, but only in that way."

It was a fine line between interfering and helping, nor was it my place to be telling Susie about Kimberley's business. But maybe she could help Kimberley and Pete with their website?

"Can you wait another half-hour or so? I'd like you to meet her."

We chatted and then right on cue Kimberley stopped her cleaning and joined us.

"Kimberley," I said, "this is Susie. She works close by. Apparently we share this table, different shifts."

"Yes, I've noticed that," Kimberley smiled. "I wondered if this day would happen."

We chatted pleasantries, and as casually as I could, which wasn't very, I mentioned Susie's line of work.

"I thought Susie might be just the person you're looking for, Kimberley. With her skills, I mean."

Kimberley's face furrowed. "That's thoughtful of you, Jackie, but Pete can't afford to pay for accountants and website managers."

Ooops. Had I overstepped my mark? "I'm sorry, Kimberley. Of course, it's none of my business."

"It's not that." Kimberley sighed and pulled up a chair. "Pete and I had an awful row last night. He insists Jimmy can do the job, but I know he can't. It's so clear to see he's not the slightest bit interested. The website is a disaster, even I can see that. If he doesn't get it done properly, Pete's going to lose what business he has."

Kimberley seemed totally crestfallen. She went on to tell Susie about the business. In fact, she poured out the story.

Finally, she stood and said, "I'm sorry, I shouldn't be ruining your lunch."

"It's okay, Kimberley," I said.

"No worries1, Kimberley," Susie said. "You haven't ruined my lunch, but I'd better be getting back to work."

"Me too," said Kimbereley and busied herself with cleaning tables and straightening chairs.

As Susie was preparing to leave, I had one more try.

"I'd just like to help in some way but if Pete is set on Jimmy managing the website, I'm not sure if there's much more that can be done. Jimmy is Pete's younger brother. I don't think I'm talking out of school in saying they lost their parents when Pete and Jimmy were young. I don't know any more than that."

Susie and I decided to have lunch together in two days' time. Kimberley again joined us towards the end of her shift. The bright-eyed and bushy-tailed young girl of a few days earlier had disappeared. I hoped it wasn't permanent.

FORTY-FIVE

Thakit

The nurse called me back from having tea with Mrs Gallagher. Lachlan was rested and wanted to talk on. He was straight into the story as if he'd just paused for breath.

"Mrs Gallagher found me lying on the floor in the morning. The ambulance was called." He took a breath and looked at me. His eyes were sharper. "Mrs G called your mother. She thought she ought to know, would like to know. Your mother was our cleaner for a long time … your mammy."

"Yes I heard. Mrs Gallagher told me."

"What else did she tell you?"

"Nothing."

"Just as well. Where was I?" Lachlan paused. "Ah yes. When your da's illness got worse, your ma worried herself sick. It was a great strain on her. Your da's illness was showing itself. She was low, I listened. She knew her husband would die of his disease soon, that there was no hope. I believe he lived longer than expected though. After the initial diagnosis he rallied on, but after a year or so he deteriorated a little every week. Every cough, every wheeze was like a shot in the head for her. She loved your da, Ryan, I have to tell you that."

Ryan. Ominous.

"We would often sit and talk in the conservatory, not about illness, death or dying, but about the garden, or just anything at all. Anything that took her away from her sadness. We got to giving each other a hug before she left for the day. One day we kissed. There was so much comfort in that kiss. It was overwhelming."

"What?" Overwhelmed understated how I felt. "You kissed? Are you about to tell me my mammy had an affair with you?"

"I'm afraid so. I was better looking back then."

What the hell did better looking have to do with it?

"I thought you were having it off with Brianna?"

"She was at work. Never mind that."

Never mind that? Who was this man? Then he carried on like he'd not kicked me in the guts.

"We both became alive. We were an escape for each other. The affair carried on for weeks. The spell broke when your father got much worse. She took leave to look after him. Time moved on, perhaps two or three years, and eventually he went into palliative care. I didn't see her for some time. She'd left my employ to care full time for him.

"After your father passed away, I offered her her old job back, but she decided against it. She'd found another. You must have been three or four years old by then. She'd failed to mention to me that she'd borne a son. I didn't even know she'd been pregnant.

"We'd been keeping in touch by phone and spoke often over the years. Then she occasionally visited me. After a decent time, I offered to marry her, but she didn't want that either. I thought it would offer her security, be company for me, as apart from Kate, I was on my own by then. We got on well and I could help her, support her. Your ma is very independent. She didn't want pity or convenience."

I'd been sitting there the whole time with my mouth zipped and my fists clenched. My ma, an affair; that was disgusting. And the person she had an affair with was sitting in front of me. Talking freely about it. And I'd not heard a word of it before. Double disgusting. I should not be hearing this from this man. It was more than difficult for me to digest. And I'd finished another whiskey.

"And the job?" To hell with not interrupting. "The one I'm doing? Why? Why won't Kate come back? Doesn't she know you were in hospital, in this wheelchair?" I was quiet, my mind still focused on the affair. "Is she ashamed of something?" I said absently.

"No. I don't know if she knows about the wheelchair. Back when she left the house in a hurry, she cut ties completely. Even Mrs Gallagher has never heard from her. That hurt her greatly, I might add. Kate might think she's in trouble for stealing all my cash and taking all the jewellery in the house, but she's not."

"She stole from you?"

"I'm not worried about that. I used to get drunk and tease her. There was only me and her in the house after Mrs Gallagher and other help had gone home. She's feisty, that Kate, just like her mother. I was ... um ... I made a pass at her. She got angry with me and pushed me away. We were at the top of the stairs by the library. She pushed me away with a mighty thrust, shall we say, and away I went. Down the stairs. She must have got scared. No doubt she thought she'd be in trouble about what happened to me."

"What happened? You mean you ended up in the wheelchair?"

"I was unconscious. Maybe she thought I was dead."

"Did you try and contact her after she left?"

"Not directly. I was in hospital for a long time and not really with it. I didn't have the capacity to sort things out in my head. I also felt very guilty that I'd driven her to leave. People tut-tutted about

Kate's whereabouts. I never told anyone, except you, now, about how I came to be at the bottom of the stairs. Mrs G figured it out and was sworn to secrecy. Though Mrs G can let her tongue slip. She's fond of a bit of gossip but swears she never mentioned the how of the stairs. For the rest of the community, I tripped."

"So, is it the jewellery Kate stole or the fact she doesn't know you're alive?" I was gobsmacked. "Couldn't she have found out?"

"Maybe. Would you if you were sixteen and frightened? Think about that."

I did and yes, I could see a young innocent girl would be very frightened. Then on top of it all, she nicked all the valuables. She would think someone was after her. And I expect she wanted distance from this uncle making passes at her.

"And you've never actually spoken with her or been in contact with her?"

"No."

"Why?"

"I didn't know how to for a long time. How I'd approach her. How to find her. At times I thought, like her father, she'd chosen to leave so I let her go.

"Anyway, when I finally came out of hospital and recovered well enough," Lachlan continued, "I put out a search. I found out she was working in a London club and she was okay. She had changed her name. She has a fascination with names. She likes to keep them rolling. If she thought she was hidden in London under a false name, she was mistaken. If I could find her, so could the gardaí. She was only sixteen and a runaway. Underage. If you remember how you felt back then, you think you're invincible. You think you can tackle the world. Especially if you're feisty enough."

"You didn't get the gardaí involved?"

"No. I could see she wanted to stay hidden. I decided to let her be."

I felt the real truth was that he was concerned for himself. If nothing else, surely the priest, if Lachlan was practising, would have had a few words.

Through the windows, I could see the day outside had moved to late afternoon and rain hovered. It was the same day as when I arrived. The same space and time, but my life had taken a giant leap to the side. I knew who Aedan was, that he had an affair with my mother and Kate was his niece.

And I was desperate for a pee with the tea and all the whiskey I'd drunk. I could, however, hold on a little longer.

"May I look?" Indicating the pictures on the wall. He waved his assent. Looking at Lachlan then, I could see his appeal. Lean, angular and tall, with an engaging smile. He was smiling in every photo. There was Lachlan with his brother, I presumed, and his parents. So that was Kate's father.

Lachlan called the nurse. "Take Ryan to the dining room and the library please." He waved his bony finger at me. "You'll find more photos there. Then go. I'm tired."

The nurse ushered me into the darkened, forgotten rooms, switching on lights as we went.

"I need a pee," I said. The nurse showed me the way and waited outside.

The house was empty, a mausoleum. Lachlan had become entombed in his own house. The library, on the other hand, was alive; he must still spend time in it. I'd missed the room on my walk around. Pictures of a young Kate and, yes, her very beautiful mother and less attractive aunt. Lachlan was right. On her own, Iris was attractive but put the sisters together and Brianna was a standout. More pictures of Lachlan. He must have been a hit with the women. But my mother? I was queasy all over again. Angular, handsome features with a twinkle in his eye. My mother fell for that? I thought she had more depth.

FORTY-SIX

Kate/Jackie

At lunch with Susie, I mentioned I wanted to help with Pete's business. Financially. What were her thoughts?

"You could be a silent partner," she said, "but an agreement would have to be drawn up legally. You'd have to have boundaries drawn up. Very specifically, in case either you or Pete and Kimberley wanted to pull out. If you did and there was no money, you could lose your investment. Depending on how much that was, it might not be viable." She was quiet for a moment. "Have you spoken with Kimberley about this?"

"No, I'm running it through my head. What's your office space like?"

"Oh, I see where you're going. Why don't you come back with me now and have a look."

As we approached the building I was struck by its beauty, (though apparently not in the eyes of developers). Brown, reddish stone with large half-circular windows alternated with a square style. Susie gave me its current predicament as we entered.

"This building is now forgotten sandwiched between the two construction sites you saw. Apparently, the owner wouldn't accept the offer, so destruction went ahead on either side. Now he or she or they, would probably never be able to sell the building. There's a supervisor who's so laid back it's hard to get him perpendicular. As long as rent is paid on time, he doesn't care. And he doesn't care about the building's upkeep either. He makes sure the lift works. He's the bin emptier on each floor and judging from his size, he probably dreads having to climb the stairs."

"I love the lift," I said. "It reminds me of those old-time buildings you see in movies set in New York."

Susie's space was huge. "This is fabulous, Susie."

"It is and the rent is really cheap. Far more space than I need. As you can imagine, I get a bit lonely from time to time. Better than being at home though."

"Have you ever thought of sharing the space?"

"I have. But I haven't been here that long, so I'm biding my time with that thought."

"You know, I'm thinking an office for Pete's business. I know they're trying to work just from the website. Kimberley mentioned they'd like an actual office but can't even begin to think about affording that. You could be their accountant and website manager ... and sharer of office space."

"I could, could I? You really go for it, Jackie."

"Ooops ... sorry."

"Go on."

"I could put in some money to set them up. Give me an interest, as well as helping a hardworking capital."

"That's a leap, Jackie."

"Yes, guess it is. Hypothetically, would you consider it? All of the above?"

"Hypothetically, yes. I'd have to check with the supervisor about subletting. Can't see a problem if they're sharing the space."

"Would he notice?"

"He's lazy, not stupid."

"Okay then. I'm eager to hear the outcome."

FORTY-SEVEN

Thakit

The pile Kate was sitting on was unbelievable. Why wouldn't she want to come home? Okay, the uncle's an arse, but she's an adult now.

As I walked to the door, I took a last look at a picture of Lachlan as a young man. He was clearly a magnet for women; again – my mother? And my father still alive. I was sickened.

Thanking the nurse and Mrs Gallagher, I walked to my car and drove to Colin's. I needed to get drunk. A couple of whiskeys or three with Lachlan, was only a start. I realised I shouldn't have driven. I left my car at Colin's garage.

As soon as Colin saw the look on my face, he wiped his oily hands, washed up and joined me. He called to his mechanic, "I'm finishing up." He rang home and told his wife he was going to the pub. Family emergency.

We didn't speak until we were sitting down, me with another whiskey and Colin a Guinness. Only at family crisis times.

"So what's the craic?"

Two more drinks and I started fuming. "Our mother was having an affair with Lachlan Mulvaney. She was his boss, Colin, our father was still alive."

Colin was quiet. Still. I wanted him to blow up, share my rant, share my bile. But that's not my brother's style.

"She was very scared, I'm sure. Our da was a very sick man; she was losing him. I'm sure she didn't set out to have an affair. Shit happens, Thakky. You can't judge a person without knowing the conditions at the time. The emotional strain she must have been under ... she had a young son who was me, at the time. And you on the way."

"You think she was pregnant with me when she was having this affair? My God, that's more revolting."

"Seems like it."

"Oh God. Imagine ... I saw that dick when I was growing inside mammy."

"Christ, Thakky ... but yeah, guess you have a point there ... What was it like? A big'un?"

"Fuck off."

When we ran out of talk of mammy, I threw in my lot about Jen and how I felt about her. I really wanted his feedback. For so long I'd been desperate to chat to him about her and now it seemed a lame way to change the subject.

"Strike while the iron is hot, Thakky, if that's what you want." He was still back on the familial situation. "Don't take it out on ma when you get home. Give her a break."

Colin's phone had been beeping the whole way through our drinking. He finally picked up. It was mammy.

"He's with me ... yeah, bit pissed ... he's okay. Think he needs to sleep it off when he gets home. Cup of tea and bed ... yes." Colin stood. "Off you go, Thakky. I'll get you a taxi. Cool off. Be nice to our mammy."

◈

She was waiting for me, our mammy, at the front door when I got out of the taxi. Expecting trouble was written all over her. Arms crossing and uncrossing, she looked like a person about to be assassinated.

"Tea and talk?" she said.

We sat. She waited for me this time.

"An affair, mammy? Da was still alive. How could you?"

She didn't miss a beat. She'd been expecting it.

"It was wrong, Ryan, I know it. And I'm sorry. But not wholly sorry."

"Why not wholly sorry?"

"Well ..." She didn't progress.

"Colin said I shouldn't judge people not knowing what motivates them. He said you would have been very scared and vulnerable at the time."

"I was, yes, I was. It's true. But I loved your da, Thakky."

"Yeah, I know you loved him." I was feeling very wobbly. I was sorry too. I couldn't scream at her as I'd intended. She looked so sad in that moment. We sat at the table, her expecting me to go ballistic, but I couldn't. Through the haze of drink, Colin's talk had taken the puff out of me.

"It's okay, ma, it's okay. All a long time ago. You know ... I'm exhausted. I have to sleep on all this."

"Of course, Thakky. Cup of tea when you wake up."

She looked more than relieved. I hadn't realised how my intended scolding could have affected her. She'd done a marvellous job with both Colin and me. It couldn't have been easy. Colin was right, I had no right to judge her.

FORTY-EIGHT

Kate/Jackie

While I mulled over the possible investment, I decided to do something I'd been putting off. My rough diamonds needed evaluating, learn if they were genuine.

Visiting the safety deposit box, I took two diamonds from the bag and made my way to an area where many jewellers worked from small spaces in old buildings similar to Susie's. They were relics of an age gone by and held a charm. I'm not sure working in them was charming. The area was the old part of town near to the pub, not far from Chinatown.

I'd bumped into a crossroads in my life. Was I even staying in Sydney? I had been quite content discovering the city and its environs, taking ferries, buses and trains to different parts. I'd gained a broad knowledge of the lay of the land. More so than the whole time I'd spent in London.

At the building I took another clunky old lift which juddered to a stop on the fourth floor. A few steps from the lift I pushed open the door. The jeweller's name was stencilled onto a frosted glass panel. Through a waiting area I saw an elderly gentleman hunched over a cluttered workbench. He looked as if he'd been born and progressed throughout his life in that spot. He didn't speak or lift his head as I approached.

"I have two diamonds I would like valued. They're rough diamonds."

He motioned for me to take a seat in the chair opposite and finished what he was doing. Cleaning a ring by the looks of it. I sat patiently.

"Show me."

Retrieving the two diamonds, I laid them out.

"Mmm," was all he said after an interminably long time. "Where did you get these?"

"My aunt."

He turned the diamonds many times. Giving each one total focus. Then back to the first and so on. Beyond an 'mmm' and a suck of his tongue, he said nothing. I wondered if that's what Cooper had done. Finally ...

"Where did you get these again?"

"My aunt."

"And where did she get them?"

"I don't know. She left them to me. She's passed on."

"Was she here in Australia?"

"No."

"Where did she live?"

Now the jeweller was beginning to annoy me. "What's that got to do with anything? Just tell me if they're genuine."

"Oh, you think they may be fake?"

"They could be."

"No, they're not."

"Okay, that's fine. What do I owe you?"

"Don't you want to know how much they're worth?"

"No. You've told me they're genuine and asked me unnecessary questions. Genuine is fine. How much do I owe you?"

"Nothing."

"Thank you."

I returned the diamonds to a pocket in my handbag and left his workshop. Clearly, the jeweller had knowledge of a heist. It would have been good to know where they came from, but maybe he didn't know that. One thing I did learn, they were real. Another thing I knew, it was not the time to cash them in.

FORTY-NINE

Kate/Jackie

Being married and settled had brought about a change in me. I hadn't realised how much until then. I thought I'd just go back to my old ways. Now I thought about it, I didn't know what those old ways were. I'd drifted from one thing to the next. From one man to the next. One situation to the next. All I'd ever done was change my location and life took me on from there. It was happening again but this time I was directing it.

And I was being foolish. A chat with pragmatic Laurel might sort me out. We caught up, talked about her latest man, her job and life in general.

"Laurel, I'd like your opinion. I've met a young woman." She looked at me with surprise. "No, Laurel, not like that. Her boyfriend is an animal trainer, hiring them out to the television and film industry. He's struggling with his website, using his younger brother to set it up and maintain it. That isn't working. Although Kimberley and Pete have known each other for years, he doesn't want her getting involved. Kimberley is a smart young thing and although she's no expert in technology, she knows the website's crap." I paused for breath.

"Okay."

"I'm thinking of investing in them. Only to help them get set up. Get the website professionally handled. He can't afford an accountant and that side of things is in need of attention too. I'd like to help them for the first, say, six months, so they can get on their feet."

"Wow. Is this what you've been doing with your time? Nothing simple then. I presume you have the funds to help them?"

"I have the funds."

"Is this all going to be made legal?"

"It's a loan and a gamble. If I make things legit, I'm going to run into some trouble, aren't I?"

"I'd say so. Birth certificate for a start. Perhaps going back to your real name ... but then you'd have to 'fess up as to the name you entered the country."

"That's what I thought."

"Why? Why bother at all?"

"Feels right. I'd like to do something for someone, make a difference."

"Oh, God help me. Save the world? Plenty of charities would love you."

"Yeah. I know. But I'd like to see this happen."

"What does, Kimberley is it, and Pete say about this?"

"I haven't mentioned it."

"Well, perhaps you should. They may think it's a bit weird, don't you think?"

"Mmm ... I hadn't thought of it like that. I've got to know Kimberley quite well."

"How do you know her?"

Even as I was telling the story, it was sounding more and more limp. I still didn't even know Kimberley's surname.

"She's the waitress where I have lunch at a pub at the other end of town." I waited for her to either roar with laughter or look at me like I was a total eejit.

"Okay, so clearly you say you know this young woman very well. However, you can't have checked out her credibility or even know if Pete is for real. Does she suspect you want to give her money?"

"No, she does not. I'm running it past you to get your reaction ... which I'm getting."

Laurel didn't say anything for ages. Just looked at me. "You're one of the more interesting stories I've met at the hotel. I'm good at judging people, as you know, but I didn't see this coming."

We were both quiet. There was no point my saying more, as I thought I knew her opinion.

After an age of silence and unable to stop, press on I did. "Saying it out loud, instead of having it in my head, helps. There is one more thing. I've met another young woman who rents an office space, a large space, on her own. She's just starting out as an accountant and website management."

"And you've spoken to her about it?"

"Yes. Hypothetically, she'd be okay with the idea."

"Okay, so it is a step further than just a thought. Well ... Jackie," she said my name, stressing the infallibility of it, "if it will give you something to do, something to get involved in and you're not going to send yourself broke, go for it. Let me know how it goes." She squared her shoulders. "Personally, I think you're mad."

Laurel had more or less reacted as I expected. It was good to speak out loud to someone totally impartial with no knowledge of any of the participating players.

Another night sleeping on crazy and time to speak to Kimberley. It had been a week or more since I'd lunched at the pub. I sipped at my wine as I waited for lunch to arrive, thinking about what I'd say. I was just finishing up when Kimberley appeared cleaning the tables.

"Hi," she said. "I thought you might have left town."

"No, not at all. Out and about getting to know the city."

"Can I join you?"

"Of course. How are things? You'd had an argument with Pete last time I saw you."

"Fine. More than fine. We've had many talks about the business. Long story short, it's time Pete took the next step. He agrees. He realises Jimmy is never going to be any use with the website, so he wants to get someone to run it. Now we just have to find someone."

"Remember Susie? We had lunch together. I think it was the last time I saw you?"

"Yes, I do. She comes in from time to time, but I've only seen her once since then."

"Did she speak with you?"

"No, we just waved."

"She's an accountant and looks after websites. She's just starting out."

"Is she any good?"

"I've no idea. I haven't a clue about websites. Would you like to talk to her? I could get her to join me for lunch and you can have a chat."

"Okay, but she'd have to speak with Pete."

"Well, first things first. She has an office space not far from here. A huge area in one of those old buildings. I don't know if an office space would help matters but I'm sure she'd be happy to share."

"Oh, we hadn't got that far."

"I'll see if Susie can join me for lunch tomorrow."

After the lunch, things went well enough for Susie and I to be invited to a barbecue at their farm that weekend. It was about an hour out of town.

Pete was a surprise. Engaging, appealing, a young man who was instantly likable. He complemented Kimberley's freshness. Her bubbly personality blended with Pete's quiet calm. Between the two of them, they prepared an impressive lunch with Blair, Kimberley's mother, part of the close family unit. When talk turned to websites, Jimmy, Pete's brother, disappeared. Susie and Pete eventually absorbed themselves at the computer and it was clear they were getting along.

Pete's rapport with his animals was also clear. His favourite and best mate was Alfie the dog. He looked like bits and pieces of different breeds, placed in a sack, shaken and hey presto, Alfie.

If all things worked out and my financial offer was taken, I felt I could contribute in some way, having experience managing small businesses both with Stanley and then Duncan. Not forgetting the photography studio.

In this peaceful place, though not necessarily quiet, due to chattering animals, the environment was quite different from anything I'd previously experienced. The air was hot and dry, the heat intense. The land fought for moisture as it lay flat and gasping. Yet there was growth. Spindly trees pushed their way through long brown grasses. The temperature was hotter, I was told, as we were so far from sea breezes. I wasn't accustomed to the harshness. It unnerved me and gave me the impression of taking no prisoners.

Strolling away from the house, my feet crunched on the short, stubbly dry grass. The stillness had a strong aroma, expectant but resigned at the same time. There was not a rustle amongst the grasses. It was hard to imagine living there. I wondered if character was determined by living in such a place – or if character chose its living conditions. Flies were something else. Kimberley had warned me about them. She wasn't wrong.

Suddenly I felt homesick. But for what and where I wasn't sure. Hawaii with its soft breezes and abundant growth? No, it wasn't there. Then, quite unexpectedly, I realised I missed Ireland. The lush green fields that rolled into rocky outcrops, wet and cold; but when the sun shone, what a lift it gave the soul. Yes, that was it. For the first time in my life, I was homesick for Ireland.

Nausea overcame me. Panic-stricken, I sat down on that dry land. This was not the time to be wanting to go home. In all these years, any desire to return had been the last thing on my mind. This was a different life, different circumstances, different times. Eventually it passed and I went back into the house.

"Susie's okay then?" I said to Kimberley.

"Yes, we think she's great. We just have to sort out the money side," she replied.

"I want to speak with you about that, Kimberley."

Pausing briefly to take a breath I was aware of something Laurel had hinted at; how they would see the loan. How self-centred I was. My offer needed to be presented clearly without appearing patronising or doolally.

"I'll get straight to the point. I'd like to lend you the money to get started. If you decide on sharing the office space with Susie, I'll pay the rent for six months. It would be a share of Susie's rent. Half. It would help her too. The same goes for accountancy and the website. It would be a loan and you can pay me back later."

Kimberley sat transfixed. "Why?"

"Good question. I'm interested. This business is something I don't know anything about. I want to see you and Pete get a chance. I've been helped along the way. I'd like to pass it on. I also need to have an interest in something. I won't interfere with how you manage your business, but I might be able to lend a hand. If you want me to. I have some experience in managing businesses, but I promise I'll only input if I'm invited."

"I don't know what to say." Kimberley was quiet. "It would have to be legally drawn up, I'm guessing?"

"No, I'm happy to do it on a handshake."

"I can't believe it, Jackie." Her face told me she was excited, but not trusting. As in, what was really in it for me. "I'll have to see what Pete says. He's not one for getting deep into debt. That's why he's been stuck. We were thinking about getting a small loan for running costs. We don't have much collateral in the eyes of the banks. We haven't tried, but Pete thinks animals might not be seen as a good investment. We don't want to put the house and land up, as it's mum's. She's offered but we both said no to that."

"Well, it's there, Kimberley, if you want. Let me know."

"How soon would that offer be available?"

"As soon as you like."

Susie and Pete emerged from the house.

"I'll speak to him tonight," Kimberley whispered.

FIFTY

Thakit

The morning after I'd been drunk, after the chat with Colin, I was very relieved I hadn't upset my ma. I had slept long and deep. Mammy had already left for work when I woke. By the time she got home I had the tea ready and was sat waiting at our table. I poured the hot water into the teapot as she walked in.

"Looks serious," she said, as she dutifully sat.

I told her everything Lachlan had told me from beginning to end. His condition and the mausoleum atmosphere of the house. The pictures I saw. Meeting Mrs Gallagher.

"She holds you in high regard, by the way." I paused for a moment as we sipped our tea. "Did Lachlan leave anything out, mammy?"

"So that's everything, is it?"

"Why? What do you mean? Is there more?" I said.

"I'm not I'm ashamed of that time. I was scared about losing your da and my future looked dubious with two little boys."

"Why me? Why did he choose me and not Colin? I've been thinking about that since I woke up."

"Why not you? Do you have family? Are you settled in your life?"

"Don't suppose he knew that before you told him, ma."

"We're not islands, son, knowledge is out there. I don't know how his mind is working right now. He must be on a lot of medication, which can muddle the brain. Going back, when your da originally got sick, Colin was a littl'un. Then you came along unexpectedly and I didn't tell Lachlan. I hadn't told him out being pregnant either. I was no longer working in the big house. We kept in touch but only by phone. He was cross with me later when I did tell him. Said I should have shared it with him. Well, it wasn't his business. I needed to deal with it in my own way, in my own time. Despite all that, Lachlan appreciated it had been a difficult time for me. Since then, Lachlan has been good to all of us, Thakky, all of us."

"Why didn't you marry him? You could have lived in luxury – though that house is not luxurious, just big."

"Marrying someone who I didn't love would not have made me happy, Thakky. Secure maybe, but security is not worth the trade-off when you don't love someone. Marrying for convenience didn't seem the answer to me, then or now. It would have been a big noose around my neck. Lachlan was generous after you came along. I had two sons to look after. With his input, we coped financially. I was very lucky in that respect. I had my boys and my independence. I missed your da, but he'd been ill for so long. I missed him, Thakky, and I missed the earlier years."

Mammy still hadn't answered my question. Was there more? I needed to know.

"Your da and I had a sexual relationship until almost the end. You coming along was a miracle."

The chat with ma left me feeling odd. Not everything had clicked into place, but taking Colin's advice I didn't want to put pressure on mammy for having an affair. Colin hadn't wanted to talk any further on the subject. Always the practical one, my brother. How I loved him. He had the ability to lighten things up, level them out. Like a giant roller flattening out the bitumen for the road ahead.

Not long after that day, Kate was found in Sydney. Lachlan's contacts once again came up trumps. He was told she was working in a business there, one she was involved in, as in helping to set it up. Lachlan said probably with his money. It seemed she'd put down roots, changed her name again. Lachlan wanted me to go over and get her, bring her home. I wondered how long she'd stay put and if I'd meet up with her before she disappeared again. I didn't care. It gave me the opportunity to go to Melbourne.

"Mind if I go to Melbourne first?"

"I'm a sick old man and you're asking if you can joyride on my money while I'm dying?"

"Erm ... yes ... that is what I'm asking."

"Is it a woman?"

"Yes."

"Well then, why didn't you say so in the first place?"

"Erm ..."

"Yes, you can."

His mind wasn't too sick to chuck me around. When I tried to tell him the story, he shooed me away. "Just go ... and bring my niece back. A reminder, in case you forget why you're over there."

The next time I spoke with Lachlan, to finalise arrangements, I mentioned how I felt about Jen. He didn't shoo me off that time. Maybe he was too sick and couldn't rustle up the energy, but I detected interest. I found myself talking to him like a father. He wished me well, supported me and hoped it worked out. He reminded me time was running out for him.

Colin was beyond being pissed off this time. But he did give me instructions on how to woo the woman I thought I loved. "Don't piss about this time, Thakky."

"She might not feel the same. We've only been emailing on a casual basis."

"You won't know if you don't try. You've got a bloody airfare to go there, don't be an arse. Pretend to yourself it's a foregone conclusion. That's if you still like her when you meet up again."

Mammy didn't fight the plans either. She was mildly interested, though reserved.

"I've never heard you mention a girl so many times. Maybe it's because you haven't seen her. She's so far away. I don't know why you couldn't have met someone who lived in Ireland. Even the other end of the country would be better. If you move there, I'll not be forgiving you."

I'd not thought about living anywhere other than Ireland. Mammy's words had put a different slant on things. Suddenly it was very serious and not entirely fun anymore. I hadn't thought beyond meeting up with Jen – I just wanted to know she liked me as much as I liked her. The thought that my feelings might change on seeing her again, also hadn't entered my mind.

Lachlan had instructed me on how to convince Kate to come home. It did occur to me he didn't know her now. She wasn't an innocent sixteen-year-old anymore. He said I was not to beat around the bush. There was no time to lose.

FIFTY-ONE

Thakit

Melboure, Australia — 2009

The day came quickly, and I was on my way. I'd never flown so far. I had plenty to read and movies to watch to keep my mind off the outcome. I couldn't focus on anything. What if? What if? The vague reminder that I was on a mission to bring Lachlan's niece back also interfered with my thoughts. I'd never felt weighed down by so much responsibility before.

The Melbourne hotel I decided on was in the city centre, so there was no pressure for Jen to invite me to stay. For all I knew, she didn't feel as I did about her. Our emails had continued as weekly chats, as friends. I could find nothing in them that gave the impression of a forthcoming serious relationship. I read them as me, and then as a stranger, and from both angles I came to the same conclusion. I couldn't tell what she felt.

So I was surprised to see Jen waiting for me as I came through customs at Melbourne airport.

"Jen, I had no idea you'd meet me. How did you know when I'd arrive?"

"You told me when you were leaving and what airline. It wasn't hard to ask the airline what time your flight was arriving."

She drove me to my hotel. As we sat in her car, I was a mess, with the butterflies fluttering about all over me. I was surprised she couldn't see them. Maybe she did but was too polite to mention it. She was also concentrating on driving.

"I have to get to work, so let's catch up tonight for dinner. Oh, unless you have other plans?"

"No, no, that would be great." She would come to my hotel. She knew a little Italian restaurant just a short walk away.

Jen was the same fun, enigmatic woman I'd met in Hawaii. I still couldn't tell if she was keen on me or if that's how she treated every man. The next night we had dinner again. This time she invited her friends along. They were welcoming but scrutinising. Were they looking at the shell Jen had found on the beach? Whatever they thought didn't interfere with us meeting every day I was there.

"I'm going to Sydney on Tuesday," I said.

"Has it been five days? The time has flown by. What are you doing in Sydney?"

"Looking for a relative. There's a sick family member who wants to see her. I'm supposed to take her home."

"Sounds mysterious ... as in strongarming."

"Yes, it does sound like that. It is, but I'm hoping it won't be difficult."

"I have a cousin in Sydney, well just outside. She's just expanded her business. I'm very excited for her. Maybe I could come up and see her and you? Oh ... unless you will be too busy. It's time I saw my cousin again in any case."

Butterflies were swarming again. She wanted to come to Sydney while I was there. That must mean something. I hadn't even kissed her or felt we'd moved on. My brother's words rang in my head. Man up.

"Do you like me, Jen? In a special way?" If that was manning up, I wasn't sure, but it was all I could muster. It sounded pathetic out loud.

"Yes, Thakky, I do. Of course I do, I wouldn't be here if I didn't. But I'm not sure if you feel that way about me. You're very laid back. You have a passing-through quality about you. As if nothing is serious."

I laughed. She looked at me quizzically.

"I'm only laughing, Jen, because my mother always says I don't take life seriously enough. I don't but I do. Life is too wonderful to scrutinise, to get bogged down in what a person should do and not do. And I've never felt about anyone like I do about you, and I don't know what I'm supposed to do. Are there procedures I should follow?"

She laughed. "Wonderful, you are so wonderful, Thakky. Really ... you really like me, in a special way?"

"Of course I do. What do you think I'm doing here?"

"Stopping by on your way to Sydney."

"You've got me there ... but I pulled out all the stops to get the extra time. The Sydney thing is getting urgent. I really, really wanted to see you and you've been on my mind since that first time on the beach. I think I fell in love with you when you beat the hell out of the ocean, although I didn't know it then."

She looked at me, smiling with her eyes and her heart. "You fell in love with me?"

"Yes ... I did. I do." I'd not even thought that word before and as it popped out of my mouth, it felt more real than if I'd just thought it.

"You snuck up on me," Jen said. "I can't think of being with anyone else but you."

She hadn't actually told me she loved me, but I hoped that would come.

I flew to Sydney the next day, taking with me a night I would never forget, and a confidence in myself I'd never experienced before.

FIFTY-TWO

Kate/Jackie

2009

A second barbecue at Kimberley's showed Pete had seriously considered my idea. He picked me up from the train station as I'd travelled alone. We arrived to find Kimberley and her mother Blair in the kitchen, cooking up a storm.

My putting up the money was taken warily by Pete and Kimberley's mother, which I respected. I reassured them I trusted my investment.

"The big question is," Pete said, "when do you want the money back?"

"As the loan is on a handshake, I trust you'll pay me back when you can."

"Why would you do that?" Pete said. "You don't know either of us very well."

"No, I don't. But I do. I've seen how you live, I've seen how Kimberley works, I've met Kimberley's mother, you and your brother. You get to know people by how they live."

"But we don't know you," Pete said.

"Ah, no, I guess you don't. But as the loan is on a handshake, you'd have to know I trust you. My marriage broke down in the States and I'm making a new life for myself here. I could go and get some job I'm not really interested in. I could look around for other investments or do nothing at all." I shrugged. "You've got under my skin for some unknown reason. I liked Kimberley instantly and as you know, we talked at the pub. It *feels* right. Not very businesslike, I know. But your business feels right to me. I have a gut feeling about you two. Besides, it's a bigger risk for me than for you. I know you'll pay me back when the time is right."

Kimberley, Pete and Blair looked at one another. Their questions seemed to have petered out.

"If you don't feel comfortable with the loan, it's okay."

They were quiet. "Of course we'd like to accept your offer but forgive us if we're wary," said Pete.

"Understood and I'm sure it's an odd gesture in these times. But I mean it."

"Yes," said Pete. "If you're sure. I will repay you but I'm not sure we'll ever know how to thank you."

Actions moved quickly from then on. Pete and Kimberley decided to share Susie's office, as it would make dealing with the website easier if Kimberley could be there too and keep her job at the pub. I could help out as well with the management side of things on a needs-only basis. I would also get one of the spaces in the office.

We all had input on how to decorate the space. Susie had minimal furnishings. Our first acquisition was a large table Pete unearthed from a friend's shed. It was a piece that would double as a desk. Cleaning it, we discovered it was ash and when polished it glowed like satin. It was positioned facing the heavy glass swing doors. Kimberley claimed the table as her reception desk where she'd work part time initially. Susie and I took the two offices either side of the central area. Light flooded in through the arched windows, which faced the park.

A couch was found and cleaned, revealing lime green fabric. So comfortable that I feared whoever sat there might never leave. Photos of Pete's animals hung on one wall space, with Susie's qualifications displayed on another.

We celebrated with bubbles. Amidst the cheering, the name B.A.Q.A.M. rose to the surface. Even when we sobered up, we liked it.

B.A.Q.A.M.
bark and quack and more
Animals for Hire

Loopy, the lopsided dog, occasionally joined us in the office. Pete's second favourite after Alfie. She was a bitzer Pete trained to do anything, although she had a mind of her own. Not fond of being conned, she'd play dumb.

Kimberley's business acumen far exceeded our expectations. With this extra business, Susie's business grew as well. She acquired more clients and found she was busier by the month.

My living arrangements changed. Laurel's aunt Coral, who I'd met on Christmas day, owned a terrace house not far from the office. She rented out a flat on the ground floor and the tenant had just vacated. Laurel had a special relationship with her aunt that reminded me of mine with my Aunt Iris.

Behind the flat lay a private square of garden where the sun shone in the morning. An outside laundry was attached to the back. The flat was small, with one bedroom, a small kitchen and a lounge room.

I loved it. Pete found me a bed and I bought a mattress. Other pieces of furniture arrived by the same route as the office – second-hand with nothing more needed than a lick of paint and a nail or two. My piece of paradise. I'd never owned my own furniture before, as Cooper's place was already furnished as was Duncan's and Stanley's. I accepted the offer of a repaired bicycle and became fit riding to and from the office. I spent time there when I was needed, sometimes to organise an event for potential clientele. Weekends or afternoons, I rode ferries.

Oliver entered my life as I dallied around the harbour often getting off at a ferry stops and exploring. Oliver ran a boat charter company. Easy going, fun, divorced, one daughter who lived with her mother. Maybe he was too easy going to be married and bring up a child – I didn't ask. The relationship was relaxed and I went along for the ride. Deeper questions about one another went unasked. We were totally in the day. No past, no future. We played in the blissful present. He stayed overnight on occasions at my place and met Aunty Coral, as I came to call her. His place was above his boatshed and tiny, where occasionally I stayed.

Worried when he went quiet for a couple of weeks, I looked in on him unannounced. I found someone else had dallied around the harbour. I didn't mind that he was bisexual or that he had other friends. Shades of Coops lingered. There was nothing binding us, but I found I didn't want to play anymore. Not out of jealousy, but from a disconnect with impermanence.

It wasn't Oliver's fault – he'd helped me change. I didn't know myself until that moment. My reaction shocked me. Not wanting to delve too deeply into my own psyche, I stopped answering his calls. He left messages suggesting I wasn't carefree at all. He felt betrayed. What emerged from the break with Oliver was an unpalatable feeling of missing Cooper. I didn't want that; no, I definitely did not want to feel any misgivings. They were not helpful. I sent a text: *Live and let live and don't annoy me.*

Monday morning, I cycled off to work.

FIFTY-THREE

Kate/Jackie

2009

After so-called Thakit Thirdplace left our office on that blustery day, Kimberley quizzed me.

"He's okay."

"He's not." She judged from my tone it wasn't a subject I cared to discuss. I needed to quell her curiosity. It was a joke from Oliver, I told her, and I wasn't amused. I added that it was probably better we lock the door when there was only one person in the office if they weren't at the front desk. The old building was seriously security challenged. Susie and Kimberley agreed with my explanation. It was safer for all of us. We didn't want Loopy getting hurt if she took it upon herself to be a guard dog. Unlikely but you never knew.

Kimberley didn't give up on the subject of Thakit, though.

"Are you keeping the cool guy away, Jackie? He looked nice … right age for you."

"Kimberley, don't say that," said Susie, "stop going on about age."

The way Susie defended me made me wonder if she thought I was old. Hell, I wasn't much older than her. I checked myself out in our full-length mirror. I looked all right – what was she going on about?

Thakit's looks were hard to judge, I suspected he was about ten years older than me. Whatever – he was as irritating as a fly.

After Thirdplace's appearance that day, I stayed in my own office when the girls were out. At lunch we locked the front swing doors and hung a sign giving the time we'd reopen. I let the phone ring to voicemail. It worked, because Thakit did not return. He didn't ring either or email the website. He clearly didn't want to leave a trace. Was he a crook? A blackmailer? Gardaí? I didn't know what extradition agreement Ireland had with Australia.

A couple of days passed. I checked my safety deposit box. Phew. All safe.

However, the peace was to be short-lived. Later that week, the doors swung open just as the girls were leaving for lunch. Thakit tailgated into our office as quick as a flash before I had time to lock the door. The girls were on their way to the lift, looked back and I waved an okay. It wasn't, but I didn't want them witnessing anything that might be revealing. He stood inside the door smiling to them, with a little wave. They waved back, a look on their faces like 'how exciting'. A thumbs-up when he turned back to me.

Here I was once again with Thirdplace in our office, having breezed in happy with himself. He had his briefcase. The same windblown trench coat. What was that – a forties Bogart look? It wasn't bad weather outside and his hair still looked windblown. I acted calm. A fake-it-until-you-make-it kind of calm.

"Kate, we need to speak," Thakit said, economic with his greeting.

"No, we don't."

"You're answering to Kate, that's a start."

I sighed.

"I know you're Kate. I have a toddler photo and the face is there."

"Is that all you have? A photo of a toddler and you're pinning that on me?"

He opened his case and showed me the photo. How I remembered that photo. I nearly choked. Me with my mammy and my da. I looked so happy, so cared for. I'd looked at the photo many times over the years while I was at the house. Sometimes I didn't believe I ever had a father. I couldn't remember when he left, I was too little, so my reminiscing must have been some years after the photo was taken. How I'd missed that picture when I left the house.

"Your face says it all, Kate. You know it's you, as I know it's you."

"Where did you get it?"

He ignored my question.

"Kate, I've followed your trail. Sometimes with difficulty. To be honest, I don't know how you remember all those names. Perhaps once one identity is used you simply step into the new one and wipe the old from your memory. Except sometimes you raise it again." He gave an annoying know-it-all arch of the eyebrow.

Thakit paused, watched my reaction. "Is that how it works?" he said. "But I don't think it's a simple process. The construct must take you quite a while, establishing a back story would take time in itself … let alone the character you arrive at. I'm thinking you have fun with it."

I couldn't speak. He'd been following me? For how long? He wasn't going to get a confession. I used the old mainstay; keep mute and let the other person do the talking. There was a long silence. He was obviously playing the same game.

"You seem to have it all figured out," I said finally.

"I have."

So bloody sure of himself, he gave me the shits. "Perhaps, Mr Thirdplace, you have followed the wrong person. Please leave me alone and go fish somewhere else for whatever you're after." I waited. Nothing. "Now please go." I walked to the door and opened it. He sat on the couch. I let the door go.

"You're not going through that sock procedure again, are you?"

He laughed, which exasperated me because I wasn't being funny. He was wearing the same shoes, but this time, bright blue socks.

"You're needed back in Ireland."

"I don't think so." There was no one left, so he must mean for an arrest.

"Someone wants to see you."

"Someone ... who?"

"All your expenses will be paid."

"So ... I'm wanted, am I?"

My tone must have been a give-away as he looked at me with suspicion. I tried to hide my fear and thought I'd succeeded.

"What's up? You look scared. What is it?" he said.

"Who wants me?"

"A relative."

"I don't have any relatives." Which was true. Uncle Lachlan was the last of my family, ... although I could have a father somewhere.

"You know what? I'm going to let you think it over," Thirdplace said. "I'll be back."

He closed his briefcase, stood and pulled the swing door with precision and billowed out. I noticed he was a man who didn't waste movement.

The gardaí had finally tracked me down. I was sure of it. Time to go. And I so didn't want to. Deep in thought, I hadn't noticed he didn't walk along the corridor to the lift. The door swung open.

"And don't think of running. I have you covered. I know where you live, as the saying goes, but it's true." With that, he was gone.

FIFTY-FOUR

Thakit

Sydney

Cruel, I know. But now the mouse had caught the cat, I decided to flick its tail. Have some fun. Kate wasn't going anywhere. She wouldn't run. She didn't want to. I could see it in her eyes. Also, she knew I had her.

Jen had occupied my mind since my visit to Melbourne. She was locked in my heart which in some ways helped me be more pragmatic with Kate. On the phone that night, Jen asked who the mysterious person was that sent me to Sydney.

"I can't tell you that, Jen. I'm sorry. The person I've been looking for and found, might run and I can't afford to lose them again. I promise I will tell you, when all this is settled. Besides," I said, "time is precious with you, Jen. I don't want to be talking work stuff."

Now I'd given Kate time to stew, I wondered if I could nick down to Melbourne and catch-up with Jen. Colin had suggested it. "If you've got a couple of days and your sugar daddy is paying, go to Melbourne. Go see her."

I checked in with Lachlan as usual, giving him the full run down.

Lachlan loved the idea of teasing her just a little bit. The man was dying, for fuck's sake, he needed some joy. But earlier he had been in a hurry. Why was he buying time? I asked him that. His reply: "Let her stew. And before you ask, no, you can't go to Melbourne again. You're working. Watch her."

That put paid to my elopement time.

I did watch her. I switched between staking her out at work, her flat and the bank. I wished I had Bart to work a shift. After I'd popped in and scared the bejeesus out of her, she skulked. It was sad to see. She wasn't the defiant Kate of before. I was sorry about that as I liked her pluck.

Mammy was right, I distracted easily. In Trinidad and Tobago, my first venture overseas, I was in awe of differences; the climate, the light, the colourful people. In Hawaii, the same. The beauty of the place and then, wham, Jen landed with a thump. I worried I wouldn't see Jen again before leaving Australia. Worrying became my distraction. Colin wasn't much help. "You'll sort it, Thakky, you always land on your feet."

Kate/Jackie

I didn't run after Thakit appeared. I was like stone, a statue that couldn't move. Held fast by what I wasn't sure. I did know I was tired of starting over. Although I locked the door and stayed out of sight at lunchtime, I was resigning myself to facing up to my inevitable fate. What was the worst? Jail for manslaughter, theft? That *was* the worst. My view of the world had changed. I'd found happy. I'd found a bright, shiny existence. Different happy to Hawaii. This happy was on my terms only. Also an ordinariness had settled. Life was good.

Overnight the coin had flipped and now I was in a dark place with no future. And worst of all, I had no energy to run. What was wrong with me? I should at least be at the airport, if not already on a plane. Where was that girl? The one with the mojo? The one I'd got to know, liked and got along with. What was it? Ten or so years since I left Ireland? That girl's spirit was fearless. She had chutzpah. I'd shone like a diamond. Naivety was a good part of it. Now here I was, lapsed like the lapsed Catholic family I'd been born into. Is this what ordinariness does to you?

After Thakit left saying he'd be back, I barely slept. I spent more time at our office, where I huddled out of sight. At home, I spent time peering out the window expecting to see him in his trench coat standing on the corner. He wasn't there, which was more frightening. I pictured myself being dragged away in chains. How embarrassing for Kimberley. How awful for the business. Bad publicity is often good for a growing enterprise, but I wasn't sure this would cut it. *Woman hunted for manslaughter found in Sydney, working in a business by the name of B.A.Q.A.M.* Cooper and Joan would eventually find out. The diamonds? The cartel would find out. Duncan might add to the charges of theft and maybe assault. The list got longer. Would my father therefore hear of it and find me and rescue me? I was out of my mind.

The time had come, I guessed. I'd never thought of final outcomes. Until I left Cooper, I thought I was in a forever life. No plans other than everyday stuff that would go on and on.

I was in my office with the door shut, keeping the gloom in. It could be contagious, and I didn't want anyone else catching it. The girls called out that they were off to lunch. I'd been expecting Thakit and not expecting him. I clung to a glimmer of hope he might disappear. With the girls out of the building, I continued to sit in my morose state, unable to move. Eventually, maybe it was only a minute or two, maybe half an hour, I pulled myself together, opening my door to lock the front glass doors.

Standing, smiling, between the doors and the desk, hair dishevelled, his coat in its usual billowed state, stood Thakit. Did his coat have an underlay that gave it that look?

The countdown had counted down.

FIFTY-SIX

Thakit

Kate looked terrible.

"You need to lock the door if you don't want me to come in, Kate."

"Do you hide around the corners waiting for the right moment?"

"Yes. Sometimes I do. Your girls are very punctual. Lunch on the dot. Mind if I sit?" I didn't wait for a reply.

Laying my briefcase on the sofa, I pulled out papers, shuffled through them and held up one sheet. For dramatic purposes, I meticulously held it with both hands between forefinger and thumb, like a delicate page of gold leaf, my other fingers splayed like a showman. Maybe I should have persevered with the acting agency. I laid the paper down and withdrew each separate sheet with the same ceremony.

I explained each: "Your uncle's birth certificate, your aunt's, your mother's and finally yours, Kate." I leaned back on the couch. "So Kate, I think you can see I do know who you are." I showed her the airline ticket in the same way. "Note the name ... Grace Katherine Mulvaney. And look ... you're booked in the posh end. And there's more."

Retrieving a recorder from my briefcase, I explained, "there's a message for you, straight from the horse's mouth." I pressed play.

Lachlan's voice. Kate turned white. She looked at the recorder, then at me.

"What is this?" she said.

"Your uncle, I believe."

"When was this recorded?"

"A few days ago."

"What?"

She stared at me. I was shocked by her shock. She'd lost all the blood in her face. It was if her whole body had washed away.

"Why do you look like that? What is it, Kate? That's outright terror. Is it his voice? It's quite shaky since you last heard him speak, I expect. He's sick."

"He's not dead?"

"Dead? No ... why do you think he's dead?"

I remember Lachlan saying Kate might think he was dead, but I didn't take much notice at the time. Now I could see that was true.

"Erm ..." her voice quivered. "A long time ago ..."

"You've thought him dead all this time?" I stifled a chuckle. Wow, I thought, that's a long time thinking you're alone on the planet. A ferocious black look glared back at me.

"Kate, I don't believe this. When did you think he died? Or rather, how long ago did you think he was no longer alive?"

Kate sat dumbstruck. Her face was a painting. Fears and acknowledgement flurried across it like a brush on a blank canvas.

"I think I'm getting it," I said carefully. "Come on, tell me. I know a good deal about you, but not, it seems, your secret fears."

"We had a fight. I left. For good. We were on the top landing in the house. He was trying to have sex with me. I struggled and fought. I was strong and angry, and I pushed with all my might.

He went head over heels down the stairs." Kate looked down at her hands as she spoke.

"I looked down and he lay at the bottom in a weird shape. Bent in all the wrong places. I ran down and stood close to him. I was scared he was mucking about and would grab my leg. I crept close and whispered his name in his ear, but he didn't answer. I pushed his arm with my foot and jumped away. He didn't move. He was silent, didn't say a word. He wasn't breathing."

"Did you check his pulse?"

She shook her head. "I didn't know to do that then. I was only sixteen."

"Then what?"

"He was dead, so I left the house, left for good."

"Not before you took the silver, then left it behind ... too heavy, I imagine. Then took all the jewellery and his cash. Don't look so shocked. I know about that. A smart thing to do, if you ask me. Safeguarding your future."

"I'd killed him. I was really scared. I didn't know what to do. He wanted so many times to have sex with me. Even before my mother died. That was the first time he'd used force though. I couldn't stay there any longer."

"He's at his end days ... that's why he sent me to find you and, believe me, it's taken time." I couldn't stand the look on her face. Was she about to cry? I changed the subject and the pace. "Jackie Chittleworth ... Chittleworth? Really ... where has that come from?

"Thakit Thirdplace? Where has that come from?"

"A dream. It was very strong and I rather liked it. I'm not an ambitious man, so first place didn't matter. Do you like it?"

"Is that true?"

"No."

Her patience had run out. "Go away, Thirdplace, you're wasting your time and mine. I don't care about any of this. I'm relieved, but I don't care if he is alive. Go."

"So all these years you thought you killed him. That you were a murderer. Wanted for manslaughter, let's say. Waste of energy, Kate. Just so you know, he lay like that all night. In the morning Mrs Gallagher arrived and heard moaning." Kate's face reddened. She was back there. "Mrs Gallagher rang an ambulance. He's been in a wheelchair ever since. Not dead, very much alive … at least at first. Now he's dying … not from anything you've done. He smoked and boozed a lot and is now paying for his pleasure."

"What about the gardaí? The stuff I took?"

"He didn't call them. He cared … cares about you, Kate."

Kate slumped in the seat behind the desk and dropped her head into her hands. I felt immensely sorry for her.

"I don't think I can go back there," she whispered, lifting her head. "I'm sorry he's sick, dying, but I thought he was already dead. It feels very weird."

"I've been searching for you for ages. You seem to slip away just when I'm about to make contact."

"Who the hell are you really?" she said.

"A man who's been following you, like I said. He employed me to track you down and bring you home. It's been interesting watching how you navigate your life. You're good, I'll give you that."

"That doesn't answer my question."

"My mother knows your uncle. She used to work at the house, cleaning."

"Huh. Lucky her. What's her name?"

"Siobhan Kelly."

"Oh." Kate was quiet. "I think I remember her name." Quiet again. "I don't want to go back there. Just because he's dying doesn't mean I have to be there."

"You're his last relative, Kate. I think he's sorry for any stress he caused you. He just wants to see you before he dies."

"I presume his dick doesn't work, so his brain's functioning with more respect."

She had a point.

"Are you so squeaky clean?" I asked.

"Don't suppose I am."

"But your ... erm ... misdeeds are not as bad as his, right?"

"Certainly feels that way," she said with a little leftover bravado.

"Let's put who's better and who's worse aside for a moment. No one's going to the gardaí? He's all the family you have. Can't you just say goodbye? He truly is sorry. Over the years, almost since you left, he's wanted to help. Knowing how impetuous you are, if you were ever in serious trouble, he wanted to be there. If not in person, then in help from afar, even if you didn't know it was him."

"You're giving me the creeps. Were you always watching me?"

"No, not always. But sometimes when I was around, he just wanted me to observe you. He'd tell me to hold off talking to you. I don't know why."

"Where was it, you observed me?"

"First place was Trinidad."

"What? I don't believe that. You were you in Trinidad?"

"Yes."

"That is just so creepy."

"That piece of jewellery, the necklace with the diamond, he got wind of it. Paid the pawnbroker a lot more to get it back. I believe he has it."

"Oh my God. That freaks me out. I so regretted selling that piece." She straightened. "I've had enough now, heard enough." After a moment, she said quietly. "But ... what about his brother? Who is my father, by the way."

"Lachlan's not heard from him. Doesn't know where he is and believes he wishes to remain unfound."

"It still means I'm not really the last member of his family. His brother has to be included."

"I've not been asked to find him or bring him home."

Kate mumbled something about she wondered why.

"Kate, you have a lot to digest. I'll give you time. But we don't have much more of it. I'm not going back empty-handed." I put all the papers back in my case in reverse, fluttering them to emphasise the game was up.

"Just one more thing. Is he paying you?" Kate said.

"My expenses ... hotels ... flights, that sort of thing."

"And you're in his will?"

"In his will? I don't know anything about his will. I'd imagine you're the only person in his will. You're going to be a rich woman, Kate, what with all the booty you've collected." I winked. I was at the door.

"So you're not tailing my father?"

"No."

Just then the girls walked in.

They looked from me to Kate. Kimberley picked up Kate's demeanour.

"Come in," I said, "We're just finishing up."

I turned to Kate. "See you soon."

FIFTY-SEVEN

Kate/Jackie

Thakit unfurled out of the office, giving his little wave and wink. I hate winks. As he twirled to wave, his coat billowed around him again. How did he do that? It was beginning to irritate me.

My uncle changed? I didn't believe it. On the upside, there wasn't much my Uncle Lachlan could do to me now if he really was that sick. Not physically, anyway. As much as I ran and moved on, his death was the stain that clung to me. It never went away. More than my mother's sudden death and more than my beloved Aunty Iris dying before my eyes. He was there, whispering in my ear, "*Katie … Kateee … come out to playee … it's your Uncle Lachie come to show you the wayee,*" in that horrible singsong fashion.

Would it bother me if he just passed away without me ever seeing him again? All the years I used my uncle as a template for anything bad that happened. Now it was like that bad energy had popped and gone up in a puff of smoke. But had it? Suppose he stayed with me until *I* died? I thought of all the vile things I could say to him in his present condition. Vitriolic hate, spitting in his face. I felt my heart race at the thought of it. Was this how I was going to live?

My life felt it had swivelled on a pinpoint. Everything; all my thoughts and emotions were built on hurt and fear. If that wasn't there anymore, what would I have? What would support me? Another fear crept in. I was no one without that backdrop, an empty shell. That scared the shit out of me. My impulse was to run again, but instead of running *from* I'd be running *to*. Running into myself. I was more scared than I'd ever been.

As I walked to the bank to check on my safety deposit box once again, I thought on what had just happened. Replayed the conversation with Thakit. I kept hitting the pause button to go over things more slowly.

"I could ring immigration," he'd said.

"You could, but you won't. You wouldn't be standing here negotiating with me."

It was ages before he spoke. "My God, all this time I was following you, I didn't realise. You really think you killed your uncle. And now you can't believe he's alive."

My face had broken into a thousand thoughts.

"That's why you keep moving. Passport to passport, running from a murder, or at least a manslaughter charge and robbery."

The pause button again. I was waiting at the lights, waiting to cross the road.

Play. When I heard my uncle on the tape, I felt the earth sink beneath me. It was him, although I hadn't heard him in years. I couldn't tell if he just sounded old or really wasn't well. It was his voice. So distinctive. A mix of polished Irish brogue with the depth of a cavern. Apparently, it was his voice that won my aunt and kept her there through thick and thin.

I was nearly at the bank, still playing and rewinding. No wonder Lachlan had picked Thakit for the job; he didn't give up. He was like a lost dog that wouldn't stop searching for home.

Replay again. "Go on. Listen," said Thakit. "I'll leave you in peace for a moment. Take it into your office. Shut the door. Listen in private."

Thakit had handed me the recording device. "You look like you're not familiar with technology." He showed me how to work it. "Just press here and rewind here if you want to listen again. Go on, take it into your office."

I'd settled into my chair. "Which is the arrow I press?" I called out, the door still open.

"The one pointing right ... dear God, how does she navigate the world?" I heard him mutter.

I pressed it.

"Hello, Katie. From this recording you can perhaps hear I'm not well. I must see you. I am dying, Katie, and I must see you before I do. Come home. Thakit will look after you. It's important. Please come home. Please, Katie."

'Please, Katie.' There it was again. Those two words sickened me. It took me back to his pleading. I could smell the drink on his breath, still hear his voice calling me through the door. *Tap, tap, tap. "Katie, Katie ... come out to play."* There had been no one to protect me. Nausea crept up from my gut. And the name 'Katie'. Only my family called me that. I hadn't heard that name for a long time.

Shudders rippled along my spine. My emotions swirled like fog. I could barely see through it. He sounded so old and sick. I had played it twice more, then walked out of my office and returned the thing to Thakit's outstretched hand.

As if my mind needed a distraction at that moment, I noticed the leather of his briefcase matched his shoes in texture and colour. What man does that?

"I can't do this, Thakit. I can't go back. I feel sick just thinking about it. What about what I stole from him?"

"You did it to survive. He's not bothered about that."

I laughed. "Here I am in Australia ... convict country ... where felons were sent who stole to survive."

"He understands why you took stuff. He's forgiven you for that."

"He's forgiven me? *Forgiven me?*" My anger surfaced. "That's a treat. Months when he tried to molest me and I had nowhere to go. I was only young when my Aunt Iris died and then later my mammy. He was the only family I had, and I was supposed to trust him. He kept saying, over and over, '*Trust me, little Katie. I'll show you about life. Prepare you.*' Have you any idea how scary that is, Thakit? I was terrified. Thank God it was a big place. Our gardener secured my room, but I couldn't stand the tapping on my door. I slept in different places around the house where he couldn't find me. If it was earlier in the evening and he had the woolly beanie on, he chased me until he ran out of puff and I ran back to my room and locked the door, jamming a chair under the door handle, just in case. Just like mammy showed me."

I was exhausted in the remembering, tears not far away.

"Could you have stayed somewhere else?" Thakit said. "Or gone to your priest?"

"Priest? That's a laugh. Not just lapsed, completely failed. As for staying somewhere else, it was suggested, but that thought was worse somehow. I didn't want sympathy. At least I was in familiar surroundings and although my mammy and my aunt weren't there in person, they were in spirit. They protected me."

"Come back," Thakit said. He held up two airline tickets. "One for you and one for me. We'll travel together."

"Have you not heard anything I've said?"

"Can you not find it in your heart to just see him, Kate?" he said in a softer tone. "He can't do anything to you now. You have every right to hate him, but do you want to live with that hate eating away at you for the rest of your life? If you see him, you can say exactly what you want to, face to face, if you choose."

For a moment I was tempted. Then my hackles stood on end and I slipped back into my defensive self where I felt strong.

"No. In your dreams, Thakit," I said. "No, no, no. *We* won't be travelling anywhere. May I suggest you take that flight this afternoon ... if there's time. There won't be any me with you, travelling anywhere."

"I'll be there. I can look after you, be by your side, if you're still frightened of him."

"Oh, fuck off," I said. "Patronising me won't work." I'd been softening to the idea but Thakit just said the wrong thing. "Look after me? Who are you? Clark Kent masquerading as Superman? Get over yourself."

"I'll come back tomorrow ... unless you'd rather see me at your place?"

Strangely there was no malice in his voice. Who was this guy? I'd just spat shite at him, and he wasn't angry. He should be spitting back at me. He sounded sincere; dare I say, caring. Something I really didn't want. I couldn't handle kindness just then. Maybe that was my flaw. I certainly didn't want to see him at home. I'd be too vulnerable. Here at least I felt secure in company. Impartial office walls surrounded me.

"No, not at home," I said.

The girls returned and saw my reaction to Thakit's visit. "Everything all right?" It was Kimberley. "You don't look so good."

I was sure they hadn't heard my bile, but the fury was swirling around me.

"Yes ... fine ... need some air." That girl was too perceptive for her own good.

Leaving the bank and my safety deposit box intact, I continued down to the Quay and the sparkling harbour. Seagulls squawked very close to me, making me jump and bringing me into the present. All these years I'd been moving around, fearful the gardaí were after me, thinking I'd killed my uncle. The full stop in my life had shifted, been rubbed out, become a colon, with brightly coloured events to follow. Although I was happy with the present life I was building, I didn't go beyond the here and now. Now I could. There was a future instead of a brick wall. The wall that had always shifted, giving me a few steps forward at a time, a few months at a time. I hadn't noticed that wall before.

Maybe for the first time I'd been confronted with my own temperament, my squished down resentments. I felt lighter. How could that be? A short time ago, I was hurling rage. Maybe I'd hurled it out of me.

The wall came down that day, down at the water's edge where the ferries bobbed about. The chains broke, the day turned bright. The water sparkled. I almost skipped.

Yes, I could do it. I could go back. I had set things up so I could run. Now I wasn't running, I was simply moving. I wouldn't be running out on anything or anyone. The business, Susie, my new dear friend Kimberley and her Pete and the animals, were set up.

It felt really weird. I was naked, vulnerable. Exposed but somehow not fearful. Could a person really change from black to white in a few short moments? Now I was eager to see Thakit, but I had no way of contacting him. I could only wait for his return.

Kate/Jackie

After my moment of clarity down at the Quay, I returned home. Watching the bobbing ferries and the squawking seagulls had done its job. After my epiphany, I was eager to meet up with Thakit. Get this thing rolling.

Considering his suggestion of meeting there, I wondered if he'd been in my house. He might have decided a bit of a snoop around would be fun. He'd find a way in, I was sure. Thakit could be sitting on my couch right now taking off his socks.

I recalled when he first came into our office. He was the weirdest man I'd ever met. I hadn't been wrong.

My flat was empty. Every room was just as I left it, absolutely nothing out of place. I checked inside cupboards and drawers; nothing disturbed. Although I gave him credit to find a way in, it would be difficult. The locks were strong. The back entrance, which required a separate key, was undamaged. There were bars on the windows. I was expecting the worst when there wasn't any. He had not snooped.

Coral must have heard me moving about as she called out. We met at the back door by the garden. Before I asked, she mentioned my cousin from Ireland had visited. Shit.

"He's so charming and an accent much like yours, though his is stronger. I do love the Irish accents," she said.

"Oh, you met him?"

"Yes, dear. He was so gentlemanly. He was hoping to see you and thought he'd try, on the off chance you'd be home. I told him I wasn't sure how long you'd be. I invited him in for a cup of tea if he wished to wait. Such a lovely young man."

Masking my face was difficult. I turned the scowl into a smile and nodded, not trusting myself to speak.

"Such a strange name though. He told me about the dream. I thought it was a wonderful story. He waited a while but then asked if I'd let you know he'd called in."

I thanked Coral for being so helpful. "I'll give him a call," I said, chafing at the bit not to yell at her.

My seagull moment of clarity had darkened. I thought perhaps his visit was his way of letting me know he had power over me. My couch, my security blanket, welcomed me and I sunk deep into it, piling cushions around me, with a cup of tea by my side. I sorted through what he said. Again. Thinking, thinking, thinking, I was exhausted. It was a habit, my slipping into darkness. It must have started way back when I left the big house. Maybe I was addicted to my fears.

I turned on the television, not knowing or caring what I watched. Tomorrow, as usual, I would go into work and see what transpires, see if he turned up. Muddled in my brain, I was vacillating between wanting to stay in Australia and giving in to return to Ireland.

FIFTY-NINE

Kate/Jackie

I rose late the next morning having slept in after watching television well into the early hours. I've no idea what I saw. I'd fallen asleep on the couch, the television playing in the background like something I was dreaming.

As I walked into our office, Kimberley said, "Thakit's been in to see you."

"What, already?" I was annoyed the way he'd ingratiated himself into Kimberley and Susie's favour.

"It's quite late, but he'll be back," Kimberley said and smirked at me.

It was much later in the day than I'd thought.

"Kimberley, please, it's not like that."

"He's persistent."

"He is that." Not wanting to explain the circumstances, I went into my office, leaving the door open. Shortly after I heard his now-familiar voice.

"Hello, girls," he called as Susie joined Kimberley at the desk. His return coincided with their going to lunch. But he knew that.

"Hello, Thakit," said Kimberley, like he was an old buddy.

From my office I could hear them talking but not their actual conversation. Looking from my window at the glimpse of park, I remembered the first time I met Kimberley at the pub and getting that feeling we would continue our friendship. To add food to flavour, her name started with my favourite letter. Then meeting Susie and her showing me around this big office space. What fun it was to set it up.

Finally I walked to the front desk in time to hear Thakit say, "Bye girls, see you later."

"So?" said Thakit. "What's it to be?" I sat at our precious table, Kimberley's front desk. "Before you answer, I have another tape." He pressed the device to play and handed it to me.

"Hello, Kate. I can't tell you how happy I am Thakit has finally spoken to you and you've agreed to come home. You won't regret it. And there'll be no trouble, I promise. I don't want to bring up the past any more than you, I imagine. It will be so good to see you. Without being too maudlin, I don't know how long I have, but not long. As soon as you can settle your affairs, please get here as quick as you can."

The tape clicked off.

"I haven't agreed," I said.

"I took the risk. I have everything ready for you. And … Kimberley wants to give you a farewell party."

"WHAT?"

"You're important to her."

"It's not for you to be telling my plans, Thakit … and before you go on … what was the idea of coming around to my home yesterday? Smarming your way into Coral's good graces?"

"A reminder to let you know time is of the essence … as you heard on the tape."

"It was very underhand. You acted like some sort of secret agent. Totally unnecessary."

"If you'd been there, it would have been fine. We could both have had tea with Coral."

"You are getting creepier. I was all prepared to return with you, but now I'm not so sure."

"And now you're pouting. So, okay, it was probably a bit off, but I have to get you home. I promised Lachlan. That's all. I believe he'll hang on until you get there."

"Shit, Thakit ... why did you have to come into my life?" I said more to myself than him. "I was having a perfectly nice time."

"Well, there it is. And Kimberley does want to throw you a farewell party."

We must have been talking round in circles for about an hour, as Kimberley and Susie returned from lunch.

"Has Thakit told you, Jackie? This weekend?" said Kimberley.

"Yes, he has. But he has no right to tell you anything. That's up to me, not him." I glared at Thakit. *Go*, I mouthed.

"See you, Kimberley, Susie. Thanks again." Thakit swirled out.

"Come on, Jackie. I'd love to travel and you're looking so grumpy," Kimberley said.

"Kimberley, her uncle's dying!" Susie said.

"He told you that?"

They nodded and said they were sorry.

"Everything will be all right, you'll see. There'll be surprises, good ones, in store for you," Kimberley said.

"Oh, there will, will there? How do you know?" I said.

"I know stuff," she said with a toss of her head as if she was making a comment about the weather. "You have to go and that's that."

I looked around and behind her. "Do you know where Kimberley's gone? She looks just like you."

"She's like that, Jackie," said Susie. "She sends me into shivers sometimes. At lunch she said there was more to the story than even you know."

Kimberley didn't know the half of it.

"Things will unfold," Kimberley said.

A young woman can gain too much bleedin' confidence.

"So how about the farewell party?" she carried on like her comments hadn't shaken me. "This Saturday, okay? A cousin of mine is coming from Melbourne too, so Saturday would be perfect. The tall man said he'll come."

SIXTY

Kate/Jackie

With a new boyfriend in tow, Susie and Frank gave me a lift to Kimberley and Pete's place. The day was cloudy but no rain predicted. It was cooler that way, out in the country where the heat could be a furnace and the flies a living hell. I wore burnt orange this time, to confuse the little buggers. On our first visit I had worn blue and the flies thought I was a pond and settled in their hundreds. Maybe this time they'd think I was on fire and leave me alone. I knew nearly everyone at the barbecue, having been out to the farm a few times.

Kimberley greeted me. "Nearly everyone's here. Pete's gone to pick up my cousin from the station. Thakit's not here yet either."

Well, that was a relief. Maybe he'd had a better offer. I could do without the lectures today. I wandered away and got into conversation with Blair.

Shortly after there was a loud kerfuffle at the gate, Kimberley saying over and over, "I don't believe it."

"Looks like Jen may have found a new boyfriend," said Blair.

She started off towards the gate. I followed, although it was of scant interest to me.

"Well, Thakit's arrived I see," I said to Blair. She didn't know him but must have known of him. He had his back to us.

Kimberley saw me. "Jackie, you'll never believe it, my cousin has brought Thakit."

What ... brought? I joined them. "My God ... Jen ... Jen from Hawaii? You're Kimberley's cousin?"

"Oh my God, you two know each other as well? This is getting bizarre," said Kimberley.

"You know Kimberley's cousin?" I said to Thakit.

"They came together," said Kimberley. "Pete just picked them up from the station. Together."

"You're *with* Kimberley's cousin?" I said to Thakit. "What ... how ..."

"Rose?" said Jen. "Good grief. Yes ... Thakit and I met in Hawaii." She rotated her startled gaze first to me then Kimberley and finally Thakit.

"How?" I said. "When?"

"When I was looking for you," said Thakit. "We met on the beach."

I was beginning to feel like a fish gasping for water.

"Hang on," said Kimberley. "Did you just call her Rose?"

Holy hell. My life was about to unravel. Thakit was going to have a field day.

"Um ... yes. Middle name."

"I can't believe you all know each other. It's amazing!"

Bloody unbelievable.

SIXTY-ONE

Thakit

Did I enjoy myself at that barbecue? Did I what!! Kimberley told me her cousin was coming and I might like her. I'd shrugged off the suggestion. Jen was the only person who interested me and she said she hoped to come to Sydney, and I hoped it was before I took Kate back to Ireland. Our last night in Melbourne still caused my heart to race. I glowed. In fact, I had trouble concentrating on my mission.

Jen had checked with Kimberley if she minded her bringing a friend. When Kate walked up with Blair, the look on Kate's face was worth its weight in all her jewels. This was going to be gripping. Kate's sunhat and sunglasses shielded her expression, but I read her mouth.

"Rose?" Jen said in surprise, peering through the covering. "You're Jackie? Kimberley's mentioned your name ... I had no idea ..." Her voice faded away in confusion.

"Oh my God, you two know each other as well ... *Rose?* What's going on?" said Kimberley.

Standing to one side, my head did the tennis-match swivel, and I was loving it.

"I decided to go with my middle name when I came to Australia," Kate said.

"Clever," I mouthed to Kate out of sight of the others.

"I needed a new start," said Kate.

"You and Cooper split up?" said Jen.

"Yes ... you know the reason."

"Yes ... yes ... I totally understand," Jen said. "Dave came back to Melbourne. It didn't work out with Cooper, apparently. He didn't say much ... embarrassed, I expect. I didn't question him. Whatever it was, was over ... as are he and I."

"Oh," was all Kate said. "But you and Thakit? When did that happen?"

"In Hawaii. Like Thakky said. We met on the beach. I was having a spit about Dave and Thakit saw me." Jen looked at me and smiled.

"You and Cooper were such a perfect pair," said Jen.

"I thought so too. Perhaps we could talk about this later," said Kate. "There's lots to catch up on, it seems."

Kimberley quickly jumped in to save the situation, "This all sounds terribly complicated," she said. "Breakups are way too nasty to be discussed openly. I'm still getting over you all knowing each other. I'd like to get my head around that first before deep and meaningfuls dull the day. Come and get a drink, Jen." Kimberley gave us drinks and shushed us over to the food. I stood by as Jen spoke with her aunt. Once their conversations finished, Jen and I wandered away.

"I'm just trying to think why I didn't know Kimberley was your cousin, but I don't think you've ever mentioned her name," I said.

"And you certainly never mentioned Rose was the person most wanted. Now I find out her name's Jackie, who I happen to know. It's all so bizarre, as Kimberley said. You need to fill me in on the details."

"I will, later, long story. You know, Kimberley mentioned I might like her cousin. Not interested, I thought. I'm only interested one person." I kissed her on the top of her head being exactly one head's distance beneath me.

"Kimberley, bless her, mentioned I might like a tall Irish man who was coming to the barbecue. Mmm ... I think she was right there." She looked up at me and gave me a big hug.

"Where are we sleeping tonight?" I said.

"Um ... I believe there's a hotel in town housing a lanky Irish man I'm thinking about."

Kate, who'd been lurking, came over as Jen and I loosened our grip. "Sorry to butt in but can I have a quick chat with Thakit?" Jen politely went to talk to Kimberley.

"Blunt, as usual, Kate. What is it?"

Straight for my jugular. "You knew about this, didn't you?"

"I did not. You are going to have to come up with something better about your name though ... maybe the truth?"

"Absolutely not. I'll go to Ireland, then come back and resume where I left off. Time will level all this out."

"Good luck with that."

SIXTY-TWO

Thakit

We sat together on the plane; all of us. Me, Grace Katherine Mulvaney, Pippa Katherine Thornton, Caroline Katherine Clark, Felicity Doncaster, Rose Katherine Havel and Jackie Katherine Chittleworth. We were all there. I was so missing Jen, I found myself pouring my heart out to the uninterested Kate.

"I hope you're not blaming me. We could have stayed," Kate said.

"I'm not blaming you."

"I don't want to talk." We were barely airborne.

"Okay. Suits me," I said.

A moment later, she said, "just before I don't want to talk, I have a question."

"Okay," I sighed.

"What was that sock thing all about, when you took off your shoes and socks in our office?"

"Just a bit of drama. I wanted to stress the point on the length of time I'd be searching for you. At one point in my life I thought of getting into acting. Did you like it?"

"No ... I don't want to talk anymore."

"Suits me. Again."

Her grumpiness was getting on my nerves and the anger mixed

in with it. She, like a ball of molten lava, hot, pitted and scratchy. Not to mention the darkness that <u>oozed</u> from her. After watching a movie, drinking champagne and eating everything that came my way, I dozed. I woke with millions of hours left of flying. I was bored. Kate was awake, glaring at nothing.

"Why are you so angry?"

"How do you know I am?"

"I can feel it. If you talk about it, you might feel better."

"I said I didn't want to talk. *You're* making me angry," she said.

"Well, take yourself off the boil, you're annoying me. I hope the glass in your window is strong; your glare could crack it."

"I've been asleep, if you hadn't noticed."

"It's like you're awake when you sleep. Steam comes out of your ears."

"If I wasn't angry before, I'm getting that way now. You think you can say what you like to me now that you have me cornered. Not Mr Nice Guy now, are you?"

"Cornered? This is first class; you're being pampered beyond measure."

"Oh, shut up. Let's go back to not talking again."

Shortly after her statement, *she* must have been bored.

"How did you meet Jen?"

"I told you. In Hawaii."

"I know that bit."

It was a story and one I liked thinking about. I started from beginning. We had so many hours ahead of us, why leave anything out?

"So arriving in Kauai ... and when I finally tried to approach you, you'd pissed off again. Then I met Joan. She's grand. Then I went back to Lachlan empty-handed with my tail between my legs."

I turned to Kate. She'd not spoken a word.

She was asleep.

SIXTY-THREE

Thakit

West Ireland – 2009

After landing in Dublin, I hired a car. We drove to the west coast, mostly in silence.

"You're actually okay, Thakit Thirdplace," Kate said unexpectedly.

That was a turn up for the books. I wondered about her change of heart. She said nothing more, nothing less.

"Okay," I said.

On the drive I noticed her interest in everything beyond the car. Her head was twisting this way and that, but at the same time, she didn't want to appear interested. The constant battle going on inside that small frame had to be as uncomfortable as a fiery furnace.

The house, her house, came into view.

"Park here," Kate said. "Let's walk the rest of the way." We stepped from the car, me following her lead. She stood still, seeming to breathe in the air, studying the house.

"It's not as bad as I remembered. It's not as dark." She paused. "I had such horrors of this place. Now instead of evil, I see serenity. It's calm. The countryside is so lush and green. After the harsh, dry areas in Australia, the rain is so nourishing ... for the soul."

Wow, I looked at Kate. Apart from her tirades in Australia, that was the longest speech she'd made to me. I realised what all this meant for her. She was terrified.

"Would you like to be alone?" I said.

"No. Can you walk in with me? Metaphorically holding my hand ... if you don't mind."

Wow again. Her vulnerability was uppermost. I'd taken control the entire journey and her reticence was strong. But now she was willing to let me in. This felt strange for me as it was her house and she needed my help to enter. How she lived alone as a young teenager in that big house with a threatening uncle, was unimaginable. I saw a totally different person stuck in circumstances that were a nightmare. Underneath the bravado, the carefree lifestyle, the impulsive nature, the suffocating memories she carried, must have bitten at her heels constantly. How courageously, she'd got her life going, even if her actions were morally flawed. She could have fallen into a heap. But this feisty young woman had carved her future and had enough forethought to ensure her financial security. Instead of a job I was doing for Lachlan, she'd become a total person to me. My feelings towards her changed in that moment.

Mrs Gallagher was there to meet her. "My little Katie," she said, hugging her tight to her bosom. "Is it really you?" Then holding her at arm's length, "God love us, it's so good to see you. And you looking so grown up and so beautiful."

Standing aside, Mrs Gallagher and I watched as Kate walked through the front door, scrutinising every centimetre of her former home. We followed. At the foot of the stairs, she looked to the floor. Mrs Gallagher explained that was where they found Mr Mulvaney.

Straightening her back and standing tall, Kate walked on.

SIXTY-FOUR

Kate

West Ireland

Thakit and I didn't talk much on that long flight back to Ireland. We flew directly to Dublin. Previously avoiding the pointy end of first or business class so as not to bring attention to myself, there I was. I tried to enjoy it, but agitation ruined my efforts. I had not killed my uncle, he hadn't reported me for stealing, in fact there really was no bad news. Instead of over-the-moon joy, I was flat. That's how I felt, numb and flat like a dead heartbeat. This helped me sleep. It was avoidance of being awake. Thakit attempted conversation from time to time, but I couldn't join him. In my waking moments, my thoughts went to Cooper. I missed him and I missed Joan, which was too bad for me.

Dublin was grey and damp when we arrived. What better greeting for my mood and homecoming? Thakit hired a car. I still could barely speak.

"Are you still mad at me?" Thakit asked.

"Thakit, it's nothing to do with you. I'm drained. I can't even think of what's coming."

"A dying man," he warned me. "A frail, non-threatening, dying man."

"I've based my whole life on anger and fear and I'm not sure what's going to fill that void."

As the house came into view, I asked Thakit to pull over. I got out of the car and stood taking it all in. I saw the young me leaving that house in the dark with a suitcase and backpack, cold and full of flight. I'd put one foot in front of the other and kept going.

The house wasn't half as threatening as the pictures I held in my memory. Sunshine flitted in and out of the clouds as if to say, 'See, take a peek, it's not so bad.'

Mrs Gallagher must have heard the car. She was already at the door with the biggest smile. I felt shy and awkward. I'd not written to her once but with her arms open she was all warmth, love and forgiveness.

Her hug was tight, "Katie," she murmured in my ear. "All these years I've been so worried." She pushed me away gripping my shoulders. "You never contacted me or asked me to help." She pulled me tight again.

"It's so good to see you, Mrs G and I'm deeply sorry. I couldn't … I was scared. I thought I'd killed him."

"I know. I thought that was so. Put it behind you. You're here now and I can hardly believe it. Run along. We've made up a bedroom in the big room behind the library. And, Katie, he's very ill."

The smell and space of the old house was overpowering. Surprisingly there was no mustiness, just a fresh smell of polish. The house was still in need of repair but at least Mrs Gallagher was caring for it in some way. I passed the stairs. To my horror, the banister was still broken from that fall all that time ago. Unless there had been another one, the break looked the same. The memory flowed so freshly into my mind. I glanced behind me to see Thakit and Mrs Gallagher still hovering. Bless them.

At Lachlan's door I stopped, breathed deeply and squared my shoulders.

"I'm here," I said as I walked in.

The sight of him made me gasp. He lay in amongst pipes and tubes. A nurse stood by. Mrs Gallagher's and Thakit's warnings had not prepared me.

If the sheets had been white, I wouldn't have seen him. Navy, his favourite colour, contrasted his pallor. The hiss of breathing, whether his or the machine's, sounded like small waves ebbing and flowing. He feebly pushed the mask aside and beamed. His now pale and watery blue eyes shone. "Katie," he said in a deep gasp, barely audible.

He waved away the nurse. I caught sight of Thakit at the door, out of sight of Lachlan. Once the nurse moved aside, a bony shaking hand reached for mine. Cool, thin and papery to the touch, I nervously held it.

"Thank you for coming." His voice shook as it tumbled over the gravel of his throat. "I'm sorry ... so sorry."

I nodded. "Don't talk, Lachlan, it's okay." And suddenly it was okay. Vengeance had no place here.

He seemed to gather strength as he tried to lift himself from the pillow. I wanted to help him but there were so many tubes, I worried I would dislodge something. As a gesture I fluffed the top of the pillow.

"I must ... I have something to tell you." He paused for breath. "Your father is here ... yes ... and your uncle." Shocked, I dismissed his confusion. "Yes, Katie, he's here, he'll be here in a minute. You must prepare yourself."

Prepare myself? I was still getting over what I was looking at. Now to see my father too. "Is he sick too?"

Lachlan shook his head.

Just then the door opened. The nurse came first, followed by a man who looked like a healthy version of my uncle. He seemed nervous, walking slowly and stopping a metre or so from me. So this was my father. There were physical differences and similarities. He had Lachlan's blue eyes before they became watery with illness. I hadn't seen this man since I was two years old and with no recollection of that time, you could say I had never seen him before. Neither of us knew what to say.

It was his voice I wanted to hear. To hear if there was any similarity to Lachlan's. To hear what had attracted and endeared my aunt through thick and thin. I'd have to wait. Lachlan's condition was the focus and there's wasn't much to be said. All the same, it did feel strange. I stood with my father on one side and my uncle on the other. From nobody to two members of my family.

SIXTY-FIVE

Thakit

If Kate needed me, I stayed outside Lachlan's bedroom. After a reasonable interval, a man I hadn't seen before, arrived. Although I had no clue as to who he was, I recognised him. It was a man I'd seen in the photos lining the library walls. Although an older version, he was still recognisable. I knew they were similar in age, but of course their health vastly changed their appearance. This man was what Lachlan should be looking like.

The nurse ushered him in and closed the door. I continued to wait, not knowing whether to stay. I'd brought Kate straight to the house and the hire car was parked out front. Should I just go home or wait? Wait for what? Kate would be staying at the house. I was just considering if it might be best for me to go when the nurse came out.

"He wants to see your mother. How quickly can you get her here? Lachlan can send a car for her if that's easier. I've just rung your mother, so she's aware she'll be picked up."

"You've rung her? Why wasn't I asked to do that? I haven't even seen her yet."

"Don't quibble, young man. We haven't time."

She was a woman not to be questioned. "I'll get her. I have a car out the front."

"I'll ring her and tell her you're on the way."

It was me who could do that, but she shooed me from the house.

Mammy was waiting at the front door when I drove up. She was all polished up. Why bother, I thought, he's not going to notice. Or could it be for me?

Before mammy had a chance to get in the car, I was out and giving her a big hug hello.

"Come on, Ryan, quickly. I believe we don't have much time."

Ryan. She wasn't in the mood for flippancy or a welcome home.

"You look nice," I said.

"Well, yes. This is important. He's passing. One must give respect."

"I know. But I've been away. I thought I might get some greeting."

"Later. Let's get there as quick as we can, save speeding."

Buffeted on two sides by a nurse and a mother on a mission, I drove with my mouth zipped.

SIXTY-SIX

Kate

Once we'd acknowledged Lachlan and not saying a word, Liam, my father, walked towards me, his arms shyly open. Matching his shyness, I walked into them. We hugged – two strangers. We stepped back and each of us gave a small smile. 'Later' our eyes said as we turned back to Lachlan.

Lachlan whispered something to the nurse, his whisper a hoarse rasp, about waiting for Thakit. Had Thakit gone somewhere? Why were we waiting, what were we waiting for and why were we waiting for Thakit? Lachlan emphasised he had something to say, so it must affect Thakit too. I could only fathom he wanted him there as they must have built up a relationship while looking for me. Tension stretched in the awkward silence.

The nurse opened the door; Thakit still hadn't arrived. I counted the chairs around the bedside and wondered who was to sit in the spare, presuming Thakit was taking one of them. I thought maybe the nurse. The priest, who I'd barely noticed until I'd been in the room for a few minutes, was standing and would continue to stand, chanting his ritual. It was very clear how timely my arrival was. Had Lachlan waited for me or was I just in time? Lachlan agitated the nurse again.

"Sir, they shouldn't be long ... don't talk ... save your strength," the nurse said.

Liam, still standing close to my side, said in a distinct whisper, "Hello, Kate."

"Hello, da." How difficult that felt. I was barely old enough to speak those words before he left. I desperately wanted to hear his voice, to speak with him, but it wasn't the moment.

We continued the silence, listening to the ebb and flow of the apparatus. There wasn't much to be said. My anger was gone. This would have been the time. The years of recitation, what I'd say if I ever had the chance. I was right there, free to say it, but the well was empty.

Finally, breaking the tension, there was a quiet tap on the door. The nurse ushered in Thakit accompanied by a woman and gestured for her to sit by my uncle's side, close enough to hear him and him her.

Silence. We all sat. I was directly opposite the stranger, Thakit seated to her left. Who was she? I looked to Thakit as he looked at the woman. Was she Thakit's mother? I compared them but could not see a similarity. Maybe there was in the chin? I had to stop staring. The room was deathly quiet except for the hiss of Lachlan's equipment and the priest's intermittent chanting. The weight of collective thoughts hung in the air. I wondered how Lachlan felt about the priest as my uncle, as far as I knew, hadn't stepped inside a church, in for ever. I suppose the priest was doing his job, doing what he could for this sinful, perhaps remorseful man.

Lachlan gestured to the woman and gave her his hand. She leant forward and whispered something. They spoke closely, inaudible to the rest of us, which finally exhausted him. The woman smiled.

Lachlan's voice, louder, raspy and erratic, spoke with the help of the oxygen:

"I had a DNA test taken, Katie. You took a lot when you left but you left behind plenty of your DNA. That gave me the proof I needed. I am your father. Not Liam."

Deathly silence. What did he just say?

"WHAT?"

As he had few words left in him, I presumed he did not have time or the energy for explanation. Had the man gone mad, lost his mind? Was he living in some realm no one else could penetrate?

Lachlan repeated. "I am your father."

I looked to Liam. "Is this true?"

Barely a whisper, Liam said, "I can't believe it, after all these years."

What the hell was going on?

Before Liam could continue, Lachlan spoke again. "Liam is your uncle, Katie."

"There it is," said Liam. Then louder. "There it fucking is. You finally admit it."

All eyes locked on Liam.

The quivering voice continued. "It's all with my solicitor, all the proof. But ..." and Lachlan paused to gather his strength, "there's more." The oxygen puffed. "Thakit is my son ... again I have DNA proof."

We all looked to Thakit and the woman I presumed to be his mother.

"WHAT?" said Thakit. He looked to his mother. "Ma?" It hit him hard. "My DNA?"

"Yes, son, the house is full of it. But I gave a comb."

"You've done all this behind my back?"

"Shush, Ryan. We'll talk about this later." She turned to Lachlan.

Then that news hit me with a double whammy. "He's my brother? You're my half-brother?"

Equalling my shock, Thakit said, "she's my half-sister?"

The nurse bent over Lachlan. She nodded.

"He needs sleep. The solicitor has details. He will give you further information."

Isn't that enough. What else is there?

Kate

We all filed out. I looked back to the dying man. Surely he'd explain himself, but he'd already closed his eyes. I knew I was being cruel, but it seemed like an easy way out for him to say he was too tired. Into the conservatory we went and sat in silence. Everyone's eyes were riveted on the garden. I could not make sense of any of it, though it was clear enough. The others must have felt the same.

Mrs Gallagher brought in tea.

"Mrs G, do you want to join us?" I said.

"No dear, I'll be leaving it to you."

Wise woman. "You know?" I said softly.

"I do." She closed the door behind her.

"What did you mean, you knew it?" I said to Liam.

"As soon as Brianna fell pregnant, I knew it. She was adamant. Threw a tantrum. She was disgusted with my suspicions." Liam paused. "Sorry, perhaps you don't know about the relationship between Brianna and Lachlan?"

We were a small party of four and Liam had no qualms in sharing the sordid details. As we were now all family, he felt free to talk. As did I.

"I do. Aunt Iris told me."

"Iris and I became the spectators, which drew us closer. We didn't talk about their goings on, it was a silent knowledge we shared."

The voice was there, though Liam's was not as cavernous as Lachlan's. Liam talked at a slower pace, which gave the impression of depth, but it didn't match Lachlan's.

"I loved you, Katie, from the get-go, but I knew you weren't mine. Although Brianna never admitted it, timing-wise you couldn't have been mine. We hadn't been having sex, for chrissakes, ages. Well, occasionally, guilt sex, hers, but not often. Now I think about it, she probably suspected she might fall pregnant. Cunning, don't you think? I can remember that time, before you were born, Katie. I remember it as if it were yesterday. I came home early and she hadn't had time to shower. I could smell him on her."

I grimaced. Thakit grimaced. Thakit's mother grimaced.

"Having a baby was not on Brianna's agenda. It was me who wanted babies. She was only focused on Lachlan. Getting pregnant as quickly as she could was like a sport to her. It was her way of saying to Iris, 'see, I've got what you want'. I'm sorry Katie, your mother was cruel.

"Finally, fed up to the back teeth, I confronted Lachlan. I wanted my wife back. More to the point, I wanted my wife. Lachlan and I had a huge row. He actually denied there was a physical affair between them. He said it was just flirting and I was overreacting. I wore him down and he admitted ... maybe once or twice, he said but nothing more.

"I couldn't fight him or Brianna any longer. I gave up waiting for Brianna to love me, as I thought she might when we married. I hoped a baby would help. I didn't worry it wasn't mine, but after you were born, their affair continued. I really think it was more her than him ... she was obsessed with him ... but it takes two. I wanted out. So I left. Brianna didn't plead with me to stay; she was annoyed, what was she supposed to do? Stuff like that. Of all things ... what would people think? But I kissed and hugged you goodbye, Katie. You were too little to remember."

"Did Lachlan agree with you that he was probably my father?" I said.

"He said Brianna told him it was impossible. Only your mother knew that truth and she wasn't telling. So he didn't believe it, or chose not to. He believed what he wanted to believe, what was convenient, until now it seems, when science has proven otherwise."

Thakit jumped in. "We need to go. This is between the two of you. And ... erm ... mammy ... we need to talk."

With my hand out, I leaned forward to shake with Thakit's ma. "I'm Kate." She took it warmly.

"Oh yeah, sorry. Forgot. My mother Siobhan," said Thakit.

"And I'm Liam, Kate's ... well, whatever."

We all stood and shook hands in comical formality. Thakit and Siobhan left. I fancied being a fly on their wall. But I had my own walls to concern me.

Once they left, I said, "Aunty Iris filled me in on the affair".

How long would it take me to process all this? I thought my reaction and Liam's reaction to Lachlan's announcement was similar. Ultimately we'd both taken off in our own directions. We'd both had similar reactions to the act of sex. Then the thought hit me. It had been my own father who'd been trying to seduce me. I felt like puking. Had he known, deep down?

"Are you all right, Kate?" Liam said. "You're quite white."

I kept my explanation brief as I told him the story.

He sat motionless, turning white with rage.

"I'm so sorry, Kate." He hugged me, the hug of a lost life together.

"Are you married?"

"Not actually married, not the ceremony, but I've been in the same relationship for a long time. I was never divorced. I never wanted to get in contact. I did know Brianna died."

"How did you know?"

"I can't remember now. Maybe it was in the paper? I'm not sure about the internet then. Anyway, getting married didn't seem to matter to either Brigitte or me. I fell in love with someone who loved me back. We have a child."

"Oh ... a boy or girl?"

"A daughter. Daisy Katherine Mulvaney-Mertens. Brigitte chose her first name and me her middle name."

"Doesn't Katherine go down through the female line?"

"Do you intend to have children?"

"I don't know." I thought of Cooper, Joan, her wish for little feet to run around the house.

"You better get a move on if you're going to." He smiled warmly.

There was time but not the person. And then was not the right time to be reminded. I wasn't in the mood to tell him about Cooper. What was the point?

"Well, in case you don't, we have the name covered."

He showed me photos. Both his wife and daughter were beautiful. I said that Brigitte looked French to my eyes.

"Belgium, that's where we live."

"How did you find out about Lachlan?"

"I've been keeping tabs on him. Although we left on bad terms, he is still my brother. And to be mercenary, I have a half-share in this house. In the end, someone contacted me. He must have kept tabs on me, or recently got someone to do a search when his health was failing. But I didn't want him to pass away with us still on bad terms. I've been here a week and spent a good bit of time with him. Limited as it was."

"And he only told you about him being my father just now?"

"Yes."

"Right to the end," I said mostly to myself. "Must run in the family." Liam looked puzzled. "Keeping tabs on family members. He must have told you my story? He's been tracking me for years."

"He has told me some but, as you can see, he runs out of energy very quickly. He was waiting for both of us to arrive and trying to save his strength on the advice of his nurse."

"What about me? I thought you were my father. I've never heard a thing from you. I used to wonder what you were like. Aunty Iris was my godsend and told me her side of the story, but she didn't know you weren't my father. Or chose not to tell me."

"Yes, that was cowardly of me. But you were so young, Kate, you wouldn't remember me anyway. And besides, how could I stay in contact with you and not your mother? I didn't want to be found. And I only suspected I was not your father. I had no proof."

"Must run in the family," I said again. "I expect he told you how I left."

"What he told me has been patchy. Mrs G, bless her, has told me her side. But I'd like to hear the full story from you."

"You will. Right now, I'm exhausted. I arrived this morning, after that long flight from Australia, and then the drive here from the airport. I think jetlag has caught up with me."

We both walked to the kitchen to return the tea stuff to Mrs Gallagher. She and the nurse were there. There was a lot for them to talk about.

"Lachlan's too tired to see anyone for the rest of the day," the nurse said. "I think it's best you see him tomorrow. Mornings are his best times."

I wondered how many of those there'd be.

"I'm exhausted too," I said. "I could sleep for days. Mrs G, will you be here tomorrow? I'm so tired I can barely keep my eyes open, and I want to spend time with you."

"Yes, dear, I will be. Your room is all made up. Sleep well."

SIXTY-EIGHT

Thakit

Despite my tiredness and jetlag, when mammy and I arrived home from visiting Lachlan, I asked Colin to come over. This time it was me who made the tea, got the biscuits out and took control of the talking table. Mammy sat.

I gave Colin a detailed account of the events at Lachlan Mulvaney's bedside and his revelations. I gave him the background, the lead up, Australia, my Jen – and although Colin knew most of what I said, and of mammy's affair, he didn't know I was the result. My dramatic side was playing out as I spaced the telling. Both mammy and Colin managed to stop their eyes from rolling.

Was I angry, disappointed, disgusted, expanded or diminished? I couldn't decide. By the end of my spiel, I was exhausted. But ultimately, none of it mattered. Which is what Colin backed up when I finally finished.

"And ...?" said Colin.

I looked to my ma, then to him. "Well ... tell me, should I be disgusted or what?" Mammy sat watching both of us. Face impassive.

"Colin, you're my hero, my big brother."

"And ...?" was all Colin said again.

"Well ... now you're only half that." I said.

"So," Colin said, "what you're saying is, since hearing those few words I have diminished as your brother. Do I no longer hold that place of hero?"

"Colin, you will never be anything else. But how do you feel about me? This is no small thing."

"You're still my whacky thakky brother. To be honest, when you told me at the pub our mammy had an affair and how you and ma had been taken care of financially, I did wonder. I was older than you when da was sick. I knew how difficult it was for mammy. As an adult, I can see how compassion by someone outside of the family would have been a comfort. Something she could cling to in the sinking ship where she found herself."

We were all quiet, thinking within our own spheres. I'd always felt there was more to mammy's telling. I said, "I knew there was a missing link, mammy. Why didn't *you* tell me?"

Mammy continued to sit in silence eventually saying, "I didn't have the proof. Besides, it didn't matter to me. You're *my* son, that is all that matters."

"Life has expanded for me and I don't know how to feel about it," I said.

"What does that mean?" Mammy said.

"Expanded because I now have two halves, a wonky and a whole."

"You're doing my head in, Ryan ... go on," said mammy.

Ryan. She was cross with me.

"Go on, Thakky, tell us in plain English what you mean," said Colin.

"Instead of one whole brother I have half a sister and half a brother, making one whole, and also half an uncle."

Mammy looked to Colin. "He was always good at maths, let him have that thought. So long as I am one whole mother and you still love us both, I don't care how you work it out."

"God help that poor Jen if she gets the whole of you full time," said Colin.

Restful sleep was beyond me that night. Too much churning in my head. But I returned the next morning to my rightful place alongside Lachlan's bed, sitting next to my newly discovered father, half-sister and half-uncle. With Lachlan's few words my life had lifted or plunged, depending on my mood. I was no longer just the person who brought Kate home; I was his son who brought home our family member. It was like a cog had slipped into place but needed oiling. Best of all, I still had my mammy and Colin.

Lachlan was noticeably frailer that following morning. It must have taken great strength to hang on until Kate arrived. When Liam, Kate and I came together at his bedside, the nurse and the priest were already there. The nurse looked grave. Her patient had visibly shrunk overnight. I held his hand, Liam stroked his head and Kate held his other hand. I wondered how she felt about touching the man she had so much vitriol towards. Her face was a mask.

Lachlan knew we were all there. He gave me the smallest movement with his hand, and I thought I detected a smile. A short time later he was able to briefly open his eyes, look at each one of us, then close them. A shudder ran through his body, his breath rattled and he passed gently away.

Nobody cried. We all sat numb, including the nurse. It seemed we sat like that for an age. I was vaguely aware of the priest. I needed to get out of there but was held down by the others and the gravity of the situation. I was suffocating.

SIXTY-NINE

Thakit

He'd pulled it off, right until the end. Lachlan had managed to get Kate home, his brother home, me in attendance, my mother farewelled – and he'd achieved it all in the midst of a debilitating illness. My biological father. I wanted to scrape the skin off from my body and start again.

After the funeral service, the crowd went back to the big house. The wake was huge. I was there with mammy and Colin. Although my attention was with them, I couldn't help but notice the reception Kate received. I saw person after person speaking to her. "You're back, Kate. It's lovely to see you." First condolences, then comments on how lucky she was to have been at his passing. Reproachful and slippery. Lack of knowledge or understanding of her circumstances were clearly not considered. Nor were her reasons for not staying in Ireland. I wondered what she'd decide to do.

"And who are you?" I was asked several times. Mammy stepped in and said we were close friends of the family. In time they would know, but not then. I didn't relish that time. Maybe no one needed to know. As it was a small village, I doubted the secret would be kept.

After the funeral and the wake and after Colin and mammy left, I spent time at the house, where Kate, Liam and I were able to reflect on Lachlan's passing and the consequence of his living. A peaceful time to get to know one another.

The day came for the will to be read. Mammy was surprised to learn she'd been called to attend.

Mrs Gallagher prepared the library. We filed in and sat at the large, highly polished, very old table. Sombre, befitting the circumstances. Books competed with the dark, panelled walls, glowering down upon us. Anticipation filled the room as we waited for the solicitor to arrive.

SEVENTY

Kate

At the reading of the will, my attention hopped from shock to shock as Mr O'Clements's legal spiel droned on in the background, a nonsensical hum. I was preoccupied, an uncle swapped for a father. A new uncle. A brother's arrival into the family. The shock, too, that if Lachlan had got hold of me and shown me how the world worked, how sick would I be feeling right now? That last sensation of him trying to kiss me, pressing himself into me, was fresh in my mind. Like I'd taken the clingwrap off a rotting bowl of fruit, the thought pungent. My own father. I was so sickened I didn't hear anything going on around me. Finally, silence interrupted my thoughts.

Liam nudged me. "Kate, where are you?"

Everyone was looking at me.

"What? ... sorry."

"You're a very rich girl," said Liam.

I looked to the solicitor. "What?"

Mr O'Clements repeated: "You own half the house with your ... erm ... uncle, Liam Mulvaney. Your ... father ... I can't keep track of this myself, your father Lachlan allowed you to keep the jewels and cash already in your possession."

Thakit chuckled. Go suck, Thakit, I glared.

"Can we pay attention until I've finished, please," said Mr O'Clements, having noticed the eye communication between Thakit and myself. "Grace Katherine Mulvaney, you also inherit a third of Lachlan Mulvaney's estate including his shares and other business dealings."

"If he had all this money, how come he couldn't fix up the house?" I said.

"Miss Mulvaney, please." Mr O'Clements again.

"Sorry."

Mr O'Clements slid sheets of paper across the table to the three of us. This listed Lachlan's shares and 'other business dealings'.

"I won't read through them. You can peruse them at your leisure. I have one more item. Mrs Siobhan Elaine Kelly, you are given a lump sum which I have been asked to pass to you on this document," sliding it to Siobhan. "These are Lachlan's precise words and which he wanted me to read out. 'As you wouldn't marry me, I'm hoping I can posthumously share a honeymoon with you. Think of me while you're away.' Mr O'Clements paused. "I have now concluded the will."

Yet again I was shocked.. He must have really been serious about Thakit's ma. When did he fit that love affair in? "Hang on," I said. "What about the others? My ... erm ... uncle?"

"That has already been read out, Miss Mulvaney."

"Oh ..." I turned to Liam. "So what did you get?"

Mr O'Clements sighed. "I'll take my leave and you can discuss this amongst yourselves."

Clearly I was not in Mr O'Clements's good books.

"Keep up, Kate," said Liam, "half the house and a third, like you, of his business dealings."

"Oh ... a third. Who's the other third?"

"Thakit," Liam said.

"Oh," I said again. "It'll be fun sorting that out." I found it difficult to navigate. And what was this thing with Thakit's mother? She sat looking as surprised as the rest of us. She seemed like a nice woman.

My brain was quickly doing the sums but I was still unsure of Thakit's age. Certainly while my mother was on the scene. How on earth did he conduct an affair while my mother was alive? From all accounts she never let him out of her sight. The sneaky bastard. He was certainly a busy man when it came to the trouser department.

"Are you okay, Kate?" said Liam.

"No, I'm not really. I've lost my uncle and gained another uncle and lost a father when I thought I just found one. Not to mention gaining a half-brother. And ..." I looked across to Siobhan, "... it doesn't matter."

Siobhan didn't miss my look. "We were a comfort to one another all those years ago, Kate. I worked here, cleaning. My very ill husband, then his death ... he helped me during a tragic time. He was good to me, to my son, my whole family in truth. A marriage would not have healed our loss and in time I felt would only have exacerbated it. I wanted my independence. To have my life with my sons. That's why I said no to his offer of marriage."

"I'm sorry, Siobhan, I ... erm ... don't deny you anything. It has nothing to do with me. I ... it's just ... there was so much going on when I was a child, and I was too young to understand it or to know anything that was happening. When confusion is all you know, it's all you know. It's like an antique wooden chest you've been using as a table, never thinking to open it to see if there's anything inside. When finally you do, it's packed full."

No more was said on the matter. It was Liam who changed the tension in the room.

"It feels very weird to be sitting in this library. I haven't been in here since I was a young man."

I looked at Liam, realising he'd spent his childhood and his teenage years in this house. I hadn't even considered that. I knew I was being awful all round, but the whirlpool was spinning so fast I was drowning.

"You're my uncle too?" Thakit said to Liam.

"Erm ... yes, I guess so."

"Half an uncle," Thakit said.

"Give it a rest, son," said his mother.

"I didn't want an ordinary life, but deep down I thought it would be," Thakit said.

"You can't have ordinary, Thakit, that's mine," I said.

"Not a hope in hell, Kate," Liam said.

SEVENTY-ONE

Kate

We sat for a while in the gloom of the library. It was raining outside. I thought of the beautiful sunshine and warmth of Kauai. My thoughts trailed to Cooper. Suddenly I missed him again. More than ever. There was a completion in my life alongside a huge hole. And Joan. How was she? Angry with me? Had she forgotten me or had I simply been dismissed? How long did it take her to reach the conclusion I wasn't coming back?

Cooper wasn't with Dave, I knew that much. What happened there? Had he really had a bisexual experience, or was there something else going on? When he got back and dug up the diamonds from the safe in the garden, and realised I'd swapped them for fakes, fury must have engulfed him. And yet, I couldn't imagine Cooper getting furious. He'd talk around it. His calm, logical, at times over-thinking attitude would have accepted it. But how did he think of me? Not just my actions, but me? I wondered if my name was written in black evil pen somewhere in their house, or there was a doll with pins in it.

"I miss Cooper," I said to no one in particular. I looked to Thakit. "I still love him," I muttered.

"That's too bad."

"Why? He's not with Dave."

"There's another woman."

"What?" I was thrown, thrashed against rocks like a garment washed Indian-style. I wasn't sure I could take any more surprises. The day kept getting more difficult to comprehend. In my head all my misdemeanours were lined up, counted and coming to fruition in whatever form was relevant.

"Yes ... a Toni. Toni with an 'i'," said Thakit.

"A Toni? How do you know?"

"I'm still in touch with Cooper's mother."

"What?"

"Could you stop saying 'what', Kate," said Liam. "Thakit, for heaven's sake, give her more than a one-liner. I also need to figure out what you're talking about."

"Her full name is Antoinette, which is what Joan calls her. When I went to see her, Joan that is, when I was looking for you, I gave her my contact details in case she heard from you. She emailed me a couple of weeks later asking if I'd found you in England yet."

"England?" said Liam.

"It's a long story," said Thakit.

"Yes, a long story," I said.

"I've a lot to catch up on," said Liam.

"Go on," I said to Thakit.

"We stayed in touch, that's all. She mentioned it first, that she didn't think you were ever coming back. It was such a shame, she said. Things hadn't worked out with Dave and Cooper. She went on to say she never did believe her son was gay or bisexual. It was that other matter, she said. The diamonds."

"What?" said Liam and Siobhan together.

"Another story," Thakit said.

"Joan knew about the diamonds?" I said. Thakit shouldn't have mentioned diamonds, or at least brought me up to date privately. I wasn't sure how much Thakit knew. He was talking like he knew a lot. Joan had risked it, mentioning diamonds in an email.

"Seems so," said Thakit. "She didn't say that much in the email. Anyway, in time Cooper met up with someone else. You think he was pining for you? He's a good-looking guy."

"How do you know?"

"I saw the four of you having dinner at the Bougainvillea."

"What?" I said.

"Stop it. Stop with the whats … everyone. Yes I know, including me," said Liam.

"Go on Thakit. What happened?" I said.

"As I said, he's a good-looking guy, in demand. Even the waitress at the Bougainvillea told me you'd nabbed him from under their noses."

"Wh…"

"No Kate, enough," said Liam.

Thakit continued. "Why would he wait? My guess is there was something else that made him believe you weren't coming back. Maybe he was on to you, Kate?"

"Do you need to be so harsh?" said Liam.

Thank you, uncle. "Who is this Toni?" I said.

"A local girl he's known for years. She recently split from her husband. Maybe they're sharing their misery." Thakit cocked his head, thinking he was cute, I expect.

"Don't look so fucking smug, Thakit," I said.

"Charming. You've been brought up well," said my newly found, change of heart, unsupportive uncle.

"Well … you weren't around," I said.

"Stop it ... stop it right there," said Siobhan and stood. "I've things to do. We've had a big day. A lot of information to process. Come on, Ryan, let's go."

"Ryan?" I said.

Thakit nodded.

"Just one thing, Thakit ... erm ... Ryan," I said as they stood, "how much does Joan know about where I've been? Where I am?"

"Getting worried, are we?" Thakit said.

Thakit's mother gave him a shove and shook her head.

"I said you weren't in England."

"Are you still in touch?" I said.

"Occasionally." Thakit shrugged and took his ma's arm and left.

"You've a lot to tell me, Kate," said Liam, "but I won't push it ... when you're ready. I need a walk. Clear my head. I'll be out in the garden somewhere if you want to join me."

I sat in that library for ages until Mrs Gallagher came to see if I was all right. She suggested I go to the kitchen for a cup of tea and some cake.

"I want him back," I said to Mrs Gallagher, who had no idea what I was talking about.

"Well, best you do something about getting him back, dear."

Thakit

Before mammy and I left for the reading of the will, I'd been surprised to be invited, even though I was now the son of Lachlan. But mammy being asked to attend was totally unexpected.

"We might inherit something," I'd said to mammy.

Whether it was her grief talking, she wasn't pleased with me.

"Ryan, you're thinking greedy. Haven't you received enough from Lachlan?"

"Just saying, ma. Why else are we invited along?"

She had no answer to that.

Since first learning of Lachlan, back when he was Aedan, my life had been turned upside down, inside out and sideways. My general inertia, as my mother liked to call it, had helped with this lopsided world I'd moved into. If I'd had a career job, I couldn't have sleuthed, travelled, met Jen.

Now I was a split personality, in a good way. Not a Mulvaney by name, I was by being. An annoying half-sister had joined my being, and an uncle. And an inheritance. Mammy had to push my jaw shut as I listened in amazement.

As we'd walked to the car, I said. "Now I can marry Jen." I couldn't believe I'd said those words out loud. They belonged in my head. Judging from mammy's look, they'd come out loud and clear. I had yet to ask Jen. But the thought was so bright, like a shining crystal had dropped into my lap. Suddenly I had things to do. Like make a plan.

On the drive home, we picked up Colin and made ourselves comfortable at the talking table. Mammy made tea and we sat in our usual seats. Mammy and I took it in turns to tell Colin all that had gone on. Colin is rare in that he doesn't interrupt. His expression remained impassive.

"I'll give you half of everything when it's sorted out, Colin."

"Don't be silly, Thakky. I'm fine."

"It isn't fine. I'm worried you might not feel the same about me now I'm a rich half-brother."

"Jesus, Thakky, will you knock it off with the half-brother thing. You're not getting off that lightly. I can still whop you if I want."

"You're both my sons and Colin has received money along the way the same as you, Thakky. Whatever Lachlan gave me, I divided between the two of you. Colin doesn't have an inheritance but all his education and help with his business came from Lachlan via me."

"Really? I always thought it was from money da left," said Colin.

"He left very little. He did leave a lot of love for both his boys."

"Lachlan really wanted to marry you, didn't he, mammy?" I said.

"He asked me a few times if I remember rightly."

"Really? How come we didn't know this?" I said.

"You're my children. You don't need to know everything about your mother. I need my privacy too."

"Well, that's been ripped to shreds," said Colin.

"It has. But you're adults now. Well, almost. My reasons for declining were always the same. I wanted my independence. And that house … it's huge and horrible."

"It is that. Even fixed up, I'm not sure I'd want to live there." I had another thought. "Did Lachlan have skinny legs too?"

"Really, son, I'm not answering that."

"I sometimes wonder where I got them from." I thought about my nose and smile. His. "Yeah, I reckon he did."

Colin became quiet, pensive. His brow furrowed. I was so worried he felt angry or left out. He raised his head.

"Who'd he leave his car to?"

SEVENTY-THREE

Thakit

"I'm going to marry her, mammy."

"I see. Does she know?"

"Not yet, I haven't asked her."

"Small detail. Where do you plan to live?"

"I haven't thought about that."

"Small detail ... If it's Australia, you're not my son."

"Thanks for your support, mammy. I love her ... very, very much. I only realised after the will was read, when I realised I had something to offer."

"So what you're saying is, a few days ago you were a person not ready to commit, with no thought to the future, and now you are. So all it takes is money to change that fundamental part of your personality?"

"Erm ... yes. Was that a trick question?"

"I love you, Thakky, but you're even more shallow than I thought."

"Mammy, don't be so cynical. I'm not shallow. I'm easy-going. Anyway, about Jen, I can't live without her and now I can give her a better life."

"That may be, but after this fanfare, start using that degree if you want a substantial life." Mammy was at the kitchen sink. She turned with her thoughtful face. "Enough thinking Thakky, time to act if you're serious. She might get swept up by someone else."

"No … that can't happen." I hadn't thought of that. "You're right, mammy. What's the time? Night-time. I'll ring this evening our time. Not very romantic, is it? Maybe I could email a picture of me with flowers."

"I think sleuthing has gone to your head, Thakky. Maybe that's your father talking."

"Which father?"

"Mmm, good point. Perhaps both of them. I've never thought about that before. You poor wretch, having inherited ideologies from two dreamers."

"Thanks mammy, for providing that gift."

My phone rang.

"Hi, Thakit." It was Kate. "Can you drive me to the shops?"

She'd been doing this a bit since we'd arrived back. Thinking was doing my head in – I thought she may be able to help.

I'd driven mammy's car to Kate's and then we got into her/their/my limo. As soon as she got in the car, she slunk into contagious gloom. This mood of hers was driving me nuts, as well as everyone else in the big house, I suspected.

"Isn't it about time you learnt to drive? I'll teach you if you like."

"Erm … I'll think about it. Is that what brothers do?"

"It's what mine did."

"I don't think I could drive this great big limo."

My mind immediately flicked to Colin sitting in the driver's seat. Now was not the time to ask. "Buy a small car." We drove in silence for a while. Then I had a thought.

"Mind if we make a small detour? It'll just be a drive by."

"No. Fine."

On the way I told her of my plan to ask Jen to marry me and mammy's frightening point that if I wasn't quick someone else might nab her.

"That's true."

"I thought of sending her an email with a photo of me holding a bunch of flowers?"

"That sounds boring."

"What would you like then?"

"Why don't you offer to fly her over? She'll either say yes or no. Unless she takes the flight and dumps you when she gets here."

"Thanks for that." I was quiet while the sense of it all digested. I didn't think Jen was that sort of person. A man could always be wrong. Colin's words rang out, *man up, Thakky*. I had to take the risk. "Access to the will could be a while. I don't want her to fly economy."

"I'll lend you the money."

"Wow, is that what sisters do?"

"What this one will."

"Wow, would you really?"

She nodded emphatically while I was driving.

"Thank you, sis."

We were nearly at my detour destination. I slowed the car, pressed the window down and hooted the horn a couple of times. Colin came out. Once out on the footpath, I crawled the car and gave a little wave. His face was priceless.

I sat in the limo while Kate did her shopping. On the drive back I said, "What are you doing about Cooper?"

She nearly cried. "I don't know. You said he's with someone but he's still my husband."

"Under a different name."

Then she did cry.

"This is not what I expected of you, Kate. I thought you were feisty and fearless. Not a loser."

"I'm not a loser," she sobbed.

"You're always on the run. Stand and fight."

After that sunk in, she said, "I don't know how," and cried some more.

This crying unnerved me. I can't bear to see a woman cry, but the steering wheel was in my hands. "Why don't you go over there, go to Kauai, or ring?"

"I'm so scared of what I'll find. I'll have to confess so much. I might be tossed in the bin like an empty wrapper."

"You won't find out if you sulk all day. Go ... with your head held high. I told you back in Australia, it's time to out the truth. Besides, whatever happened to the long line of Katherines you talk about? The ones who've been so feisty, given you strength? Letting them down, aren't you?"

"I have no one to talk it over with, there's no one left."

"What do you think you're doing now?"

SEVENTY-FOUR

Kate

After Lachlan passed, my emotions rode a wild ride. Up, down, turn right, turn left. They wouldn't settle. Grief was shared with Liam and Mrs Gallagher. But was it grief or relief? What lay heavy on my soul was the loss of Cooper.

My husband had been creeping into my thoughts, renewed after meeting Jen at the barbecue. As the days moved along, I found myself wanting to talk with him, be with him.

Jen was delighted to fly to Ireland. Thakit brought her over to the big house one day. Like everyone, she was amazed at its size. Talking with her, I had to tread carefully as I wasn't sure if Thakit had done his big proposal yet.

"How is Kimberley?"

"She sends her love. They're doing so well. She misses you. I hear Susie and her boyfriend have become very much part of Kimberley's family."

"I think of them often and I'm in touch by email but it's good to hear directly. And what of Dave? Have you been in touch?"

"Very briefly. He wants us to stay friends ... why, I can't imagine. It's over. What we had was a mess, so what's the point? I don't dislike him and after I had it out with him about the diamonds, there wasn't much more to say."

"Has he met someone?"

"I think he's just exploring his coming out at the moment."

"Do you know what happened over there?" I said. "With the diamonds?"

"Not sure. I still have my two and he has none."

So, she hasn't discovered they're fakes yet.

Jen continued. "Seems Cooper took the bag to get valued, gave Dave a bunch of fakes and vanished ... I keep going to call you Rose. I can't get used to your change of name. Is Kate the real one?"

"Yes ... yes it is." Thinking of Thakit's words about revealing the truth was all good and well but it wasn't the time. "I've had a few names, Jen. And yes, Kate is my real name. Grace Katherine Mulvaney. Thakit's filled you in on what's been going on here?"

"It's all so amazing."

"It is that."

"And have you been in touch with Cooper?"

"No."

"You said he didn't leave you a letter?"

"No."

"Was it because of my letter you decided to leave?"

"Yes, I guess it was."

"Maybe you should have given him a chance to state his case. He's so nice. Well, not what he did to Dave but that's a twisted story anyway. But you two seemed so well suited."

She'd said that before at the barbecue. I could feel the tears well up and I did not want to blubber.

"Thakit said you wanted to be back with him." She wasn't letting me off the hook.

"I do. But to be honest, Jen, I don't know what to do. He's met someone else."

"But he's not married again."

"He can't. We're still married."

"Well, then. Reclaim your husband. Go get him back."

"You're not the first to say that."

She noticed my discomfort. "I believe there's a big family lunch. I'm really looking forward to it."

I was less than enthusiastic. I walked her to the door just as Thakit drove up to take her home. He got out of the car and gave her a big hug before coming over to me.

"So, sis, what's it to be? Have you decided to go to Kauai?"

I shrugged. It upset me to see them so close. Things like that had never bothered me before. "Have you proposed yet?" I whispered close to his ear.

"Tonight."

SEVENTY-FIVE

Kate

Mrs Gallagher was on my case. "Stop moping, Kate, you're acting like a little girl. No, I take that back, you never acted mopey when you were younger. Now give me a hand."

The house was abuzz. Mrs G had formed a work party. She didn't trust or want professional cleaners. Liam, his wife Brigitte, their daughter Daisy and me, would be sufficient. No one was getting a free lunch. She worked me like a draft horse. The big dining room was to be thoroughly cleaned, thoroughly dusted, everything in wood to be polished and the room decorated. She bullied energy into me and was having the time of her life doing it. I was on ladder-climbing duty to the highest shelves. Dust in those remote regions had created its own ecosystem. With the activity going on in the house, we must have been upsetting a large breeding programme.

Since I'd left the house at age of sixteen, and with Lachlan in his wheelchair with no interest in the household, Mrs Gallagher had not bothered hiring a cleaner when the last one left. She also had no intention of taking up those duties herself. The gardener was still employed in memory of Iris who had loved the garden. When things got too bad, Mrs Gallagher called on him to come in and fix something. He was still the same gardener who'd moved me downstairs when Lachlan became so obnoxious. I was reminded how good he'd been to me. He was also in the sights of Mrs G, with her emphasis on making the garden even more beautiful. He was unimpressed. Unlike Mrs Gallagher, he said, he'd never let the garden go.

In his will, Lachlan made provision for Mrs Gallagher to keep the house in order and do the cooking for as long as she liked. When she was no longer able to work or did not wish to, she could continue to live there. Her husband had long since passed. Now she was active in running things again, she referred to the house as her house. Whether in future anyone would be living in the house was another matter. More than likely a member of the growing household would be in residence at some time.

But what was I to do with my life? I had no idea. A return to Sydney was probable. Though my Sydney life was becoming more distant as each day passed. It did lay like an elusive escape if nothing else turned up. Was Kauai a possibility? Thakit's words circled; I should stop running from and march towards.

My uncle Liam was feeling dislodged too, I could see. He'd revisited his childhood and his reason for leaving. But since his family arrived, his spirits had lifted. The house had such a strong energy. Its potent force affected all of us. My relationship with Liam was elastic. It stretched and retracted as we both tried to seek out the other to build something. We overworked it or underworked it. He was overjoyed to be released whenever Daisy bounded up to him.

With all the hard work, it seemed Mrs G had been right – I came back into a happier version of myself. My mojo returned. I went to bed exhausted but fulfilled. Come morning, I bounced down the stairs with double joy as the banister had finally been fixed. Liam's doing. That memory was now just that and not a physical reminder.

As the house filled with people, the atmosphere in it lifted. Mrs Gallagher even corralled Thakit and Jen into action. Was this how it might have been in its heyday? We had two more days to the lunch.

Mrs Gallagher had been instructed by me, no one else was to touch Aunt Iris's room. That was mine. Closing in on the big lunch, I was busy with the polish; sweaty, smelly and smeared with the stuff, hair pulled back haphazardly, wearing no make-up and dressed in the oldest clothes I could find.

Mrs Gallagher knocked tentatively on Aunt Iris's door.

"Katie, dear, you have two visitors waiting in the dining room."

"Who?" I looked up, shocked. I wasn't expecting anyone. Mourners had finished calling some time ago.

"Can't say, dear." She swiftly turned and left.

Wiping the excess polish down my jeans, I moved my sticky hands to fix my hair, but only succeeded in spreading further polish. I was a picture of dishevelment.

SEVENTY-SIX

Kate

Still working on my appearance, I absently entered the room. I saw a man and a woman with their backs to me surveying the dining area.

"Can I help you?"

Turning, their initial response was shock, presumably at my appearance, but this quickly changed to huge smiles. I stared, stunned to the point of gormless.

"Cooper ... Joan ... is it really you? How ... what ...?"

Before I could utter one more nonsensical word, I sat on the floor as my legs gave way. Looking up at them, I continued gormless. I wasn't sure why they were here. I stood as they walked over, their arms outstretched. Their hugs were ferociously tight while the tears ran down my face.

"I ... what ... how ... I mean ... what are ... how did you find me?"

"You should have told me Ireland wasn't England," Joan said.

"Nice place you've got here," Cooper said.

Slumping on the nearest couch, I waited for the tirade. Accusations, recriminations, surely I deserved them.

"So, Rose, Pippa ... er, Kate. You look ...," said Cooper.

"Stop there, son."

Cooper continued, ignoring his mother. "That look is good. Is this the cool look young wealthy Irish women are wearing these days?"

Cooper was back.

Before thinking of the consequences of how they got here, how they found me, more than any other time that I could remember, I wanted him, passionately. The smell of him when he hugged me had set me off. My eyes moved to Joan. Equal to Mrs Gallagher, I'd never been so glad to see anyone.

"I'm sorry," I stammered, "I know I have so much to explain but I love you both so much."

"You think we're here for retribution?" said Cooper. "Nah, there were a few things I wanted to do to you, but I got over that. I've missed you."

He missed me. My heart leapt. "How did you find me?"

"I received an email in my inbox," said Joan, "from Thakit. 'Why don't you both come over? If Kate won't put you up, I'm sure we can find somewhere.' That's what he wrote. He did mention your real name."

"Oh ... Thakit did that? When?"

"The other day," said Joan.

"Of course you can stay," I said.

"Sure you've got enough room?" said Cooper.

"We'll manage," I said with a laugh. How good it was to hear his voice.

Just then Mrs Gallagher walked in carrying a tray.

"We have spare rooms, don't we, Mrs G?"

"Plenty enough."

Piled on the tray was a pot of tea with a jug of milk, a sugar bowl, a mound of warm scones, cream and jam, all contained in Aunt Iris's finest bone china, along with Aunt Iris's delicate silver cutlery.

Joan, so excited to see the tea arrive, clapped. "Proper Eng ..."

"Mom ... Irish."

"Yes, yes ... proper Irish tea."

My eyes were doing all the talking as I sat staring at Cooper. I couldn't believe he was actually in front of me. Cooper being Cooper. In real life. No longer in my imagination.

"I'll fill you in," he said.

"Please," I said.

Mrs G had taken the tray into Aunt Iris's room. Moved the polish and set the tray down. But before that she'd found one of Aunt Iris's crocheted tablecloths and placed it on an occasional table. We helped ourselves to scones and tea and settled in.

"First things first. I got home to find you'd gone. To England, Mom said, but you'd be back. I didn't believe that for a moment. Once she realised you weren't coming home, Mom cried. Yes, my happy mother cried and spluttered what Jen had told her, that Dave had returned to Australia, something to do with work. But my mom found Dave's letter to Jen. Torn to shreds. My resourceful mother stuck it back together."

"Why didn't you tell me what you planned to do?" I said.

"I didn't want to tell you too much. We still worried the cartel would be on to us, if you remember. And I didn't think you'd take off, Rose. First sign of trouble and you're off. But then the real reason was the diamonds, wasn't it?"

I looked across at Joan.

"It's okay, Mom knows everything. Although you might not think it, Mom's not squeaky clean either."

"Cooper, you know what I've told you about that mouth of yours," Joan said. "Besides you don't know all my personal details, so don't be a know-it-all."

Genuine shock smudged Cooper's face. "What the hell else have you done?"

I looked to Joan who sat so composed.

She put a finger to the side of her nose. "What you don't know, you don't need to know. You do not need to know everything about your mother."

"Well, I hope I'm your son."

"Very funny."

Cooper resumed. "I didn't know Dave had told Jen that gay story, although I guess it was his first foray into coming out. I took advantage of his affections before I left, especially when he told me about the second bag of diamonds."

"What?"

SEVENTY-SEVEN

Kate

"A second bag. What second bag?" I said.

"Well, don't your eyes light up at the thought of even more diamonds," said Cooper. "After finding the first bag accidentally in the boot of the rental car, Dave searched the car thoroughly and found a second. He didn't tell Jen. How mean is that?"

How mean is that, I thought. No reasonable person would ever think to do that.

"He had a second bag ... and it wasn't fake. I planned to be home in a few days. You couldn't even wait a few days." Cooper opened his hands like he was holding scales, weighing up each conclusion he thought I'd made: 'Diamonds all for me?'" Up one side. "'Husband turned gay?'" Down the other side. "Mmm ... all the diamonds just for me. The scales tipped heavily, didn't they, Rose?"

I felt shame, then defiant – wow, my mojo was back. We were both opportunists. "You'd gone weird," I said, "I knew you were up to something. The diamonds came between us, didn't they?"

"I knew something had," said Joan. "No good comes of bad things."

"Says who? Now they've brought us back together," Cooper said, glancing at his mom. "I hope. Know what mom said when I told her the full story?"

I shook my head, fearing the worst.

"'She's a naughty scoundrel ... what pluck. So what are you going to do, Cooper, she said. Best woman to come into your life. You're two peas in a pod. Get out and find her. Or I will.'

She was the one who got me to see the funny side. She's amazing, my mom."

"But you didn't ... go out and find me."

"Yeah, like you're so easy to find."

"But you've met someone else. An Antoinette," I said.

"Pshaww," said Joan.

"Yes, we're good friends, go back a long way. Maybe if you, or as it happens, Thakit, hadn't intervened, we might have gone somewhere."

"You're not in love with her?" I said.

"No ... I'm not."

"Hoorah for that," said Joan. "No ... don't get me wrong, son, she's a lovely girl."

The pause was so pregnant it could have given birth.

Joan gazed out the window, entranced by the garden, looking totally preoccupied by its lushness, watching the rain fall. But I knew she wasn't out there. She was as sharp as a tack and was in here following every detail.

"All these years I've wanted to visit England," she said, "and Buckingham Palace, not knowing this gem was lying in wait for me. All thanks to that dear boy Dave."

Cooper stifled a laugh.

Joan turned and faced me. "And ... we have visited Buckingham Palace. I have finally seen it, Rose. Cooper took me on a tour. We watched the Changing of the Guard, we stood outside Buckingham Palace and I watched everything. I have to tell you, Rose, I am now in heaven."

"It's Kate, mom ... and I have to tell you, Kate, I had to borrow the Queen's horses to drag her away."

"And ... Ro ... Kate, dear," Joan said, "I'm now in a country called Ireland. To be more precise, the Republic of Ireland." She laughed. "Who would have thought?" Joan dug into her bag and brought out her mobile phone.

"Not now, Mom."

"I've spent time in London but never seen much of it, Joan. I'd love to see all your pictures." Delight filled her face. "All thanks to Dave," I said, repeating Joan's words. "How did you leave him," I said to Cooper. "What happened? Are you bisexual?"

Joan snuffled her laughter.

"Joan, he could be ... you don't know," I said.

She shrugged a reply.

"It was a tiny bit naughty playing him along," Cooper said. "He knew something was up when I wanted a room to myself and when I didn't answer his constant knocking on the door. I'd taken a sleeping pill, I said to him next morning. I told him I'd checked his second bag of diamonds and they looked of good quality. In fact, they are brilliant. That cartel knows its stuff. I said the next day we'd go to a source I knew to get the full value. While I was with Dave, I rang the source ... but only pretended to. 'They'll see us tomorrow.' We did some sightseeing, with him making more intimate overtures. Time I left, I thought. Another night alone. I said I wasn't feeling very well. Food I'd eaten. I'd meet him downstairs the next morning for breakfast. I could see he was disappointed. I checked out early. As the diamonds were so hot, I wasn't going to take the risk of trying to sell any. Instead, I came home to find my wife had left me."

"That was mean, Cooper," I said.

"That's a bit rich coming from a thief and ... and a marriage absconder and I don't know what else. But Dave's one of those guys who believes what he wants to believe."

"Did you leave him with anything?"

"I didn't get around to it. I didn't see him. He'd probably taken a couple anyway."

Cooper reminded me of somebody. Who could it be? Me? "So that eased your conscience?"

"Yep. And you're not in a position to judge anybody."

He was right. I looked to Joan but she was still busy pretending not to listen, looking at the garden.

"Tell me, Kate, what's going on here? Your uncle died, Mrs Gallagher told us. I'm sorry for your loss. Was he very old?"

The whole story poured out of me once again. "There's more, Cooper, but I haven't the energy right now."

Joan piped up just then, "I knew you had family, dear, everyone does."

It occurred to me Cooper might have something sinister in store for me. Maybe I was safe in Joan's presence. "What schemes have you for me, Cooper? Some type of justice to lay on me?"

He lumbered very slowly off the chair, making it a gargantuan effort.

"Pippa ... Rose ... Kate," he said, unhurriedly dipping to bended knee, "will you renew our marriage vows?"

I didn't see that coming. Cooper stood. Just in time, as I took a gigantic leap up and wrapped my arms around him, nearly bowling him over. He grabbed me and twirled me in circles. I heard Joan clapping in the background. Mrs Gallagher came in wondering what all the noise was about. She beamed and Joan gave her the biggest hug. "They're married and going to be married again," said Joan.

Released from Joan, Mrs Gallagher raised her arms. "Well give thanks to all the little people. Now I hope I won't be seeing that moping face anymore."

"I'm still in love with you, even though you're a charlatan," Cooper whispered in my ear.

"And I'm still in love with you … you lay charlatan. I've missed you so much."

Cooper put me down and in front of Joan and Mrs G, asked if I'd live with him in Hawaii, have kids and take holidays here.

"Oh yeah," I said.

"And promise me you'll include me in all your charlatan ways," he said.

"If you promise me the same."

"I hope not," said Joan, "you'll need to set an example to all those tiny feet you'll be bringing into my world."

SEVENTY-EIGHT

Thakit

Jen finally arrived in Ireland and it was time for the big question. I didn't think she would have travelled all his way just to ditch me. When I'd asked her to fly over her response was out before I had chance to take my next breath.

"Yes."

"I'm buying you a business-class ticket. How quickly can you get here?"

"How quickly do you want me there?"

"Now?"

"Done."

"Really?"

"Of course ... long, lanky stick insect."

Grand. She really did still love me.

Jen took to her surroundings as the proverbial duck to water and our friends and neighbours took to her in equal measure. Not to mention Colin and his family. My nephews loved the funny way she spoke. Jen was so comfortable with us and our way of talking, we thought there might be Irish ancestors she didn't know about. Something to check out later.

The only thorn was mammy. A mother who was very hesitant

to warm to a future daughter-in-law. An infiltrator into her family. Someone threatening to take away her son to live in a far-flung land. Mammy was friendly in a courteous, sleuthing way. Jen let her be. I discovered quickly how smart Jen was. Before I even mentioned how to handle my mother, she'd worked it out. She helped in the house but didn't overdo it. She returned the friendly and courteous manner but didn't try to endear herself. Neighbours and friends did that. When they popped in for a sticky beak, leaving mammy to make coffee and tea full-time like she was working in a café, they plied Jen with questions and liked her answers. She made them laugh with her accent and her brusque ways. When the visitors left muttering to mammy how overjoyed she must be, little by little the praise slithered through mammy's protective skin. Colin and his family helped with this too. When mammy finally accepted her, Jen acted as if she never expected any other outcome.

The night I proposed I took her to dinner in a romantic, cosy, typical Irish pub. The restaurants were too over-the-top and I knew she'd be suspicious. I didn't want her to expect my proposal. For some reason I think she knew what I was about though. I expect it would be pretty bloody obvious to anyone who was only slightly more clued up about romance than me. After I asked the question, she smiled sweetly, keeping me waiting. I nearly died of embarrassment.

"Stick insects don't go red, Thakky … of course I'll marry you."

There she goes again, with her dour sense of humour.

"Shall we have two, maybe three children?"

"I love you, Mrs Thirdplace. As many as you want."

"Ah, that brings me to a request I have. I hope this doesn't upset you."

Oh God … be brave now Thakky.

"Would you mind if I keep my surname?"

"You prefer Jen Douglas to Jen Thirdplace? Why would that be?"

"Jennifer Mary Douglas, actually."

"You can call yourself anything you want. Mrs I-Got-Lucky, if that suits you."

My Jen's face changes to serious.

"As we're having a prenup ... there is something else I've always wanted to ask."

Shite, here it comes.

"Do you use coloured drops in your eyes? That blue ... it can't be natural."

"Bugger off ... 'course I don't."

Neither of us had carried the romantic gene.

"A natural crazy blue-eyed boy ... wow."

She moved in very close, then hugged and kissed me.

"Thakky, I adore you."

When we arrived home that night, mammy was wringing her hands, waiting at the door. She could tell by the smiles we were to wed.

"Where will you live?" was her first question.

"Siobhan, there's no need to worry, we can live in both countries. It's all possible. Besides, I'll feel right at home in both places ... it rains all the time there too. Don't tell anyone I told you that though."

Mammy looked at her like she was bonkers. She didn't always get Jen's remarks or her accent. Neither did I. Mammy does have a sense of humour but she struggled with Jen's comments, never knowing whether she was taking the piss or not. The same as me. I'm not sure mammy was convinced we wouldn't leave her forever, but she kissed us both and said all the traditions must be upheld. She went upstairs muttering about all the things she had to do.

I called out on her way up the stairs. "Mammy ... she doesn't want the surname Thirdplace. She's going to keep her own name."

"Well thank the lord for that," she muttered. "No one in their right mind would change their name to Thirdplace."

We decided on the official wedding in Ireland and a second informal one in Melbourne. Jen's parents had tragically died a few years before but there were relatives and friends to appease, including Kimberley and Susie and their incumbents. Jen's immediate family, one brother and his wife and children, would fly over to Ireland.

At the lunch in the big house, Jen and I, mammy, Colin and his family arrived to find Kate, Cooper and Joan well entrenched, along with Kate's and my Uncle Liam, his partner Brigitte and their daughter Daisy. Flowers adorned the hallway and dining room thanks to the faithful gardener, who also came with his wife. French champagne sat in silver buckets that had lain unused for years. All the best crockery, cutlery and glassware, dragged from cupboards, had been washed to shine and sparkle. Mrs Gallagher prepared the best spread you'd ever seen. She wanted no help but was told she must join us at the table, eventually sitting only after everyone was served.

Sometime later in the day, Colin managed to find his way into the garage where the big black car sat purring. Colin, lost to all, was secretly watched caressing and polishing it with his sleeve.

Jen nudged me. "Stick insect, I never expected to marry into money."

"I never expected to have any."

We were filled with good cheer, helped along by the bottles of bubbles.

The rain had stopped, the sun shone. It felt like the 30th of February, the glorious day when Ireland has no rain. Grand indeed.

Acknowledgements

A huge thank you to the team at Independent Ink. Ann Dettori, Daniela Catucci and Renée Bahr.

Also a massive thank you once again to my editor, Victoria Steele.

I'd also like to thank someone whose name I don't know. I visited Ireland to attend a writer's retreat. Catching the ferry from England I took the bus from Dublin to Galway. A Hugh Jackman concert had just ended and the bus was packed. A woman sat next to me and we struck up a conversation. We talked nonstop on the two-hour trip, she mostly filling me in about Ireland. She was enormously informative. As her stop was before mine and about to get off, I asked what she did. 'Associate Professor of Literature,' she said. 'That's why I've been telling you all this.' Wow. It was 2019 so my memory of what she looked like has faded plus she may well have moved on. What university? Her name? That two hours was more educational than the writers' retreat. A great big thanks should she ever read this book.

 Born in England, Pamiela moved with her parents to New Zealand, aged seven. After school years, including an unorthodox remote boarding school, Pamiela started her own travels, aged nineteen. Four years passed before returning to New Zealand and a few months later she moved to Sydney, where she now lives. A chance glamping holiday on a small, remote island in the Great Barrier Reef started the writing of her first novel. Now living near the beach, she loves to swim and snorkel. The sea inspires her writing.